Bigfoot: Shadows in the Timberline

by Ethan Blackwood

Bigfoot: Shadows in the Timberline
© 2025 Ethan Blackwood
All rights reserved.

For B.A.B. – You know who you are, and I'd follow you through any adventure on Earth.

Chapter 1: Arrival

The rain had started somewhere around Olympia, a typical Washington drizzle that thickened incrementally the further north Elise drove. By the time she passed the peeling, moss-stained sign for the Olympic National Forest, it was a deluge, hammering the roof of her rented Subaru Outback, turning the dense walls of Sitka spruce and western hemlock on either side of the highway into blurred, near-monochromatic barricades. The wipers fought a losing battle, smearing arcs across the windshield that barely cleared before the next sheet of water descended. Visibility dropped to maybe fifty feet. It felt less like driving *through* a forest and more like being swallowed by it.

Dr. Elise Holloway gripped the steering wheel, her knuckles white against the worn leatherette. This was the price of admission, she supposed. Remote assignments demanded remote travel, and "remote" was practically Bluffs End's middle name. Population: 312, give or take. Main industries: logging (waning) and rumour (thriving, apparently). Location: clinging precariously to the ragged edge of the Olympic Peninsula, where the jagged coastline met the impenetrable forest, miles from anywhere resembling civilization.

She glanced at the passenger seat. Her field kit – sturdy, waterproof Pelican cases containing sampling equipment, weatherproof notebooks, GPS units, high-resolution cameras, and bioacoustic recorders – sat securely buckled in. Beside it lay a manila envelope, thick and slightly damp despite her efforts. Inside was the non-disclosure agreement she'd signed electronically weeks ago, printed out for good measure, alongside the skeletal mission brief provided by the Kestrel Foundation.

"Preliminary Ecological Assessment – Uncharted Drainage Basin, Olympic Peninsula." That was the official title. Dry, bureaucratic, purposefully vague. The details were scant: Establish baseline data on flora and fauna in a region lacking previous scientific survey due to accessibility challenges. Deploy sensor arrays (camera traps, audio monitors). Collect geological and hydrological samples. Standard fieldwork, albeit in a challenging environment.

Except it wasn't standard. Not really.

The Kestrel Foundation wasn't a household name like the WWF or Nature Conservancy. They were private, well-funded, and intensely secretive. Their communication had been routed through encrypted channels. The stipend offered was significantly higher than typical academic or NGO fieldwork grants. And then there was the addendum, buried in conditional clauses – the secondary objective, delivered verbally during a secure video call with a clipped, authoritative voice that introduced itself only as "Mr. Graves." *"Maintain vigilance for, and thoroughly document if encountered, evidence pertaining to unconfirmed primate speciation endemic to the region."*

Unconfirmed primate speciation. A euphemism as delicate and transparent as gauze. They meant Bigfoot. Sasquatch. The big, hairy ghost of the deep woods.

Elise snorted, a humourless puff of air fogging the inside of the windshield. As a wildlife biologist specializing in primate behaviour and ecology – mostly Old World monkeys and apes in Africa and Asia – she'd learned to maintain a healthy scepticism towards cryptids. Fieldwork was gruelling enough without chasing myths fuelled by blurry photos and campfire stories. Yet, the Kestrel Foundation was pouring serious money into this, equipping a multi-disciplinary team for a month-long deep-woods expedition under the thinnest of cover stories. Either they were incredibly eccentric and wealthy believers, or there was something more to it. Something they weren't putting in writing.

Graves hadn't elaborated. Questions were deflected with practiced ease. The mission was the mission. Stick to the protocols. Report findings directly. Maintain absolute discretion. The 'unconfirmed primate' angle was treated as a low-probability contingency, a scientific curiosity to keep an eye out for, nothing more. But the intensity in his voice, the precision of the language, hinted otherwise.

She adjusted her glasses, pushing them higher on her nose. The truth was, part of her *was* intrigued. Not by Bigfoot – that was preposterous – but by the secrecy, the resources, the location itself. Uncharted valleys in the Olympics were rare beasts these days. What ecological secrets might such a place hold? Perhaps an isolated subspecies of marmot, an undiscovered orchid, a unique fungal network? Those were the possibilities that fuelled her professional curiosity, the real reason she'd accepted this bizarrely clandestine assignment, justifying the slight unease that prickled beneath her scientific detachment.

The highway narrowed, the tarmac degrading into chip seal scarred with potholes full of murky water. She slowed the Outback, navigating the uneven surface. According to the GPS, which was thankfully still getting a satellite lock beneath the thick cloud cover, Bluffs End was less than ten miles away. The trees pressed closer now, their massive trunks slick with rain, their lower branches draped in thick, velvety moss like ancient shrouds. The air filtering through the car vents smelled intensely of wet earth, decaying needles, and resin. It was the smell of a forest that had stood for centuries, indifferent to the transient concerns of humans.

Finally, a sign appeared through the grey curtain: *"Bluffs End. Pop. 312. Watch For Logging Trucks."* It was hand-painted, the lettering faded, riddled with what looked suspiciously like pellet marks. Beneath it, someone had crudely spray-painted, *"Turn Back."*

Charming.

The town emerged abruptly from the trees, not so much built *in* the landscape as grudgingly permitted *by* it. A single main street sliced through a cluster of weathered buildings huddled between the relentless forest and a steep, mist-shrouded bluff that plunged towards an unseen shoreline. The architecture was utilitarian Pacific Northwest gothic: clapboard storefronts with sagging porches, corrugated iron roofs weeping rust-colored tears, frame houses needing paint. A gas station with antique pumps stood sentinel at one end, opposite a diner optimistically named "The Fog Horn." A tavern called "The Loggers' Rest" occupied a prime spot, its neon sign flickering weakly in the gloom. Tiedeman's General Store looked like it hadn't changed its stock since the 1970s. Everything seemed damp, subdued, closed-in.

Few people were visible. An old man in stained overalls huddled under the gas station awning, smoking a cigarette and watching her approach with eyes narrowed against the rain. A figure bundled in yellow rain gear hurried across the street from the store, head down. There were pickup trucks parked haphazardly, mostly older models, mud-splattered and dented. Several bore the logo of defunct logging companies. The overall impression was one of slow decay, a community clinging on long after its primary reason for existing had dwindled.

Elise pulled into the gravel lot of the "End of the Trail Motel," a single-story, L-shaped structure painted a depressing shade of brown. It looked less like the end of the trail and more like the place trails came to die. Several vehicles were already parked there – a newer model black SUV with tinted windows that screamed 'federal agent' or 'private security,' a beat-up Ford Ranger pickup that looked like it wrestled bears for fun, and a sensible, slightly muddy Jeep Cherokee. Her team, presumably.

She cut the engine. The sudden silence was broken only by the drumming rain and the distant, mournful groan of what might have been a foghorn out on the water, hidden by the impenetrable mist clinging to the bluffs. Taking a deep breath, she mentally reviewed the roster provided by Kestrel:

- **Graves:** Mission Lead (Ex-Military). The voice on the phone. Presumably the owner of the black SUV.
- **Boone:** Tracker/Wilderness Expert. Possibly the Ford Ranger?
- **Nora:** Local Guide/Logistics. (No vehicle specified, maybe lived locally).
- **Jules:** Field Technician/Communications. (Jeep?)
- **Levi:** Medic/Geologist. (Also Jeep?)
- **Elise Holloway:** Wildlife Biologist/Ecological Lead. (Her rented Subaru).

A diverse group, assembled for... an environmental assessment. Right.

She unbuckled her seatbelt, pulled the hood of her rain jacket over her head, and braced herself. Time to meet the colleagues she'd be spending the next month with incommunicado in the deep wilderness. First impressions mattered, even on hush-hush potentially mythical creature hunts disguised as science.

As her boots hit the sodden gravel, the door to the motel office creaked open. A woman stood silhouetted in the dim light filtering from within. She was taller than Elise, built solid, with sharp features framed by dark, rain-plastered hair pulled back severely. She wore practical, waterproof gear – canvas trousers tucked into sturdy boots, a dark green oilskin jacket zipped high.

Her eyes, deep-set and watchful, scanned Elise from head to toe with an unnerving lack of expression.

"Dr. Holloway?" The voice was low, slightly rough, carrying easily over the rain. It held the flat, no-nonsense cadence of someone accustomed to the local environment.

"Yes," Elise confirmed, pushing her glasses up again as raindrops spattered the lenses. "And you must be Nora?"

The woman gave a curt nod. "Nora Tallsalt. Graves isn't here yet. Stuck haggling for permits down in Forks, last I heard. Should be here by evening. The others are in the common room. Got your key." She held out a key attached to a large, worn wooden fob carved crudely into the shape of a pine tree. Number 7.

"Thanks." Elise took the key. The wood felt smooth, almost oily. "Rough drive."

Nora's gaze flickered towards the wall of forest looming behind the motel, then back to Elise. A ghost of something – irony? Resignation? – touched her lips. "It only gets rougher from here, Doctor." There was no warmth in the statement, just fact.

"So I gather," Elise said, trying for a neutral tone. "The briefing materials emphasized the terrain difficulty."

"Briefing materials." Nora made a small sound, almost a scoff, quickly suppressed. "They tell you about the valley? The one that ain't on the maps?"

"They mentioned an 'uncharted drainage basin'," Elise quoted carefully.

Nora nodded slowly, her eyes holding Elise's. "There's reasons things stay uncharted 'round here, Dr. Holloway. Reasons maps leave places blank." She paused, letting the rain fill the silence. "People go into those woods back there," she gestured vaguely eastward with her chin, towards the deepest, darkest part of the forest visible through the deluge, "especially up past the old logging tracts, into the Hollows… sometimes they don't come out. Happens."

Elise felt a chill that had nothing to do with the damp air. This was the cageyness the outline mentioned. Delivered directly, without preamble. "Logging accidents? Exposure?" she offered, keeping her voice level, scientific.

"Sometimes," Nora conceded. "Weather turns fast. Ground gives way. Easy to get lost, break a leg. But sometimes… it's something else." She didn't elaborate. Her expression was closed, like a suddenly barred door. "Keys in the room. Drop your gear. Team's meeting in Room 1. End of the hall. Used to be the manager's suite, now it's our common room. Smells like mildew and regret, but it's dry."

With another curt nod, Nora turned and disappeared back into the dim recesses of the office, the door sighing shut behind her.

Elise stood for a moment in the drumming rain, the key heavy in her hand. *Something else.* The local warnings weren't just whispers; they were delivered face-to-face with unsettling conviction. She shook her head, trying to dispel the unease. Folklore was common in isolated communities, especially ones bordered by vast, imposing wilderness. It was a way of understanding the unknown, coping with disappearances that might simply be tragic accidents in treacherous terrain. Still, Nora's words lingered.

She quickly retrieved her essential gear from the Outback – her laptop bag, the Pelican case with her sensitive recording equipment, and a smaller duffel with immediate necessities. Lugging it towards Room 7, she noticed the curtains twitch in one of the other occupied rooms. Someone was watching. Bluffs End wasn't just remote; it felt… watchful. Suspicious.

Room 7 was exactly as expected. Functional, bordering on bleak. Two double beds with thin, patterned comforters, a scarred wooden desk and chair, a buzzing mini-fridge, and an ancient, boxy television bolted to the wall. The air was thick with the smell Nora had described – mildew, stale cigarette smoke, and damp carpet. A single window looked out onto the unrelenting curtain of rain and trees. Home sweet home for the foreseeable future, or at least until the expedition launched.

She dropped her bags, peeled off her drenched jacket, and ran a hand through her short, damp brown hair. Looking in the smudged mirror over the dresser, she saw a woman in her late thirties, pragmatic rather than pretty, with intelligent hazel eyes currently shadowed by fatigue and a growing sense of disquiet. She looked like what she was: a scientist out of her element, dropped into a situation that felt increasingly less like a standard field study.

Squaring her shoulders, she grabbed her waterproof notebook and pen. Time to meet the rest of the team. She locked her room carefully, pocketed the key, and walked down the covered walkway towards Room 1, the rhythmic drumming of rain on the roof her only accompaniment.

The door to Room 1 was slightly ajar. Muffled voices drifted out, punctuated by the clink of ceramic mugs. Elise paused, took another breath, and pushed it open.

The 'manager's suite' was marginally larger than her room, dominated by a long folding table covered in maps, printouts, and portable electronic devices charging via a tangle of cables plugged into a power strip. The same depressing décor prevailed, augmented by stacks of expedition supplies piled against one wall – dehydrated food packets, climbing ropes, first aid kits, water filters, solar panels. The air hummed faintly with the sound of charging electronics and smelled strongly of coffee.

Three people looked up as she entered.

Closest to the door, leaning back in a chair with his muddy boots propped carelessly on another, was a man who could only be Boone. He fit the 'tracker' archetype almost perfectly. Mid-forties maybe, lean and weathered, with sun-creased eyes the color of faded denim. His brown hair was shaggy, receding slightly at the temples, and a few days' worth of stubble shadowed his jaw. He wore worn jeans, a flannel shirt under a canvas vest, and had an air of relaxed competence, like he was deeply familiar with being uncomfortable. He held a steaming mug and offered Elise a slow, easygoing nod. His Ford Ranger, no doubt.

Sitting at the table, hunched over a laptop displaying complex topographical software, was a younger man, likely Jules. He looked to be in his late twenties, wiry, with restless energy. He had dark, close-cropped hair, wore technical outdoor gear that looked brand new, and peered at the screen through stylish, rectangular glasses. He gave Elise a quick, distracted smile before his attention snapped back to the elevation lines on the map display. Definitely the Jeep Cherokee.

Standing near the coffee percolator, carefully checking the contents of a large, professional-looking medical kit, was the third man – Levi. He appeared to be somewhere between Boone and Jules in age, solidly built, with neatly trimmed brown hair and a clean-shaven, serious face. His movements were precise, methodical. He wore practical cargo pants and a fleece jacket. When he looked up, his eyes were calm and direct. He gave Elise a polite, reserved nod. Also the Jeep Cherokee, she guessed, co-owned or co-rented.

"Dr. Holloway," Boone said, his voice a low drawl that contrasted with Nora's clipped tones. He didn't get up. "Pull up a patch of gloom. Coffee's fresh, if you trust the machine. Name's Boone."

"Elise," she replied, stepping further into the room and letting the door click shut behind her. "Good to meet you." She moved towards the table, setting down her notebook.

"Jules," the younger man offered, tapping a final key before turning his full attention to her. "Field tech, comms, drone pilot extraordinaire – weather permitting, which it currently is not." He gestured towards the rain-lashed window with a wry grin. "Levi handles the rocks and the stitches."

Levi closed the medkit with a quiet snap. "Medic and geologist," he clarified, his voice steady. "Welcome, Doctor. Glad you made it through that downpour."

"Just barely," Elise admitted, pouring herself a mug of the dubious coffee. It smelled burnt, but it was hot. "Is Nora joining us?"

"Came and went," Boone said, taking a sip from his mug. "Dropped off the key, gave her standard 'don't piss off the woods' speech, vanished back into the mist. She's local Tallsalt tribe. Knows this area better than her own reflection. Doesn't mean she likes talking about it. Especially not to outsiders."

"She seemed… direct," Elise said carefully.

Boone chuckled softly. "That's Nora. Direct as a falling tree. If she tells you not to step somewhere, you'd be wise to listen."

Jules swiveled in his chair. "So, you're the primate expert, right? Kestrel was pretty specific about needing someone with your background."

Elise took a tentative sip of the coffee. It tasted like despair. "My PhD focused on behavioral ecology of Cercopithecinae in Central Africa, and I've done post-doc work on gibbon vocalizations in Southeast Asia," she explained, keeping it factual. "This biome is new territory for me, but ecological principles are broadly applicable." She decided against mentioning the 'unconfirmed speciation' angle just yet. Let Graves handle the formal briefing.

"Right," Jules said, though he looked faintly disappointed, as if expecting stories of charging silverbacks. "Well, this assessment should be interesting. The satellite imagery shows some seriously anomalous geological features in the target valley. Major fault lines, unusual mineral signatures according to the initial remote sensing data Levi's looked at."

Levi nodded. "The topography is rugged, unstable. Significant erosion potential. That alone makes access difficult, which likely explains the lack of previous survey work." He spoke with the precision of a scientist, focusing on verifiable data. Elise found his approach grounding.

Boone stretched, his chair creaking ominously. "Forget the geology. The ground's shaky 'cause it wants to swallow you whole. Place has bad energy. Always has."

Elise raised an eyebrow. "Bad energy?"

Boone met her gaze squarely, his easygoing manner momentarily replaced by something serious. "Call it what you want. Locals have stories going back generations. Things you hear at night. Things you glimpse between the trees. Shadows that move too fast. Places where the birds don't sing." He shrugged, the seriousness receding. "Maybe it's just the wind whistling through the crags. Or maybe it ain't."

Jules rolled his eyes, but Elise noticed he didn't entirely dismiss Boone's comment. Levi remained impassive, carefully arranging charging cables on the table.

"The foundation mentioned access will be challenging," Elise said, steering the conversation back to logistics. "Have they provided detailed route plans?"

"Graves has the final route," Boone answered. "He's meeting with the Forest Service, smoothing feathers. We're technically operating under a research permit tied to the university – the cover story has layers, apparently. But the real entry point is off-trail, starting from an old, decommissioned logging road way back east."

"Decommissioned means 'likely impassable without considerable effort'," Levi added dryly. "Expect creek crossings, washouts, deadfall. We'll be earning that stipend."

"Hence Boone," Jules grinned, jerking a thumb towards the tracker. "He's supposedly part-man, part-mountain goat, part-bloodhound."

Boone ignored him, finishing his coffee. "Just means I know how to read the damn woods, unlike some tech-heads who can't find north without a satellite." He gave Jules a pointed look, though there was no real malice in it.

The dynamic was becoming clearer: Jules the enthusiastic techie, Levi the calm professional, Boone the seasoned cynic grounded in practical experience. And Graves, the unseen leader, pulling the strings. Elise wondered how her own scientific approach would mesh with this group, especially Boone's more intuitive, anecdotal style.

"Well," she said, deciding to contribute something concrete. "My focus will be on transects, setting up camera traps and bioacoustic recorders along promising gradients. I'll need input on trap placement to maximize coverage while minimizing habitat disturbance."

"Happy to help plot potential hotspots based on terrain and water sources," Levi offered.

"And I can help lug the gear," Jules added cheerfully. "As long as Boone doesn't make me carry the heaviest pack again."

Boone grunted. "Builds character."

They spent the next hour discussing equipment checklists, preliminary map reconnaissance, and potential challenges – weather, terrain, gear malfunction. The conversation stayed within the bounds of a normal, albeit difficult, ecological survey. No one mentioned Bigfoot. Yet, the undercurrent was there – in Boone's oblique warnings, in the excessive preparations, in the very existence of this secretive, high-budget expedition to an uncharted valley known locally for disappearances.

Around four o'clock, Elise decided to brave the rain again and visit Tiedeman's General Store for a few personal supplies – extra batteries, some chocolate, maybe a local map not dependent on satellite signals. The excuse was flimsy; mostly, she wanted to gauge the town's atmosphere herself, away from the contained bubble of the expedition team.

Pulling her hood back up, she stepped out into the relentless grey. The rain had eased slightly, but the air was still cold and heavy with moisture. The main street was even quieter than before. The lights inside The Fog Horn diner cast a warm, inviting yellow glow, a stark contrast to the gloom outside. On impulse, she decided coffee and maybe a slice of pie was a better goal than batteries.

Pushing open the diner door, she was met with a blast of warm air smelling of frying bacon, old coffee, and damp wool. A bell jangled overhead, announcing her arrival with unnecessary enthusiasm. The diner was small, classic Americana: booths with cracked red vinyl seats, a long formica counter with spinning stools, faded photos of logging crews and prize-winning fish tacked to the wood-paneled walls.

Two men sat at the counter, both clad in plaid flannel and suspenders, nursing mugs of coffee. They stopped talking mid-sentence and turned to look at her, their expressions guarded, incurious. Behind the counter, a stout woman with tightly permed grey hair and formidable forearms wiped down the surface with a damp cloth. Her eyes, magnified by thick glasses, were sharp and missed nothing.

Elise felt a prickle of awareness, the distinct sensation of being an outsider under scrutiny. She slid onto a stool at the far end of the counter, dripping water onto the linoleum floor.

"Coffee, black," she said to the woman, offering a polite smile that wasn't entirely returned.

The woman poured a mug from a glass carafe on a hotplate and slid it towards her without a word. Elise wrapped her cold hands around the warmth. The silence stretched, broken only by the hiss of the rain outside and the hum of the ancient coffee machine. The men at the counter hadn't resumed their conversation; they seemed to be listening.

"Heard you folks are heading up into the back country," the woman said finally, her voice flat. She wasn't asking a question.

"Yes," Elise confirmed. "Doing some environmental study work for a foundation." She kept her tone light, professional.

The woman snorted softly, resuming her wiping. "Foundation folk. University types. Forest Service. Always pokin' around where they ain't welcome."

One of the men at the counter shifted on his stool. "That valley back there... best left alone," he muttered, not looking at Elise. He had a deeply lined face and eyes that looked permanently weary.

"Something bad in those woods," the other man added, his voice low. "My cousin's boy, Danny? Went deer hunting up past the old Cougar Creek cut five years back. Never came home. Found his rifle, pack was torn to shreds. No sign of him."

"Bears?" Elise asked quietly, trying to sound sympathetic rather than dismissive.

The first man shook his head grimly. "Warn't no bear. Tracks they found… too big. Wrong shape. Sheriff wrote it off as 'lost, presumed deceased.' But folks 'round here know."

"Know what?" Elise prompted gently.

The woman behind the counter slammed a clean mug down. "Know that some places… you just don't go," she said sharply, her eyes fixing on Elise. "That valley, the one the loggers called the 'Hollow Ground' back in the day before they pulled out? It ain't natural. Things live there. Old things. Things that don't like bein' disturbed." Her voice dropped lower. "You wanna do your 'study'? Fine. Stick to the marked trails. Stay outta the deep timber, especially after dark. Don't go looking for trouble, 'cause up there… trouble *will* find you."

The warning hung in the air, heavy and sincere. It echoed Nora's words, Boone's insinuations. This wasn't just rumour; it was deeply ingrained local belief, born from disappearances and things left unexplained.

Elise finished her coffee quickly, the burnt taste barely registering now. She paid, leaving a generous tip, acutely aware of the eyes following her as she pushed back out into the rain. The warmth of the diner felt a hundred miles away.

Back in her motel room, the gloom seemed to have deepened. She unpacked her gear methodically, laying out instruments, checking batteries, organizing field notebooks. The scientific process, the familiar routine, was a comfort, an anchor against the unsettling tide of local folklore and the mission's inherent strangeness.

She sat at the desk and opened her laptop, intending to review topographic data, but found herself staring at the blank screen instead. *Things that don't like being disturbed. Tracks too big.* Nonsense, of course. Anthropomorphic projection onto natural predators or simple, tragic accidents in a dangerous wilderness. Bears, cougars, treacherous terrain, sudden storms – the Olympics had plenty of real dangers without invoking shadowy monsters.

And yet... the Kestrel Foundation. Graves. The 'unconfirmed primate' addendum. The insistence on secrecy. The team composition – a tracker known for his intuition, an ex-military leader, a tech expert, a medic. It felt over-equipped for a simple environmental survey. It felt... prepared. For what?

She pulled out the manila envelope again, rereading the sparse lines of the official brief. *"Preliminary Ecological Assessment..."* It seemed thinner now, more transparent. What lay beneath the carefully worded scientific objectives? Was Graves simply a wealthy eccentric chasing a legend? Or did the Kestrel Foundation know something? Had they received credible evidence, something beyond fuzzy videos and campfire tales, prompting this expensive, clandestine operation?

A gust of wind slammed rain against the window, rattling the glass. Outside, the forest stood immense and silent, soaking up the fading light. The mist swirling around the bluffs seemed thicker, hiding the world beyond the town's edge.

Elise shivered, despite the room's stagnant air. She was a scientist. She dealt in data, evidence, observation. But here, on the edge of the known world, in a town steeped in fear and guarded by an ancient, indifferent wilderness, the line between scientific inquiry and something far older, far stranger, felt disturbingly blurred.

The expedition hadn't even begun, and already the woods felt like they were watching. Waiting. And for the first time, Elise allowed herself to consider, truly consider, the possibility that the 'unconfirmed primate speciation' wasn't just a wild contingency. What if it was the entire point? What if they were walking into a place where myths had teeth?

She pushed the thought away, closing her laptop with a decisive click. Speculation was useless. Tomorrow, Graves would arrive. The briefing would happen. And then, they would go into the woods. Whatever secrets the Kestrel Foundation held, whatever mysteries hid in that uncharted valley, they would confront them soon enough.

But as she sat there, listening to the rain and the profound quiet of Bluffs End settling into night, Elise couldn't shake the feeling that they weren't just going to study the wilderness. They were walking willingly into its oldest, darkest heart. And Nora's final words echoed in her mind: *Trouble will find you.*

The thought kept her awake long after the lights in the End of the Trail Motel blinked out, leaving only the oppressive darkness and the endless, whispering rain.

Chapter 2: The Briefing

Morning arrived not with sunlight, but with a subtle lessening of the oppressive grey. The rain had subsided overnight, leaving behind a world sodden and dripping. Mist clung stubbornly to the trees and ghosted over the gravel lot of the End of the Trail Motel, muffling sounds and adding another layer of isolation to Bluffs End. Inside the common room, the air was thick with the re-stewed aroma of coffee and the low hum of electronics.

Elise had slept poorly, haunted by fragmented dreams of shifting shadows and echoing footsteps just beyond the reach of firelight. She joined Jules and Levi at the long table, nursing a mug of the motel's corrosive coffee. Jules was already engrossed in calibrating a handheld sensor device, murmuring specs under his breath, while Levi methodically cleaned and checked a compact satellite phone – one Graves was supposedly bringing prototypes of. Boone's chair was empty; through the window, Elise saw him outside talking quietly with Nora near his truck. Their conversation looked serious, their body language mirroring the damp gloom – heads bowed slightly, gestures economical. Whatever local knowledge Nora possessed, she seemed to be sharing it directly with the man most attuned to the woods.

"Morning," Elise offered, trying to inject some normalcy into the charged atmosphere.

"Morning, Doctor," Levi replied, looking up briefly. "Sleep okay?" His tone was neutral, but his eyes held a hint of professional assessment, the medic checking for signs of stress.

"Fine," Elise lied, pushing aside the lingering unease. "Just eager to get the official brief."

Jules looked up from his device, grinning. "Yeah, waiting for the man himself. Boone said Graves is ex-Special Forces or something. Bet he arrives in a black helicopter, rappels down."

Levi gave a small shake of his head. "His file listed 'advanced field operations and logistical management'. Could mean anything from supply sergeant to something more kinetic. Best not to make assumptions."

"Still betting on the helicopter," Jules muttered, returning to his calibration.

They didn't have long to wait. Around 8:30 AM, the crunch of tires on wet gravel announced a new arrival. It wasn't a helicopter. The black SUV Elise had noted yesterday – a late model Chevy Suburban with government-style tinted windows – pulled smoothly into a spot near the office. The driver's door opened, and a man emerged who seemed to command the space around him simply by occupying it.

This had to be Graves.

He was perhaps fifty, trim and fit, with close-cropped grey hair cut with military precision. He wore expensive, high-performance outdoor gear – Arcteryx jacket, tactical pants – that looked practical yet subtly screamed 'budget no object'. His face was sharp-featured, his jaw set, his eyes pale blue and unnervingly direct. They scanned the motel layout, Boone and Nora by the truck, the common room window, assessing everything with swift, practiced efficiency. There was an air of contained energy about him, a tightly coiled stillness that suggested impatience with inefficiency and zero tolerance for bullshit. He moved with an economy of motion, retrieving a heavy-duty Pelican case and a sleek aluminum briefcase from the back of the SUV.

Boone and Nora walked over to meet him. From the window, Elise couldn't hear their words, but the interaction was brief. Graves nodded curtly, gestured towards the common room, and then strode purposefully towards the walkway, leaving Boone and Nora to follow a step behind. Boone's expression was unreadable; Nora's was etched with a familiar stony reservation.

The door to Room 1 opened, and Graves filled the entrance. His gaze swept over Elise, Jules, and Levi, lingered for a fraction of a second on the haphazard arrangement of gear, then settled on the table.

"Doctor Holloway, Mr. Jensen, Mr. Clarke," he said, his voice exactly as Elise remembered from the call – clipped, authoritative, devoid of warmth. He nodded fractionally to each in turn. "I'm Graves. Apologies for the delay. Permitting bureaucracy is its own special kind of hostile environment." He placed his cases on the only clear section of the table. "Boone, Nora, join us. Close the door."

Boone ambled in, taking his usual chair, while Nora stood near the entrance, arms crossed, her presence a silent, watchful weight in the room. Graves remained standing, commanding attention without raising his voice.

"Right," Graves began, opening the aluminum briefcase. It wasn't filled with papers, but with neatly recessed slots containing a projector, a laptop slimmer than Jules', and several encrypted hard drives. "Let's dispense with the preamble. You've all received the baseline ecological assessment parameters from the Kestrel Foundation. That work is essential, and your scientific findings will be meticulously documented and submitted through the agreed channels."

He paused, letting that sink in, his eyes meeting each of theirs in turn. "However," he continued, his tone dropping slightly, becoming more intense, "that is not the primary operational driver for this expedition. It is the necessary cover for a more sensitive, more urgent investigation."

He connected his laptop to the small, powerful projector, which whirred to life, casting a bright square onto the grimy paint of the opposite wall. Jules leaned forward, intrigued. Levi sat a little straighter. Boone watched Graves, his expression still carefully neutral, but his eyes sharp.

Graves clicked a key, and an aerial map appeared on the wall – high-resolution satellite imagery, far clearer than anything publicly available. It showed the dense, convoluted terrain east of Bluffs End, a chaotic tapestry of green ridges and shadowed valleys. He used a laser pointer to indicate a specific area deep within the forest, a convergence of steep-walled canyons and densely forested basins noticeably absent of logging roads or any sign of human intrusion.

"This," Graves stated, circling the area with the red dot, "is our Area of Operations. Designated AO 'Hollow.' Approximately fifteen square miles of uncharted, unsurveyed territory. Officially, it doesn't exist in detail on any geological or forestry map due to extreme terrain and inaccessibility. Unofficially, it's been studiously avoided for decades."

He switched the image to a topographical overlay, highlighting the dramatic elevation changes, the sheer cliffs, the narrow choke points. "Access is via decommissioned logging spurs here," he pointed to a spot miles away, "followed by an arduous trek through dense undergrowth and unstable slopes. We establish a base camp here, deploy sensor grids, and conduct systematic exploration of the primary valley system."

So far, it sounded like a difficult but plausible research expedition setup. Then Graves changed the image again. This time, it was a series of blurred, obviously copied documents – missing person reports.

"Our primary objective," Graves said, his voice hardening, "is to investigate, locate, and if possible, ascertain the fate of multiple individuals who have disappeared without explanation within or near the AO over the past fifteen years."

He brought up the first file: A hiker named Sarah Jenkins, missing since 2009. Last seen heading towards the old Cougar Creek trail, near the edge of the AO. Search teams found her abandoned campsite, food untouched, sleeping bag still rolled. No sign of struggle, no tracks indicating animal attack, no trace of her.

Second file: Two surveyors, Marcus Bellweather and Alan Choi, contracted by a timber company in 2014 to do preliminary boundary work near the southern edge of the AO. Their vehicle was found locked on a disused spur road. Their equipment was located a mile further in, neatly stacked. No sign of them.

Third file: A geology student, David Chen, conducting independent thesis research on unique rock formations on the AO's western ridge in 2018. His advisor reported him missing when he failed to check in. His field notes were found near a creek bed, the last entry describing 'anomalous bio-acoustic phenomena' and a feeling of being watched. No sign of him.

Fourth file: Daniel 'Danny' Clarke, vanished in 2019. Graves paused, his gaze flicking briefly towards Levi. "No relation," he clarified coolly, though Elise saw Levi tense slightly at the shared surname. "Local hunter. Went missing near the northern perimeter. Rifle and damaged pack located. Extensive search yielded nothing. You may have heard locals mention this case." He nodded towards the man mentioned in the diner yesterday.

"Total of five individuals," Graves summarized, the laser pointer sweeping across the names. "Officially listed as 'lost/exposure' or 'unresolved disappearances.' Unofficially..." He let the word hang. "Unofficially, the pattern, the location, and certain recovered evidence fragments which were suppressed from public reports, suggest something else."

The room was silent except for the hum of the projector and the distant drip of water outside. Elise felt a knot tighten in her stomach. This wasn't just folklore anymore. These were documented cases, recent disappearances, linked directly to their destination. The mission suddenly felt far more dangerous, the 'ecological assessment' cover absurdly thin.

"Suppressed evidence?" Jules asked, his earlier excitement replaced by a frown. "Like what?"

Graves hesitated for a fraction of a second. "Fragments of material exhibiting unusual tensile strength. Trace organic samples that defied easy categorization by state labs. Let's leave it at that for now. The point is, there's a consistent pattern of vanishings centered on this valley, lacking clear explanations."

Boone finally spoke, his voice quiet but resonant in the tense room. "So Kestrel ain't paying top dollar for us to count spotted owls. They're paying us to figure out what happened to these folks. Or maybe find out if what happened to them is gonna happen to us."

Graves met Boone's challenging gaze. "Our operational security protocols, equipment, and personnel expertise are significantly higher than those of recreational hikers or standard search and rescue teams, Boone. We are prepared for contingencies. The objective is reconnaissance, investigation, and data collection, not confrontation."

"Contingencies," Boone repeated softly, his tone skeptical. "Good word."

Graves ignored the implied criticism and changed the image on the wall. It now showed a series of stills – grainy, low-light images captured from game cameras or hiker photos, notoriously ambiguous. A dark shape moving behind trees. An unnaturally large impression in mud. A fleeting silhouette against a moonlit ridge. The usual 'cryptid' fare Elise had seen debunked countless times online.

"Which brings us," Graves continued, his voice regaining its neutral, professional tone, "to the secondary objective, which the Foundation believes may be directly linked to the primary." He looked directly at Elise. "Dr. Holloway, your expertise was specifically requested due to persistent, albeit unverified, reports emanating from this region for decades. Reports concerning sightings of a large, bipedal primate unknown to science."

There it was. Bigfoot. Sasquatch. Not just a whisper, but an official secondary objective, linked potentially to disappearances.

Elise felt a strange mix of vindication and disbelief. So the rumours, the secrecy, the budget – it *was* about this. Yet, presented so baldly, linked to missing persons, it felt both more absurd and more chilling.

"With all due respect, Mr. Graves," Elise said, choosing her words carefully, forcing her voice to remain steady and scientific, "the evidence for such a creature existing, particularly a primate of that projected size in a North American Holocene ecosystem, is nonexistent in the established scientific record. Anecdotal accounts, footprint casts of dubious origin, and blurry photographs are not data."

Graves nodded curtly, seemingly anticipating her skepticism. "Understood, Doctor. And the Kestrel Foundation is not asking you to 'believe.' It is asking you, as part of this team, to apply rigorous scientific methodology to *verify or refute* these claims. Your secondary objective is to document, analyze, and collect verifiable evidence *if, and only if,* encountered. High-resolution imaging, audio recording, environmental DNA sampling if possible, scat or hair analysis – your standard biological survey toolkit, applied to a unique potential subject."

He keyed another command, and a highly detailed 3D rendering of a primate skull appeared – large sagittal crest, heavy brow ridges, powerful jaw. It looked like a composite, blending features of *Gigantopithecus blacki* with other pongids. "Foundation analysts," Graves said coolly, "have theorized that if such a relict hominoid or pongid relative exists, this isolated, resource-rich valley system offers the most plausible habitat niche for its survival undetected. Deep, inaccessible terrain, ample food sources, minimal human encroachment until recently."

Elise stared at the skull rendering. As a biologist, her mind immediately cataloged the inconsistencies, the ecological improbabilities. A breeding population would require significant numbers, a huge territory, massive caloric intake. Where was the fossil evidence? The confirmed genetic material? Yet… Graves presented it so calmly, backed by the Foundation's resources, linking it to real disappearances. What if…? No. Stick to the facts.

"So," Jules interjected, looking from the skull rendering to Graves, a flicker of awe or perhaps nervous excitement in his eyes. "You're saying... you think *Bigfoot* is responsible for those people disappearing?"

"We are investigating the disappearances," Graves corrected firmly. "And we are investigating the *possibility* of an undocumented species in the AO. Correlation is not causation, Mr. Jensen. We gather data; we do not jump to conclusions. However, the possibility of an unknown, potentially territorial large predator – primate or otherwise – cannot be discounted given the circumstances."

Levi spoke, his voice calm and practical. "What are our rules of engagement if we do encounter large, potentially aggressive fauna? Unknown or otherwise?"

"Standard wilderness protocols apply," Graves answered immediately. "Avoidance is primary. Deterrence secondary – noise, light. Defensive measures only as a last resort and only under direct threat to life. This is a scientific investigation, Mr. Clarke, not a hunting party. We are equipped with non-lethal deterrents – high-lumen strobes, acoustic projectors, bear spray. Lethal force," his eyes briefly scanned each of them, "is authorized *only* in an undeniable, life-threatening scenario, and its use would necessitate immediate mission abort and extraction, assuming communication is possible. Our priority is data collection and team safety."

Elise felt a measure of relief at the emphasis on non-lethal methods, though the mere mention of lethal force authorization underlined the perceived seriousness of the potential risk.

She looked towards Nora, who had remained silent, her expression unreadable, arms still crossed. "Nora," Elise asked directly, "you know this area, the local stories. What do the Tallsalt legends say about this valley, about these disappearances?"

Nora unfolded her arms, her dark eyes meeting Elise's. Her gaze was heavy, steeped in generations of coexistence with the forest and its mysteries. "Our stories don't talk about 'undocumented primates,' Doctor," she said, her voice low and steady. "They talk about the *Stick-shí'nač* – the Forest People, the ones who watch from the shadows. They are guardians of the deep places. Old. Powerful. They tolerate the edges, the logged lands, the places humans have scarred. But the deep valleys, the sacred groves... those are theirs."

She paused, her gaze sweeping over the maps and the photos on the wall. "The Hollow Ground, we call it *snaxʷalxʷ čał* – the place where echoes stay. It's where the guardians are strongest. They don't like intruders. They don't like noise, or disrespect. Disappearances..." She shrugged slightly, a gesture not of indifference, but of grim acceptance. "Sometimes people get lost. Sometimes the weather takes them. And sometimes... they ignore the warnings. They push too far into places they weren't meant to be. The Stick-shí'nač... they enforce boundaries."

Her words fell into the room with a weight that scientific jargon couldn't replicate. It wasn't presented as myth, but as established fact within her cultural understanding of the landscape. Graves listened impassively, neither endorsing nor dismissing her statement.

"Thank you, Nora," Graves said formally. "Your cultural knowledge and terrain expertise are invaluable assets. Adherence to Leave No Trace principles and minimizing our environmental impact is paramount." He reframed her warning into procedural terms.

He spent the next thirty minutes outlining operational details: communication protocols involving the prototype sat phones supposedly capable of penetrating dense canopy (Jules looked skeptical but intrigued), data handling procedures (all raw data encrypted, uploaded directly to Kestrel servers via timed burst transmission), emergency rally points, medical evacuation plans (reliant on Graves' sat phone connection to a private Kestrel asset), chain of command (Graves, then Boone, then Levi).

Questions were fielded with crisp efficiency. Jules asked about drone deployment restrictions (visual line-of-sight only, weather dependent, minimal flight time to conserve power and reduce noise signature). Levi inquired about specific geological hazards noted on the topo maps (Graves confirmed awareness, emphasizing cautious route selection). Elise asked about sampling protocols for potential eDNA collection (Graves provided surprisingly detailed guidelines, suggesting the Foundation had considered this thoroughly).

Boone asked only one question. "This Kestrel Foundation. Who are they, really? All this gear, the secrecy, the suppressed reports... This ain't some rich folks' hobby club."

Graves' expression tightened almost imperceptibly. "The Kestrel Foundation is a private entity dedicated to investigating complex environmental and scientific anomalies through discreet field operations. Their funding sources and full charter are confidential. Our focus is the mission they've assigned us." It was a non-answer, delivered with absolute finality. Boone held his gaze for a long moment, then leaned back, folding his arms. He didn't look satisfied, but he didn't push further.

Finally, Graves switched off the projector, plunging the room back into the ambient grey light filtering through the window. The absence of the bright images seemed to make the room feel smaller, more claustrophobic.

"Gear check and final packing this afternoon," Graves instructed. "Load out tomorrow morning, 0600 sharp. Vehicles staged at the trailhead by 0800. From there, we're on foot. Radio silence except for scheduled check-ins or emergencies. Any critical issues, raise them now. Otherwise, prepare yourselves. We're entering an environment that demands utmost focus and discipline."

He began packing his equipment back into its cases with swift, precise movements. The formal briefing was over.

The team members looked at each other, a new tension humming between them. The mission parameters were clear now, far stranger and more dangerous than the cover story suggested. Disappearances. A potential cryptid. Suppressed evidence. Local legends of powerful forest guardians.

Elise felt her initial skepticism warring fiercely with a burgeoning, uncomfortable sense of... possibility. Not belief, not yet, but an acknowledgment that *something* unusual was happening in that valley, something that warranted this level of secrecy and investment. Her scientific mind still screamed 'improbable,' but the combined weight of the disappearances, the local conviction, Nora's gravity, and the Foundation's commitment was hard to dismiss entirely. And beneath the skepticism, the intrigue remained, stronger now. An uncharted valley potentially holding secrets far older than logging maps? A genuine ecological enigma, even if it wasn't Sasquatch? As a field biologist, the lure of the truly unknown, the chance to explore a place outside the established lines of scientific knowledge, was potent. It was a dangerous curiosity, perhaps, but it was there.

Jules looked simultaneously thrilled and nervous, already fiddling with comms gear, likely imagining the data streams they might collect. Levi maintained his professional calm, but his gaze kept drifting towards the topo maps, assessing risks. Boone's expression was grimly accepting, as if the briefing had merely confirmed what he already suspected. And Nora... Nora just looked weary, like someone about to guide outsiders into a place she respected deeply and feared rightly, knowing they likely wouldn't grasp the true nature of the risks until it was too late.

Graves snapped his briefcase shut. "Dismissed until 1600 hours. Be ready." He gave a final, curt nod and left the room as abruptly as he had entered it, leaving the rest of them in the heavy silence, the unasked questions, and the undeniable weight of the mission they had just formally accepted. The woods outside dripped, waiting. The Hollow Ground beckoned.

Chapter 3: Into the Woods

The departure from Bluffs End happened under a shroud of predawn grey, the same colour as the exhaust fumes puffing from the idling engines of Boone's Ranger and Graves' imposing Suburban. The rain had held off, but the air hung thick and cold, carrying the pervasive scent of damp earth and woodsmoke from a lone chimney somewhere in the sleeping town. Lights flickered on in a few houses, casting pale yellow rectangles onto the wet pavement, but mostly Bluffs End remained dark, seemingly indifferent to their leaving.

Inside the common room, now stripped bare of the maps and sensitive equipment, the atmosphere was muted but charged. Final gear checks were performed with grim efficiency under Graves' watchful eye. Packs, already bulging, were weighed, straps adjusted, contents double-checked against the master list. Elise hefted her own pack – a serious internal frame model loaded with her personal gear, share of the communal food and shelter, plus the specialized bio-sampling kits, weatherproof camera housings, and bioacoustic recorders. It felt brutally heavy, a dead weight pulling at her shoulders even before the trek began. Forty-five pounds, maybe fifty? She'd carried similar loads before, but never with such a palpable sense of entering the unknown, compounded by the cryptic briefing and the lingering warnings.

Jules was practically vibrating with nervous energy, re-coiling cables with obsessive neatness, while Levi calmly repacked his already immaculate medical kit for the third time. Boone moved with his usual economy of motion, cinching down gear on his pack, his face set in familiar lines of weathered competence. Nora Tallsalt stood slightly apart, watching the proceedings, her oilskin jacket dark against the gloom, offering no commentary but missing nothing.

"Load out in five," Graves announced, snapping shut a waterproof case containing sensitive electronics. "Vehicles depart 0600 precisely. We have a hard schedule to maintain."

Boone glanced up from adjusting a strap. "Schedule won't mean squat if someone twists an ankle pushin' too hard on slick ground before we even hit the real rough stuff, Graves."

Graves' gaze sharpened. "The schedule incorporates contingency time, Boone. Discipline and maintaining pace are crucial in the initial stages. We need to make Camp One before nightfall."

"Camp One ain't goin' nowhere," Boone countered mildly, but with an underlying firmness. "Best get there in one piece. This ain't a forced march."

"It's an expedition with objectives and a timeline," Graves clipped back. "Adhere to the pace I set." He turned away, effectively ending the discussion, and began supervising Jules and Levi loading gear into the Suburban.

Elise exchanged a quick look with Boone. His expression was unreadable, but she sensed the friction – Graves' rigid adherence to military-style planning versus Boone's deep-seated understanding of wilderness rhythms, where pushing too hard could be more dangerous than falling slightly behind schedule. It was a conflict brewing even before their boots hit the trail proper.

The loading was swift and practiced. Personal packs went into the vehicles for the drive to the trailhead; heavier communal gear like ropes, emergency shelters, and bulk rations were divided between the Suburban and the Ranger's truck bed, covered securely with tarps. Elise climbed into the back seat of the Suburban alongside Levi, her own field kit tucked securely at her feet. Jules rode shotgun, already tapping away at a ruggedized tablet displaying offline maps. Graves drove, handling the large SUV with confident precision. Ahead of them, Boone pulled out in his Ranger, Nora beside him in the passenger seat, guiding the way.

They rolled through the silent main street of Bluffs End, past the darkened diner and the general store, the only sound the swish of tires on wet pavement. As they passed the town limits sign – *"You Are Now Leaving Bluffs End. Drive Carefully."* – Elise felt a definitive sense of crossing a threshold. Behind them lay the last outpost of tenuous civilization; ahead lay… the Hollow Ground and whatever secrets it held.

The highway tarmac quickly gave way to paved logging roads, then gravel ones marked with company acronyms and section numbers. They drove east, deeper into the foothills, the mountains bulking larger ahead, their peaks hidden in low-slung clouds. The forest grew denser, taller, the trees pressing in on either side. After an hour, Boone's Ranger turned onto a much narrower, unpaved track, barely more than two ruts overgrown with grass and encroaching salmonberry bushes. This was clearly one of the 'decommissioned' spurs Graves had mentioned.

The ride immediately became punishing. The Suburban's suspension absorbed the worst of it, but the vehicle rocked and lurched violently over deep potholes, washouts, and slick, muddy patches. Branches scraped against the tinted windows with sharp screeches, like claws trying to find purchase. Levi gripped the door handle, his knuckles white. Even Jules put down his tablet, bracing himself. Graves navigated it all with intense focus, his jaw tight, making small, precise adjustments to the steering wheel.

They crawled along like this for another forty-five minutes, penetrating deeper into an area that felt utterly deserted. No sign of recent logging, no tire tracks other than their own faint impressions disappearing behind them. Just the endless, dripping green wall of the forest. Finally, Boone's Ranger ahead pulled over in a slightly wider, boggy clearing choked with ferns and devil's club. The track ended here, dissolving into impenetrable undergrowth and the rising slope of the mountainside. This was it. The end of the road.

"Alright," Graves announced as he cut the engine. The sudden silence roared in Elise's ears, broken only by the frantic hammering of a woodpecker somewhere nearby and the slow drip of water from saturated branches. "Gear out. Packs on. Fifteen minutes to final prep. Check water bladders, secure loose straps. From here, we move."

The air outside was cold and startlingly fresh, thick with the complex perfume of moss, decaying leaves, resin, and wet earth. Unloading the gear felt different now. The packs seemed heavier, the equipment more vital. This wasn't practice; it was the start. Every ounce counted. Elise swung her pack onto her back, grunting softly at the weight settling onto her hips and shoulders. She adjusted the straps, tightening the hip belt until it bit comfortably, transferring the load. Around her, the others did the same, movements efficient, minimal chatter.

Nora conferred briefly with Boone, pointing towards a barely visible game trail leading uphill into the tangled vegetation. "Follows the old skidder track mostly," Elise heard her say to him. "Gets steep quick. Watch for loose scree on the south faces after the first ridge."

Boone nodded, scanning the dense woods ahead with narrowed eyes, already reading the landscape. Graves strode over, checking his GPS unit against the map displayed on Jules' tablet.

"Route confirms," Graves stated. "Due east-northeast for three klicks, follow the ridge spine, then descend towards the creek drainage identified as Point Alpha. Maintain single file, five-meter interval. Boone, you take point with Nora. I'll take rear guard. Communications check."

Jules held up a rugged handheld radio. "Comms check, Graves."

Graves clicked his own radio clipped to his pack strap. "Graves, loud and clear. Standard rotation check-in every thirty minutes. Any deviation, immediate report. Move out."

With a final nod from Boone, he and Nora melted into the undergrowth, moving with a fluid quietness that belied the difficult terrain. Elise fell into line behind Levi, with Jules ahead of him. Graves brought up the rear.

The moment they stepped off the remnants of the road and into the true forest, the world changed. The thin grey light dimmed instantly under the dense canopy of towering Douglas firs, Sitka spruce, and western red cedars. The ground underfoot was a spongy, uneven carpet of moss, decaying needles, and tangled roots slick with moisture. Immense ferns brushed against their legs, soaking their pants below the knee. Progress was immediately slower, more demanding. They weren't hiking *on* a trail; they were pushing *through* the wilderness.

The first hour was a relentless uphill climb. The barely-there game trail switchbacked steeply, forcing them to use hands occasionally to pull themselves up over mossy logs the size of small cars or navigate sections where the earth had sloughed away, leaving muddy, treacherous footing. Elise focused on her breathing, finding a rhythm, placing her feet carefully, intensely aware of the weight on her back. Sweat beaded on her forehead despite the cool air, plastering strands of hair to her temples. The sounds were of exertion – heavy breathing, the rhythmic crunch of boots on detritus, the swish of Gore-Tex, the occasional clink of gear.

Boone and Nora moved steadily ahead, occasionally pausing to scout the path or wait for the others to catch up, but setting a pace that was challenging yet sustainable. Graves, at the rear, was a silent, driving presence. Elise could feel his impatience whenever the line slowed to navigate a particularly difficult obstacle. A couple of times, his clipped voice came over the radio: "Maintain interval. Pick up the pace, Jules."

Jules, clearly less experienced with this kind of terrain despite his technical gear, was struggling slightly, his breathing already ragged. Levi, just ahead of Elise, moved with a steady, enduring pace, seemingly unfazed.

Around mid-morning, they crested the first ridge. The trees thinned slightly here, allowing fractured glimpses of the surrounding landscape through the shifting mist. Rolling waves of forested mountains stretched out in every direction, an ocean of green and grey fading into invisibility. There was no sign of civilization anywhere – no roads, no clear-cuts, no distant towns. Just wilderness, vast and humbling.

"Ten minute break," Boone called out, dropping his pack onto a mossy boulder. "Check your water. Eat something if you need it."

Elise gratefully shrugged off her pack, her shoulders screaming in relief. She leaned against a massive cedar trunk, its bark rough and deeply furrowed, and drank deeply from her water bladder's tube. The air here felt thinner, cleaner. She pulled out her weatherproof notebook and pen, her fingers stiff with cold, and began making observations, forcing her scientific mind to engage.

"Elevation approx. 1200m. Dominant species: Pseudotsuga menziesii, Thuja plicata, Abies amabilis transitioning on upper slope. Understory thick: Gaultheria shallon, Vaccinium spp., Polystichum munitum abundant. Heavy epiphytic load – mosses, lichens (Lobaria, Usnea). Signs of deer browse moderate. Corvidae present (Steller's Jay call noted). Overall old-growth characteristics high."

She scanned the immediate area more closely. A fallen giant lay nearby, covered in a thick shroud of moss, already host to a new generation of hemlock saplings sprouting directly from its decaying trunk – a nurse log, cradle of the future forest. She knelt, scraping away a small patch of moss to examine the wood beneath, noting the tight grain indicative of slow, old growth. This forest felt ancient, untouched by the saws that had levelled so much of the Peninsula's lower elevations.

"Something interesting, Doc?" Boone asked, settling onto a log nearby, pulling out a chunk of jerky.

"Just noting the ecosystem structure," Elise replied, making another entry. "Classic climax community characteristics. Incredible biodiversity in the cryptogams."

Boone chewed thoughtfully, his eyes scanning the surrounding trees. "It's old ground up here. The loggers couldn't get their machines this high easily, so they left it. Mostly." He nodded towards a distant slope where the tree canopy looked subtly different, younger. "They cherry-picked the best cedars back in the fifties, dragged 'em out with mules, some say. Before the valley access got properly cut off by that big landslide downriver."

Graves strode over, consulting his GPS. "Five minutes remaining on the break. We need to cover another four klicks before midday."

Boone shot him an unreadable look but merely nodded. "Path drops down from here. Follows the feeder creek. Gets boggy in the flats."

As they started the descent, the character of the forest changed again. The slope was steep and slippery, littered with loose rocks hidden beneath moss and decaying leaves. They moved carefully, using trekking poles for balance, sometimes half-sliding down sections. Elise saw Jules stumble, catching himself just before falling. Levi offered a steadying hand without breaking stride.

Down in the nascent creek valley, the air grew heavier, cooler. Giant sword ferns formed dense thickets taller than a person. The ground became saturated, their boots sinking slightly with each step. The creek itself was a fast-flowing ribbon of crystal-clear water tumbling over moss-covered stones, the sound a constant rushing murmur.

It was here, following the creek through a grove of enormous, ancient cedars dripping with moisture, that Elise first noticed it. The silence.

The normal sounds of the forest – the chatter of squirrels, the calls of varied thrushes and winter wrens that usually echoed through these woods, the buzz of insects even on a cool day – were absent. Not just subdued, but *gone*. The only sounds were the rush of the creek, the drip of water from the canopy high above, and the noise of their own passage. It was unnatural, deeply unsettling. The air felt heavy, watchful.

Elise slowed her pace instinctively, straining her ears. Nothing. Not even the wind seemed to penetrate this grove, though the treetops far above swayed slightly. She glanced around. The others seemed focused on the footing, navigating the boggy patches and tangled roots. Had they noticed?

She risked a question over the short distance to Levi. "Hear that?" she asked quietly.

Levi paused, listening. His brow furrowed slightly. "Hear what? The creek?"

"No," Elise whispered. "The lack of anything *else*."

Levi cocked his head, listening more intently. After a moment, he gave a small shrug. "Maybe the dense canopy? Or the sound of the water drowns it out?" He offered rational explanations, but his eyes held a flicker of uncertainty.

They pressed on. The silent grove extended for perhaps half a kilometre, following the creek. The massive cedars stood like ancient sentinels, their bark deeply grooved, their lower branches thick as tree trunks themselves, draped in heavy curtains of moss. The place felt... contained. Separate. Like they had stepped into an area cordoned off by unseen boundaries.

Elise scanned the trees, the ground, looking for any biological explanation. Different soil composition? Unusual plant community suppressing other life? She saw nothing obvious. She made a note in her book: *"Segment along Creek Alpha approx. 0.5km exhibiting significant reduction in avian and small mammal activity/vocalization. Auditory dead zone? Environmental factors unclear. Subjective feeling of stillness."*

As they finally emerged from the silent cedar grove into a more mixed forest with younger trees and more light penetrating the canopy, the ambient sounds gradually returned. A Townsend's chipmunk chittered indignantly from a branch overhead. The distant call of a pileated woodpecker echoed through the trees. The transition was palpable, like surfacing from underwater.

Elise glanced back towards the grove. It looked dark, forbidding. Boone had paused too, looking back with a thoughtful expression. He caught her eye and gave a slow, almost imperceptible nod. He'd noticed it too. He didn't need scientific instruments to tell him something was off about that place.

The tension between Boone and Graves continued to simmer throughout the afternoon. Graves constantly pushed the pace, checking his GPS, consulting his schedule. Boone moved at a pace dictated by the terrain, pausing often to scan ahead, check tracks (though they saw no sign of anything larger than deer), and assess potential hazards.

"We're losing light," Graves' voice crackled over the radio around 3 PM. They were navigating a steep, muddy section littered with fallen logs. "Need to pick it up if we're going to make the designated campsite."

"Designated campsite's on the map, Graves," Boone's reply came back, calm but firm. "Reality on the ground says this section needs care. Rushing here gets someone hurt. Found a decent flat spot half a klick back, sheltered by that rock outcrop. Good water source. We should take it."

"Negative," Graves snapped back instantly. "We stick to the plan. Press on."

"Plan didn't account for this new deadfall," Boone countered. "It adds time. Better to make camp safely while we have light than push into unknown terrain after dark trying to make up for lines on a map." There was a pause, then Boone added, his voice dangerously quiet, "Or you can take point and lead us through it faster yourself."

Another charged silence hung over the radio channel. Elise held her breath. Finally, Graves' clipped voice returned, tight with control. "Proceed to the alternate site you identified, Boone. Set up camp. I will verify the position."

Boone didn't acknowledge, just moved on. They backtracked slightly, then followed Boone into a sheltered area beneath a granite overhang, near a small, clear tributary feeding the main creek. It was a well-chosen spot – relatively flat, protected from the wind, with good access to water and plenty of downed wood for a fire.

Setting up camp was a practiced affair, despite the simmering tensions. Two lightweight four-season dome tents were erected quickly – Elise sharing with Nora (though Nora looked like she'd prefer sleeping under a tree), Jules with Levi. Boone opted for a minimalist tarp shelter set slightly apart, facing the woods. Graves claimed a small one-person tent, positioned with strategic oversight of the camp perimeter.

As twilight began to deepen, turning the forest into a realm of grey shadows, Boone and Levi got a small, efficient fire going in a pre-existing rock ring, its flames casting flickering light on their weary faces. The smell of woodsmoke mingled with the scent of rehydrating ration packs being prepared over portable stoves. Exhaustion warred with adrenaline and unease.

Elise found a relatively dry log near the fire and pulled out her notes, trying to organize the day's observations. Flora, fauna, terrain... the silent grove. That stayed with her. A localized absence of sound in an otherwise thriving ecosystem. Why? She glanced towards Boone, who was sharpening his knife by the firelight, his movements deliberate, his eyes constantly scanning the darkening woods beyond the fire's reach. He knew these forests. He'd sensed the wrongness too.

Graves sat apart, hunched over his satellite communications gear, attempting to make the scheduled check-in with Kestrel, his face illuminated by the faint glow of the screen. The forest pressed in around their small circle of light, immense and indifferent. The sounds of the wilderness returned with the darkness – the gurgle of the nearby creek, the rustle of wind in the high canopy, the distant hoot of an owl. Normal sounds. Yet, after the unnerving silence of the cedar grove, even the normal felt charged with potential, as if masking something else hiding just beyond the edge of hearing, just beyond the flickering firelight.

They had made it through day one. They were deep inside now, committed. Elise zipped up her jacket against the deepening chill, the dampness seeping into her bones. They were miles from the nearest road, days from Bluffs End. The real journey into the Hollow Ground had just begun, and the wilderness already felt like it was testing them, watching them, measuring their intrusion. The tension within the group was palpable, a brittle thing in the vast, dark quiet of the Olympic night.

Chapter 4: Whispers and Tracks

The meager warmth of the campfire did little to push back the profound darkness that pressed in from all sides. Beyond the flickering perimeter of orange light, the forest was an impenetrable wall of black, stitched together with the silver threads of the creek's murmur and the occasional sigh of wind high in the unseen canopy. Dinner had been a quiet affair – reconstituted dehydrated meals eaten mostly in silence, the physical exhaustion of the day settling heavily on the group. The earlier tension between Boone and Graves simmered beneath the surface, unspoken but palpable in the way Graves kept slightly apart, reviewing digital maps on his tablet, while Boone methodically cleaned his cooking pot by the water's edge, his movements economical, his senses seemingly attuned to the surrounding night.

Jules, despite his earlier struggles on the trail, had perked up slightly, attempting conversation about potential signal reflection off the granite overhang for Graves' comms gear. Graves offered only curt, noncommittal replies, clearly focused on his own tasks. Levi checked bandages on a small blister Elise hadn't even realized she'd acquired, his touch gentle but professional, before retreating to quietly journal in a waterproof notebook. Nora sat impassively by the fire, sipping tea from a battered tin mug, her gaze distant, as if listening to something only she could hear.

Elise tried to focus on her own notes, organizing the day's biological observations, but her mind kept replaying the experience in the silent cedar grove. The complete absence of normal forest sounds... it defied easy explanation.Localized atmospheric conditions? A migrating flock having just passed through? Possible, but the stillness had felt *absolute*, heavier than mere absence of sound. It had felt like a presence. She shook her head, forcing the thought away. Stick to observable phenomena.

By nine o'clock, deep fatigue pulled at them all. One by one, they banked the fire, secured the food stores against nocturnal scavengers (a standard precaution Graves insisted upon with military rigor, stringing the bags high between two trees well away from the tents), and retreated to their shelters. Elise crawled into the tent she shared with Nora, the confines feeling both secure and slightly claustrophobic. Nora was already zipped into her sleeping bag, seemingly asleep instantly, though Elise suspected the older woman was simply conserving energy, remaining aware. Elise shimmucked out of her damp outer layers, pulled on dry thermal base layers, and slipped into her own bag, the synthetic insulation slowly warming against the pervasive damp chill.

Sleep didn't come easily. Every rustle outside the thin nylon walls sounded magnified – the drip of condensation from leaves, the scurry of some tiny creature in the undergrowth, the groan of wood as a tree settled. The weight of the wilderness felt immense, pressing down. She found herself listening intently, straining her ears against the gentle sounds of the night, her scientific mind trying to categorize every noise, yet unable to fully relax. She thought about the missing persons Graves had detailed. Sarah Jenkins, the surveyors Bellweather and Choi, David Chen, Danny Clarke… had they camped near here? Had they listened to these same forest sounds on their last night? The thought sent a chill creeping up her spine that had nothing to do with the temperature.

She must have drifted off eventually, lulled by the creek's relentless murmur, because the sound that woke her was distinctly *different*.

It wasn't loud. A low, resonant *whoop*, almost like an owl's call, but deeper, carrying a strange vibrational quality that seemed to buzz in her bones. It came from somewhere up the densely wooded slope behind their camp. Elise's eyes snapped open in the pitch darkness of the tent. She lay perfectly still, holding her breath, straining to hear. Was it an owl? A great horned owl, perhaps? The pitch was lower, though, richer. And there was a second part to it, a strange, drawn-out sigh that followed the whoop, something that definitely didn't fit any owl call she knew.

Silence returned, broken only by the creek and Nora's steady breathing beside her. Elise waited. Minutes ticked by. Maybe she'd dreamt it? Or misinterpreted a common sound distorted by sleep and the unfamiliar environment?

Then it came again. *Whoop… hhhhaaaaaaaaahhhhhh.* Clearer this time. Definitely not an owl. Definitely not a bear or a cougar. What animal made a sound like that? It echoed subtly, making the direction hard to pinpoint precisely, but it felt… large. It wasn't aggressive, not a roar or a growl, more like a signal, or perhaps just a respiration.

Beside her, Nora shifted slightly. Was she awake too? Elise didn't dare whisper a question.

She waited again, adrenaline prickling her skin. Her heart beat a heavy rhythm against her ribs. Ten minutes passed. Fifteen. Nothing. Maybe it had moved on? Or maybe it was just some weird acoustic effect, wind funneling through rocks, mimicking a vocalization? She tried to rationalize it, grasp onto a logical explanation. Primatologists often encountered strange, unidentifiable sounds in dense forests; nocturnal animals, echoes, wind – they could all play tricks on the ears.

Just as she was starting to convince herself it was nothing, a different sound cut through the night, much closer this time. A sharp *crack*, like a thick branch snapping decisively under heavy weight. It came from the edge of the clearing, maybe thirty yards away, towards the tree line Boone faced in his tarp shelter.

Elise froze. That wasn't wind. That was weight. Significant weight.

She heard a faint rustle from Boone's direction outside. He was awake. Likely had been since the first whoop.

Another sound followed the snap – a low, guttural throat-clearing noise, a phlegmy *hhrrrrmmm*, startlingly close. It was followed by a heavy *thump*, as if something massive had shifted its stance or dropped something heavy.

Silence again. But this silence felt different. Charged. Expectant. The feeling of being watched intensified tenfold, no longer a vague unease but a near certainty. Something large was out there, just beyond the dying embers of the fire, observing their camp.

Elise strained her eyes, trying to peer through the thin tent fabric, but saw only impenetrable blackness. She could hear her own blood rushing in her ears. She didn't dare move, didn't dare breathe too loudly. How close was it? What was it doing? Why wasn't it attacking? Why wasn't it making more noise?

After what felt like an eternity but was probably only five minutes, another sound drifted through the night, further away now, back up the slope where the first whoop had originated. It was a series of rapid, low clicks, almost like wooden blocks being struck together, *tok-tok-tok-tok*. Then, silence descended once more, a silence that felt profoundly empty, as if whatever had been there had finally withdrawn.

Elise lay awake for hours after that, every nerve ending firing. She didn't hear the strange sounds again, but sleep was impossible. The forest outside the thin nylon walls no longer felt neutral; it felt actively inhabited by something unknown and potentially powerful. Eventually, the first faint hints of predawn grey began to seep into the sky, painting the tent fabric a lighter shade. Only then did exhaustion finally claim her, dragging her into a brief, uneasy sleep filled with indistinct, looming shapes.

She woke fully to the sounds of the camp stirring. The metallic click of a camp stove being lit, the murmur of low voices. She felt groggy, unrested, the night's events clinging to her like the damp morning mist swirling outside. Nora was already gone from the tent. Elise quickly dressed in her still-damp hiking clothes, the cold fabric clammy against her skin, and crawled out.

The others were gathered near the rekindled fire, faces drawn and tired in the pale light. Jules looked particularly pale, nervously stirring instant coffee into a mug. Levi stood watching the tree line, his usual calm replaced by a guarded alertness. Graves was already packed, consulting his GPS, but his eyes kept flicking towards the woods. Boone stood beside Nora, talking quietly. They both looked towards Elise as she approached.

"Morning," she managed, her voice rough. "Did, uh… did anyone else hear anything unusual last night?"

Jules' head snapped up. "You heard it too? The… the whooping sound? And the cracking noises?" His voice was a hushed, anxious whisper.

Levi nodded slowly. "Woke me up around 0200. Strange vocalizations. Unidentifiable. And yes, movement near the perimeter later on."

Graves lowered his GPS. "Standard nocturnal activity," he stated flatly, though his eyes lacked conviction. "Could be deer, elk, bear moving through. Sounds carry strangely in these valleys, echo off the rock faces."

"That warn't no deer, Graves," Boone said quietly, his voice firm. He turned fully to face the group, his expression grim. "Heard it plain as day. Couple of 'em, sounded like. One up the ridge, one circled closer. Snapped that dead branch right over there." He pointed towards the spot Elise had estimated. "Stood there for a good few minutes. Listening. Breathing."

"Breathing?" Elise echoed. "You heard it breathing?"

Boone nodded. "Low and heavy. Like a big bellows. Then it moved off, joined the other one back up the slope. Heard 'em moving through the brush, tryin' to be quiet but too damn big."

Nora added her observation, her voice low. "The Tallsalt elders say the Stick-shí'nač often communicate with whoops and wood-knocks, especially at night. Signals. Warnings." She looked around the circle of tired, tense faces. "They know we're here. They're watching us."

Graves radiated impatience. "Folklore and speculation won't help us. We stick to facts. We heard unidentified sounds. We maintain vigilance. Pack up, we move out in twenty." He turned away, clearly intending to shut down the discussion, projecting an aura of control over a situation that felt increasingly uncontrolled.

Elise watched him, a flicker of doubt igniting within her. Was his dismissal genuine belief, or was he trying to maintain morale, to suppress fear? Or did he already know what was out there? The memory of the suppressed evidence from the missing persons files resurfaced. *Trace organic samples that defied easy categorization...*

Boone ignored Graves' dismissal and exchanged another look with Nora. Then, grabbing his water filter and bottle, he headed towards the small tributary creek that ran near the campsite, about fifty yards away through ferns and brush. "Gonna top off water before we head into drier country," he called back.

The others continued packing, the earlier quiet replaced by a nervous energy. Jules kept glancing over his shoulder towards the woods. Levi meticulously checked the tension on his pack straps, his movements precise but his gaze distant.

A few minutes later, Boone's voice cut through the morning air, sharp and urgent. "Graves! Doc! Get over here! Now!"

Instantly, everyone froze. Graves, Elise, Levi, and Jules exchanged alarmed glances, then simultaneously dropped what they were doing and hurried towards the creek, crashing through the wet undergrowth. Nora followed close behind, her face impassive but alert.

They found Boone kneeling on a narrow strip of damp, sandy earth right at the water's edge. He wasn't looking at them; his attention was fixed entirely on the ground in front of him. He pointed, his finger trembling almost imperceptibly.

"Look," he breathed.

Elise pushed forward, her heart suddenly pounding again. And then she saw them.

Pressed deep into the soft sand, just inches from the gurgling water, were footprints. Three of them, forming a clear stride pattern leading away from the creek and disappearing into the firmer, mossy ground beyond.

They were enormous.

Elise's breath caught in her throat. Each print was easily eighteen inches long, maybe longer, and significantly wider than any human foot. They were undeniably humanoid in shape – a distinct heel impression, a broad midfoot, and five clear toe imprints fanned out at the front. The depth of the impressions spoke of immense weight.

"Sweet Mother..." Jules whispered, his face losing all color. Levi knelt beside Boone, examining the tracks intently, his scientific detachment visibly warring with shock.

"Bear?" Graves asked sharply, stepping closer, his eyes narrowed, scanning the tracks and the surrounding area.

"No goddamn bear," Boone replied without looking up, his voice tight with conviction. "Look at it, Graves. Look close." He pointed to the clearest print. "Five toes, not the staggered five of a bear track. Clear ball-of-foot pressure ridge. Heel strike. See that slight bulge in the middle? Midtarsal flexibility maybe, like apes have, lets the foot flex more on uneven ground. Bears walk flat-footed or on the balls, totally different morphology. And the stride," he indicated the distance between the prints, "close to six feet. Whatever made this was bipedal, heavy as hell, and had one hell of a long leg."

Elise knelt down too, her scientific training kicking in despite the shock. Boone was right. These were definitely not bear tracks. Black bears, the only species native here, left distinct tracks – smaller overall, claw marks usually visible (none here), a different toe arrangement, and a much shorter stride length even when bounding. Could it be a deformed bear? Possible, but unlikely to produce such clear, consistent, humanoid prints. Could someone be hoaxing them? Out here? In the middle of nowhere, anticipating their exact route, managing to fake tracks this large and deep without leaving any other sign? The logistics seemed impossible.

She took out her camera, her hands slightly unsteady, and began photographing the tracks from multiple angles, including a scale marker from her kit for reference. "Incredible definition," she murmured, forcing herself to think analytically. "Substrate is perfect... damp sand over firm base. Minimal erosion yet."

"Any hair? Scat?" Levi asked, scanning the immediate vicinity methodically.

Boone shook his head. "Clean. Like it just came down for a drink and moved on." He looked up at Elise, his eyes intense. "You still thinkin' 'bear,' Doc?"

Elise hesitated, staring at the huge, eerily human-like print preserved perfectly in the sand. Every instinct screamed that this was impossible, defied established biology. And yet... the evidence was right there at her feet. Solid, measurable, undeniable. The sounds last night, Nora's legends, the disappearances, Boone's conviction, and now this. It formed a chain of converging evidence that was becoming increasingly difficult to dismiss.

"It's... anomalous," Elise conceded carefully, avoiding a direct answer. Her skepticism was wavering, badly shaken. "The morphology doesn't match any known North American mammal. The size, the implied weight, the bipedal gait... It requires further analysis." It was a weak, scientific hedge, and she knew it.

Graves knelt beside Levi, examining the prints with unnerving calmness. He pulled out a small measuring device from his pocket and took precise dimensions, recording them on a waterproof notepad. He showed no surprise, no shock. His expression was focused, almost clinical, as if he'd expected this. Did he know more than he let on during the briefing? Was this confirmation for him, not revelation?

"Interesting," Graves said coolly, standing up and pocketing his notepad. He took his own series of photos with a specialized high-res camera from his pack. "Document it thoroughly, Dr. Holloway. Note the location coordinates precisely. We need to keep moving. Daylight is burning."

"Keep moving?" Jules exclaimed incredulously. "After *this*? Shouldn't we... I don't know, be more careful? Set up more defenses? Maybe rethink charging deeper into this valley?"

"The objective remains unchanged," Graves stated, his voice leaving no room for argument. "We gather data. These tracks are data. Highly significant data, potentially. But they do not alter the mission plan. Maintain situational awareness. Pack up. We depart in ten minutes."

He turned and strode back towards the campsite without waiting for a response, leaving the others staring after him, then back down at the enormous footprints. The sense of being watched, which had permeated the night, now felt oppressively present even in the broadening daylight. It was as if the forest itself had confirmed their fears, leaving its signature in the sand as a clear, silent message: *You are not alone. You are intruders.*

They worked quickly to break camp, but the atmosphere was thick with tension and barely suppressed fear. Every snap of a twig in the surrounding woods made Jules jump. Levi moved with his usual efficiency, but his eyes constantly scanned the trees. Even Elise found herself glancing nervously into the shadows, half-expecting to see large, dark shapes moving just beyond her line of sight. Boone and Nora were watchful, quiet, moving with an intensified alertness born from lifetimes spent reading the nuances of the wilderness.

As Elise shouldered her heavy pack, settling the weight, she looked back one last time towards the creek, towards the impossible footprints already beginning to soften slightly at the edges as the sun climbed higher. The sounds in the night, the tracks by the water – they were data points, yes. But they felt like more than that. They felt like the beginning of something, a first direct contact, a crossing of a line. The forest no longer felt merely indifferent; it felt sentient, aware of their presence, and possibly, hostile. The scientific expedition was rapidly transforming into something far more primal: a journey into the territory of the unknown, where the rules of ecology might not be the only ones that applied.

Chapter 5: Old Wounds

The rest of the day's trek unfolded under the heavy shadow of the discovery at the creek. The air of scientific curiosity or even adventurous challenge had evaporated, replaced by a brittle, hyper-alert tension that thrummed through the small group like a plucked wire. Every shadow seemed deeper, every rustle of leaves louder. Jules practically jumped out of his skin when a grouse exploded from the undergrowth near his feet, earning a sharp, stabilizing glare from Graves. Levi moved with his usual steadiness, but Elise noticed his hand hovered more frequently near the large can of bear spray clipped prominently to his pack strap. Nora and Boone were living embodiments of vigilance, their eyes constantly sweeping the dense forest, missing nothing, reading the subtle language of bent ferns and disturbed moss that Elise was only beginning to decipher.

Their pace, despite Graves' occasional clipped reminders about the schedule, was noticeably slower. Caution dictated every footstep on the increasingly treacherous terrain. They negotiated slippery log crossings over fast-moving streams, scrambled up steep inclines slick with mud and decaying leaves, and pushed through dense thickets of devil's club and salmonberry that snagged clothing and scraped skin. The physical exertion was immense, but it was the psychological weight – the awareness of the giant tracks, the memory of the night's sounds, the pervasive feeling of being watched – that truly drained them.

Elise found herself reassessing everything. The silent cedar grove now felt less like an ecological anomaly and more like a deliberate absence, a place avoided by normal wildlife for reasons she couldn't fathom. The sounds Boone described – the breathing, the closeness – replayed in her mind, overlaying the memory of the *whoop-sigh* she herself had heard. And the tracks… eighteen inches long, bipedal, immense weight. How could established science account for that? Hoaxing seemed logistically impossible out here. Misidentification? What known animal could leave such a print? The questions gnawed at the edges of her scientific certainty, leaving uncomfortable vacancies.

She kept glancing at Boone. His initial grim conviction after finding the tracks had settled into a quiet, focused intensity. He moved through the woods with an assurance that spoke of deep familiarity, yet there was a sadness in his eyes now, a haunted quality that hadn't been there before. He seemed less the laconic tracker and more like a man returning to a place heavy with painful memories.

They made camp relatively early, well before dusk painted the sky in bruised shades of purple and grey. Graves, perhaps sensing the frayed nerves of the team or maybe recalculating based on the slower pace forced by caution, agreed readily when Boone identified another suitable spot – a small, defensible shelf of relatively flat ground tucked against a sheer rock face, overlooking the confluence of two small creeks. It offered good visibility downstream and limited approach routes from above.

The routine of setting up camp offered a small measure of comfort, the familiar tasks grounding them against the swirling unease. Tents were erected, water filtered, gear stowed. Jules immediately began setting up perimeter sensors Graves had provided – small, camouflaged motion-activated cameras and seismic detectors – placing them strategically around the camp edge under Graves' direction. It was meant to be reassuring, but the act of setting tripwires and electronic eyes only served to underscore the perceived threat.

As darkness fell, thick and absolute under the heavy clouds, Boone once again built a fire. Tonight, no one objected. The circle of light, however small, felt essential, a necessary bastion against the encroaching blackness. The flames crackled merrily, casting dancing shadows on the weary faces gathered around it, but the mood remained subdued. Dinner was another round of rehydrated meals, eaten with little appetite. Conversation was sparse, functional – comments about the dwindling water supply in someone's bladder, a query about the next day's anticipated terrain.

Graves, after ensuring the sensor network was active and attempting another brief, apparently unsuccessful satellite uplink, retreated slightly from the main fire circle. He sat on a folding camp stool, meticulously cleaning a high-powered tactical flashlight, his expression closed off, radiating a solitary, self-contained authority that discouraged interaction.

Jules nervously checked the receiver unit connected to the perimeter sensors, his eyes darting towards the dark woods every few seconds. Levi sat calmly, patching a small tear in his gaiter with needle and thread, but his stillness felt watchful. Nora had accepted a cup of tea from Elise but said little, her gaze fixed on the flames, her thoughts clearly elsewhere, perhaps on the stories of the Stick-shí'nač and their ancient claim to this valley.

Elise found herself sitting near Boone, who was poking the fire with a stick, sending showers of sparks into the night air. The silence stretched, thick with unspoken fears and the ever-present sounds of the forest – the gurgle of the creeks, the drip of water from mossy branches, the far-off hoot of an owl (a normal one this time, thankfully).

Trying to break the heavy quiet, Elise spoke, keeping her voice low. "You seem to know this area really well, Boone. Even off the main trails."

Boone continued stirring the embers for a moment before answering, his gaze still fixed on the fire. "Spent a lot of time in these hills. Grew up not far from here, down towards the coast. My family... we hunted, fished, logged a bit. The woods were our backyard."

"Is that how you got into tracking, guiding?" Elise prompted gently.

He finally looked up, his eyes reflecting the firelight, making them gleam unnervingly in the dimness. There was a weariness in his gaze that went beyond physical fatigue. "Partly," he admitted. He tossed the stick into the flames, where it quickly caught. "Learned to read sign from my dad, my uncles. But this particular stretch..." He gestured vaguely towards the dark valley stretching out below their campsite. "Got to know this area more intimately than I ever wanted to."

He paused, picking up another stick, stripping the bark slowly with his thumbnail. The others around the fire had fallen silent, listening, though pretending not to. Even Graves seemed fractionally less engrossed in his flashlight maintenance.

"My younger brother, Liam," Boone said, his voice rough with emotion held long in check. "He disappeared up here. Twenty-two years ago."

Elise felt a sudden lurch in her stomach. Twenty-two years. Before the disappearances Graves had listed, but part of the same unsettling pattern that seemed to hang over this place.

"I'm so sorry, Boone," she murmured, the inadequacy of the words starkly apparent.

Boone gave a short, humourless laugh, the sound swallowed quickly by the night. "Yeah. Sorry covers a lot of ground, don't it?" He took a deep breath, the firelight catching the harsh lines etched around his eyes. "We were kids. Teenagers. Me, seventeen. Liam, fifteen. Thought we were tough shit, knew the woods like the back of our hands. Came up here for a weekend campout, bit of trout fishing. Just us two. Up past the old Hemlock Falls trail, near the headwaters of this creek system." He gestured again towards the darkness. "Not far from where we found those tracks this morning, maybe a mile further up the drainage."

The proximity sent another chill through Elise. This wasn't just general history; it was rooted *here*.

"It was late September," Boone continued, his voice becoming distant, lost in memory. "Weather turned nasty, unexpected early snow squall blew in overnight. Woke up to four inches on the ground, visibility down to nothing. We decided to pack it in, head back down. Figured we could follow the creek, easy enough."

He stared into the flames, his knuckles white where he gripped the stick. "We got maybe halfway back towards the main trail when… when it happened. We were crossing a blowdown section, lots of big old fallen cedars jumbled together like pickup sticks, covered in wet snow. Slippery as hell. I was ahead, picking the route. Heard Liam yell out behind me. Not like he was hurt, more… surprised? Startled?"

"I turned around, expecting to see him slipped or tangled up. He was maybe twenty yards back. But he wasn't looking at his feet. He was staring off into the trees, perpendicular to the creek, his face pale as the snow. And he just… whispered my name. 'Boone…'"

Boone's voice cracked slightly. He cleared his throat, looked away from the fire towards the impenetrable blackness beyond their camp. "Before I could even ask what was wrong, something moved in the trees where he was looking. Big. Dark. Fast. Just a blur between the trunks, half hidden by the falling snow. Wasn't a bear. Too tall, moved wrong. And then… Liam just vanished."

"Vanished?" Jules whispered, leaning forward, his fear momentarily overcome by horrified curiosity.

"One second he was there," Boone said, his voice flat, devoid of inflection now, as if recounting the story had worn away the raw edges over the years, leaving only the hollow ache. "Standing by a big mossy stump. The next second, the snow swirled thick for just a moment, I heard this... this awful, choked-off sound, like a gasp cut short. And when the snow cleared a second later, he was gone. Just gone."

He paused, the only sound the crackling fire and the relentless rush of water. "I yelled his name. Scrambled back as fast as I could, heart pounding out of my chest. Took me maybe thirty seconds to get to the stump where he'd been standing. There were tracks."

"His tracks?" Elise asked quietly.

Boone shook his head slowly, his eyes haunted. "His tracks leading up to the stump, yeah. Clear enough in the fresh snow. But leading away from it... there was another set. Mixed in with his, like something had grabbed him, dragged him sideways off the logjam and into the dense timber."

He looked around the fire, meeting their eyes one by one. "They were huge. Like the ones we saw today. Bigger, maybe, or maybe it just seemed that way because I was seventeen and terrified outta my mind. Bipedal. Deep impressions, even in the soft snow on top of the logs. They went straight into the thickest part of the forest, where no person could move that fast, let alone dragging someone."

"Did you follow them?" Levi asked, his voice low, practical.

"Tried to," Boone said bitterly. "Crashed through the brush, yelling Liam's name till I was hoarse. Followed the tracks for maybe a hundred yards. They went down into this steep little gully, choked with ferns and devils' club. Then... they just stopped. Like whatever took him just... stepped out of the world. No broken branches beyond that point, no more tracks, nothing. Just silence. And the snow kept falling, covering everything up."

He fell silent, breathing heavily, lost in the nightmare of that memory. The campfire crackled, consuming the stick he held forgotten in his hand.

"I panicked," he admitted after a long moment, his voice barely audible. "Turned around, ran hell-for-leather back down the creek towards the trailhead, stumbling, falling. Took me hours. Got back to the truck just before dark, half frozen, babbling like an idiot. Called the sheriff."

"They searched?" Elise asked softly.

"Oh yeah," Boone nodded, a weary cynicism in his voice. "Search and Rescue, volunteers, dogs, even a chopper when the weather cleared a couple days later. Combed those woods for a week. Found our campsite. Found the spot by the logjam where Liam... where he vanished. Found my tracks leading away in a panic. But they never found him. Not a scrap of clothing, not a drop of blood, nothing. And the tracks I told them about?" He gave a short, sharp sigh. "By the time the main search teams got up there, the snow had melted mostly, rained hard too. What little sign was left, they dismissed. 'Bear sign,' the SAR leader told my folks. 'Probably scavenged after the boy got lost and succumbed to exposure.' Easier than admitting they didn't have a clue."

He tossed the smoldering end of the stick into the heart of the fire. "But I know what I saw. I know those weren't bear tracks. And Liam didn't just wander off and die of cold. He was taken. Something took him."

He looked directly at Elise then, his eyes burning with a conviction forged in trauma and years of brooding. "That thing... the creature people whisper about, the thing that leaves those prints... it lives here, Doctor. In this valley. In these deep woods. It's smart. It's strong. And it doesn't like people invading its territory. My brother learned that the hard way. Those folks Graves listed? I'd bet my life they learned it too."

His words hung heavy in the cold night air. The campfire seemed to shrink, its light feeble against the immense darkness and the weight of Boone's story. Jules looked physically ill. Levi stared into the fire, his brow deeply furrowed. Nora met Boone's gaze with a silent, profound understanding that transcended words. Even Graves looked momentarily thoughtful, though his expression quickly reverted to impassive efficiency.

Elise felt a deep wave of empathy wash over her. Boone's grief, his certainty, the raw horror of his experience – it was powerful, undeniable. It painted the warnings, the tracks, the strange sounds, in a starkly personal and terrifying light. Her scientific mind still wrestled with the implications, the lack of congruence with established biological paradigms. The idea of a giant, undiscovered primate hiding in these woods, responsible for abductions... it was still fantastically improbable according to her training.

But looking at Boone, hearing the tremor in his voice, seeing the conviction in his haunted eyes, she couldn't dismiss his experience as mere folklore or misidentification fueled by grief. He had *been* there. He had *seen* the tracks. He had lost his brother in this very wilderness under terrifyingly strange circumstances. His instincts weren't based on supposition; they were forged in trauma, honed by years of living with the unresolved horror and the conviction that something unnatural dwelled here.

Her respect for him deepened immensely. He wasn't just a gruff tracker; he was a survivor, carrying a burden that had shaped his life and his relationship with this landscape. Whether the culprit was a literal Sasquatch or some other unexplained phenomenon didn't negate the validity of his fear, his caution, his profound understanding of the danger they might be in.

She still couldn't bring herself to fully *believe* in the Bigfoot theory, not in the way Boone clearly did. Her scientific framework wouldn't allow that leap without more concrete, verifiable evidence beyond tracks and sounds. But Boone's story had irrevocably shifted something within her. It grounded the abstract threat, gave it a human cost. It made her acknowledge that knowledge wasn't just about data points and peer-reviewed papers; it was also about lived experience, instinct, and the deep, often terrifying wisdom held by those who knew a place intimately, especially a place capable of swallowing people whole.

She looked away from Boone, towards the impenetrable wall of darkness surrounding their small camp. The forest seemed quieter now, listening. Boone's story hung in the air, a chilling testament to the valley's history. Old wounds had been opened, bleeding into the present, staining their supposedly scientific expedition with the undeniable colours of loss, fear, and the profound, terrifying unknown. Whatever lurked out there, myth or monster, the danger felt acutely real. And Boone's instincts, she realized, might be their most valuable asset, whether Graves acknowledged it or not.

Chapter 6: Trail Cam Footage

The dawn after Boone's story broke heavy and subdued. The shared vulnerability, the raw honesty of his trauma, had subtly shifted the group dynamic. While Graves maintained his professional distance and pushed the schedule, there was a newfound quiet respect for Boone, even from Jules, who seemed to have shed some of his nervous energy in favor of a more sober caution. The forest itself felt different too, imbued with a heavier sense of history and potential menace now that Boone's loss was laid bare amongst them.

The day's trek took them deeper still, descending from the rocky shelf into the main valley system Graves had designated as AO Hollow. The terrain became even more challenging – dense pockets of old-growth cedar and hemlock where sunlight barely penetrated, steep-sided ravines choked with ferns and devils' club that required careful hand-over-hand descents using roots and rocks for purchase, and stretches of sucking bog where progress slowed to a crawl.

Elise focused on her work, deploying the first set of scientific instruments. With Boone's grudging but expert advice on placement – near game trails, potential water sources, areas showing signs of animal passage – she carefully mounted weatherproof camera traps onto sturdy tree trunks. These were high-resolution, motion-activated units capable of capturing stills and short video clips in both daylight and infrared night vision. Simultaneously, she set up several bioacoustic recorders – sensitive microphones programmed to record ambient soundscapes at specific intervals, hoping to capture not just potential anomalous vocalizations, but baseline data on the valley's overall biodiversity, or lack thereof. Documenting the silence was as important as documenting the sounds.

Jules assisted her, his technical skills proving invaluable in syncing the devices and ensuring optimal field of view and sensitivity settings. He worked with a focused intensity, the previous night's fear channeled into the task. "These units have pretty good range," he murmured, adjusting the angle on a camera overlooking a well-used deer trail. "If anything bigger than a squirrel moves through here, day or night, we should get *something*."

Graves observed the placement process, occasionally offering curt suggestions based on his own assessment of likely travel corridors and potential ambush points. His perspective was disturbingly tactical, Elise noted, less focused on ecological principles and more on surveillance and potential threat vectors. It reinforced her growing suspicion that this 'ecological assessment' was merely a convenient, deniable framework for a very different kind of operation. What was Kestrel *really* after? Confirmation of the creature? Capture? Containment?

Boone and Nora scouted ahead, marking the trail and assessing the route, their communication often non-verbal – a shared glance, a subtle hand signal indicating treacherous footing or a clear path. Elise felt increasingly reliant on their expertise, recognizing that her scientific skills were secondary to their deep, intuitive understanding of this wilderness when it came to basic survival and navigation.

By late afternoon, they reached the designated location for their primary base camp. It was a relatively level area nestled in a grove of slightly younger alder and maple, near the main fork of the valley's primary creek – a wider, slower-moving body of water here than the tumbling tributaries they'd followed earlier. The site felt slightly more open than the oppressive density of the higher slopes, though the valley walls still loomed steep and shadowed on either side.

Setting up base camp was a more involved process. Larger communal tents were erected, a designated cooking area established away from the sleeping quarters, and a more robust system for securing food stores implemented. Graves directed the setup with his usual efficiency, while Jules immediately began work on establishing a local network hub to wirelessly receive data downloads from the deployed cameras and sensors within range.

"Got four cams and two audio monitors within direct line-of-sight ping," Jules reported to Graves, tapping away on his ruggedized laptop inside the command tent – essentially a larger dome tent housing Graves' comms gear and Jules' tech station. "We should start getting buffered data packets overnight."

"Good," Graves grunted. "Prioritize motion triggers from Zone Alpha – the creek crossing where the tracks were found – and Zone Beta, the silent grove."

Elise overheard this from just outside the tent flap. Graves already had designations for the key locations. He was thinking strategically, pinpointing areas of interest based on their unsettling experiences. This wasn't random scientific sampling; it was targeted surveillance.

The first night at base camp was thick with anticipation. Despite the exhaustion, sleep came fitfully for Elise. Boone's story echoed in her mind, mingling with the memory of the tracks, the eerie silence, the strange night calls. Every snap of a twig outside felt ominous. The perimeter sensors Jules had deployed offered a thin veneer of technological security, but the vast, unmonitored wilderness pressing in felt overwhelming. She found herself listening intently, straining for any unusual sound, wondering if the bioacoustic recorders were capturing anything beyond the wind and water.

Morning brought relief in the form of routine – hot coffee, ration packs, the mundane tasks of camp life. But the underlying tension remained. All eyes kept drifting towards Jules' workstation in the command tent.

It was mid-morning when Jules let out a low whistle. "Graves? Doc? You guys are gonna want to see this."

Elise's heart gave a sudden jump. She hurried towards the command tent, Levi and Boone close behind. Nora remained near the creek, seemingly uninterested in the technological findings, her focus on the tangible signs of the forest itself.

Inside the dim tent, Jules swiveled around from his laptop, his eyes wide behind his glasses. Graves stood beside him, peering intently at the screen, his usual impassivity momentarily broken by a flicker of intense interest.

"Camera Trap Four," Jules said, his voice hushed with excitement and maybe a little fear. "Zone Beta corridor – the approach to that weird silent cedar grove. Motion trigger logged at 03:17 AM."

He tapped a key, and a short video clip began playing on the screen. The footage was infrared, monochrome green and black, depicting the rain-slicked ferns and mossy trunks of the forest floor under the dense canopy. For the first few seconds, nothing happened. Then, from the right side of the frame, something moved.

It was fleeting, maybe only visible for three or four frames, partially obscured by ferns and a thick cedar trunk. But it was undeniably there. A massive silhouette, moving upright, bipedal. It swung a heavy-looking arm as it passed, disappearing behind the cedar before the camera could get a clear lock. The scale was hard to judge precisely without reference, but it was *tall*, significantly taller than a human, broad-shouldered, and seemed to move with a powerful, fluid gait despite its bulk.

Jules replayed the clip. Once. Twice. Three times.

The silence in the tent was absolute. Everyone stared at the blurry, indistinct shape moving through the ghostly green landscape of the night forest.

"Holy shit," Jules breathed finally. "Is that… is that *it*?"

Elise felt her mouth go dry. Her scientific skepticism battled fiercely with the visual evidence on the screen. Blurry? Yes. Obscured? Definitely. Conclusive proof? No. But it wasn't a bear. It wasn't a deer or an elk. The movement, the upright posture, the sheer implied size… it aligned unnervingly well with the tracks, the sounds, Boone's decades-old sighting.

"Enhance section four-delta," Graves ordered, his voice tight. "Can you stabilize the frames, clarify the outline?"

Jules' fingers flew across the keyboard. "Trying… IR resolution is limited, and the motion blur is significant. It passed through the trigger zone fast." He manipulated the image, zooming in, adjusting contrast. The shape remained stubbornly indistinct, a hulking shadow defined more by its movement against the background than by clear features. "That's about the best I can do, Graves. It's… suggestive, but not definitive."

"Suggestive," Graves repeated, his eyes narrowed, fixed on the screen. He seemed less disappointed than calculating, as if this blurry glimpse confirmed a privately held hypothesis.

Boone, who had remained silent until now, spoke quietly from the back of the tent. "Suggestive enough for me." His voice held a grim vindication. "That's how they move. Fast. Keep to cover. Never give you a clear look unless they mean to."

Levi stared at the screen, rubbing his jaw thoughtfully. "The size is considerable. Estimating height based on surrounding flora… possibly eight feet? Maybe more? And the width across the shoulders… massive." He shook his head slowly. "It's… extraordinary."

Elise forced herself to speak, clinging to scientific rigor. "We need to be cautious. Pareidolia is a factor with low-resolution, ambiguous images. It *could* be a confluence of shadows, maybe a known animal distorted by the angle and IR lighting... though," she admitted honestly, staring at the replay again, "the bipedal motion is hard to reconcile with anything common."

"Pareidolia doesn't leave eighteen-inch tracks, Doctor," Graves said coolly, turning away from the screen. His brief flicker of interest had vanished, replaced by his usual controlled mask. "This footage, combined with the tracks and the auditory events, significantly increases the probability of the secondary objective parameter." He looked at Jules. "Log it. Encrypt it. Prepare it for burst transmission on the next scheduled uplink window. Maintain continuous monitoring of all active sensors."

He turned to the rest of them. "This changes nothing in terms of immediate protocol. Maintain vigilance, adhere to safety procedures. Dr. Holloway, continue deploying sensors as planned. Boone, continue scouting the primary valley route. We stick to the plan."

He exited the tent, leaving the others bathed in the faint green glow of the screen displaying the endlessly looping clip of the shadowy figure.

The reaction among the remaining team members was fractured. Jules seemed energized, caught between fear and the thrill of being part of a potentially historic discovery. "Proof," he kept murmuring, watching the clip again. "Maybe not court-of-law proof, but... damn."

Levi was more circumspect, analytical. "The lack of clear features is problematic. But the biomechanics... the apparent fluidity of movement despite the size... fascinating. And disturbing."

Boone watched the screen with a somber intensity. For him, it wasn't proof of existence; it was confirmation of the enduring presence that had haunted him for over twenty years. The creature wasn't just real; it was *here*, active, watching them. There was no triumph in his expression, only a deep, weary concern.

Elise felt caught somewhere in the middle. The footage chipped away another significant chunk of her skepticism. Seeing *something* moving, something large and upright, captured by their own equipment in the very area they were investigating... it tipped the balance further away from dismissal. But it wasn't the clean, undeniable evidence her scientific training craved. It was a ghost on a screen, a Rorschach test in infrared.

And Graves… his reaction was the most unsettling. His lack of surprise, his immediate shift back to operational footing, his focus on securing the data… Elise's suspicion solidified into near certainty. Graves knew more than he was telling them. The Kestrel Foundation knew more. This wasn't just about confirming rumors; it felt targeted. What was Graves' personal stake in this? Why the ex-military secrecy? What were the 'suppressed evidence fragments' he'd alluded to back in Bluffs End?

She looked back at the screen, at the massive silhouette melting back into the shadows of the infrared forest. Awe, fear, scientific curiosity, and a growing distrust of their leader churned within her. The expedition had crossed another threshold. They now had a fleeting image, a technological whisper confirming the tracks and the sounds. They weren't just searching anymore. They were documenting contact. And the feeling that they were profoundly intruding, stepping into a place governed by ancient rules and powerful, unknown inhabitants, intensified with every passing hour. The sense of being watched was no longer just a feeling; it was a documented event, played on a loop in the dim light of the command tent.

Chapter 7: The Disappearance

The atmosphere in base camp following the capture of the trail cam footage was a strange cocktail of dread and electric discovery. The fleeting, shadowy image became an obsession, replayed countless times on Jules' laptop screen in the command tent, pored over, debated. For Jules himself, the initial shock had morphed into a feverish excitement. He saw the indistinct shape not just as confirmation, but as a personal vindication of the mission's worth, a tantalizing glimpse into the unknown that bordered on the holy grail for a tech enthusiast dropped into the heart of a cryptid hunt. He spent hours analyzing the grainy infrared frames, running algorithms to sharpen edges that refused to sharpen, attempting trajectory calculations based on blurry movement, chattering excitedly about sensor sensitivity and optimal placement for the *next* capture.

"If we could just deploy a wide-angle Lidar unit near that same corridor," he theorized to anyone who would listen, eyes gleaming behind his glasses, "we could get a full 3D point cloud map! Imagine! Actual dimensional data, not just a fuzzy picture!"

His enthusiasm felt jarring against the palpable anxiety that gripped the others. Elise found his relentless tech-optimism unnerving, bordering on reckless. It felt like he was seeing the data points but ignoring the creature they represented – the creature that left eighteen-inch tracks and potentially lurked just beyond the firelight, the creature Boone believed had taken his brother. Levi remained professionally calm but doubled his vigilance during his watches, meticulously checking the perimeter sensor feed whenever he passed the command tent. Boone grew quieter, more withdrawn, his eyes constantly scanning the dense treeline surrounding the camp, his hand rarely far from the heavy sheath knife on his belt. Nora, too, seemed more somber, often found standing near the creek, looking upstream into the deepest part of the valley, her expression unreadable but heavy.

Even Graves seemed affected, though he masked it behind a veneer of operational focus. He spent more time conferring with Jules over the sensor data, scrutinizing maps, and attempting satellite communication uplinks, his jaw perpetually tight. The mission had clearly crossed a threshold for him too, though his internal reactions remained opaque.

The second morning at base camp, Jules's excitement boiled over into impatience. One of the audio monitoring units deployed further up the valley, beyond the range of the camp's local wireless network, had failed to send its scheduled 'heartbeat' signal confirming operational status.

"Unit Seven isn't checking in," Jules announced during the brief morning meeting near the fire ring, gesturing at his tablet. "Could be anything – battery drain faster than expected, software glitch, maybe just atmospheric interference blocking the long-range signal check. But," he added eagerly, "it's also located in that narrow ravine leading towards the northern ridge. Prime funnel point. If anything is moving along that ridge system, it'd likely pass through there. Could have captured some amazing audio."

Graves frowned at the map display on Jules' tablet. "Zone Gamma. Steep terrain. Estimated two klicks north-northeast. Too far off our primary survey axis for a full team detour."

"Exactly!" Jules jumped in. "But one person could nip up there quickly, check the unit, swap the battery, maybe reposition it slightly for better signal, grab the local data log, and be back by midday. Quick in, quick out. Minimal disruption to the main schedule." He looked directly at Graves, practically vibrating with eagerness. "I can do it. I know the gear inside out. I can navigate by GPS waypoint, stick to the route."

Elise felt a prickle of unease. A solo excursion, even a short one, felt profoundly unwise given the recent events. "Is that really necessary, Jules?" she asked carefully. "The unit might just come back online. Maybe wait a day?"

"But if it recorded something significant last night…" Jules argued, his eyes bright. "And if the battery *is* dead, that data could be lost if we don't retrieve the internal storage soon! This could be crucial!"

Levi cleared his throat. "Solo travel in this terrain carries significant inherent risk, regardless of technical navigation aids. A slip, a fall… communication is unreliable."

Boone spoke up, his voice flat. "Bad idea, Jules. That ravine… it's tight, lots of overhangs, easy places for something to wait. And you ain't exactly wilderness-savvy, no offense. Stick with the group."

Jules flushed slightly at the implicit criticism but turned pleadingly to Graves. "Sir, I'm confident I can handle it. It's a straightforward waypoint route. Retrieve vital data, check equipment integrity – it falls under operational necessity, doesn't it?"

Graves considered it for a long moment, his gaze sweeping over the map, then Jules, then the surrounding forest. Elise expected him to concur with the others, to prioritize safety. His decision, when it came, was chillingly pragmatic.

"Alright, Jensen," Graves said curtly. "Standard solo recon protocols apply. You take a radio, GPS unit with the waypoints locked, sidearm," – Elise's eyes widened slightly; she hadn't realized they carried firearms beyond potential deterrents – "and basic survival kit. Check in via radio every thirty minutes on the hour. Maintain strict route adherence. No deviations. If you encounter *any* sign of the primary subject or any other significant threat, do *not* engage. Retreat immediately and report. You have until 1300 hours for return. If you miss the 1300 check-in, we initiate search protocols. Understood?"

Jules beamed, seemingly oblivious to the gravity underpinning the instructions. "Understood, sir! Absolutely. Won't let you down." He practically scrambled to gather the specified gear, excitement overcoming any lingering fear he might have felt.

Boone watched him go, shaking his head slowly, his expression dark. "Kid's gonna get himself killed chasin' data points," he muttered under his breath to Nora, who merely nodded grimly, her eyes following Jules' rapidly retreating figure as he plunged into the undergrowth, heading north along the creek bed.

The mood in camp shifted perceptibly after Jules' departure. The remaining five continued with their assigned tasks – Elise and Levi processing water samples and documenting nearby flora, Boone doing a close-perimeter sweep for recent animal sign, Graves coordinating via radio while Nora quietly maintained the camp area – but an undercurrent of anxiety flowed beneath the surface. Every thirty minutes, Elise found herself glancing towards the command tent, waiting for the crackle of the radio confirming Jules had checked in.

10:00 AM. Graves' voice, clipped, professional. "Jensen, report." A pause. Then Jules' slightly breathless voice crackled back, tinny but clear enough. "Jensen reporting. Making good time. Approximately one klick north. Terrain is manageable, creek is easy crossing here. All clear." "Acknowledged. Maintain vigilance," Graves replied, clicking off.

10:30 AM. Another check-in. Jules sounded closer to the target area. "Near waypoint Beta. Entering the ravine system now. Steep but clear path. No issues." "Acknowledged. Proceed with caution," Graves responded.

11:00 AM. Graves initiated the call. "Jensen, status." Silence. Only the faint hiss of static. Graves repeated the call. "Jensen, report status." More silence. Graves frowned, adjusting the frequency slightly. "Jensen, this is Graves. Respond." Nothing.

Elise felt her stomach clench. Levi looked up from the microscope he'd set up to examine algae samples. Boone paused his perimeter check, turning towards the command tent, his body suddenly tense.

"Could be the ravine walls blocking the signal," Levi suggested, though his voice lacked conviction. "Or he's focused on the monitor, maybe inside a deeper section."

Graves tried again, his voice harder now. "Jensen, immediate response required." The radio remained stubbornly silent.

Thirty minutes dragged by like hours. The normal camp sounds – the gurgle of the creek, the chirping of a winter wren, the rustle of wind – seemed amplified, mocking their strained silence as they waited. Every snap of a twig from the surrounding forest drew tense glances.

11:30 AM. Graves tried the radio again, multiple times. Nothing. The static hiss felt malevolent now.

"He's missed two check-ins," Levi stated quietly, stating the obvious.

Boone strode towards Graves. "Somethin's wrong. He's overdue. Radio silence ain't like him, not when he was so keen. We need to go now."

Graves checked his watch, his face a cold mask. "Scheduled check-in was missed at 1100. He has failed the 1130 follow-up. Agreed. Standard procedure is to wait one full hour cycle before initiating search, allowing for technical faults or minor delays."

"One hour?" Boone exploded, his voice tight with anger. "Graves, we found tracks eighteen inches long yesterday! We heard God knows what the night before! We don't wait an hour! If something's got him, an hour is a death sentence!"

"We adhere to protocol, Boone," Graves snapped back, his eyes like ice chips. "Panic serves no purpose. There could be rational explanations. Equipment failure. Minor injury delaying him. Crossing dead zones."

"And there could be a six-hundred-pound gorilla-man tearin' him limb from limb!" Boone retorted, stepping closer to Graves, his fists clenching. "My brother vanished up here! You think I'm gonna sit around waiting for 'protocol' while another kid disappears?"

Nora stepped quietly between them, placing a calming hand on Boone's arm, though her eyes held a silent warning for Graves. "Boone is right, Graves," she said, her voice low but firm. "The forest does not wait for schedules. If Jules is in trouble, time is everything. We go now."

Graves hesitated, looking from Boone's furious face to Nora's steady gaze, then at the anxious expressions of Elise and Levi. Perhaps he recognized the potential for mutiny, or perhaps even his rigid adherence to protocol had limits when faced with the stark possibility of losing another team member. "Fine," he conceded curtly, his voice sharp with barely contained frustration. "Gear up. Search team. Boone, you have point. Navigate via Jensen's intended route coordinates. Levi, medkit ready. Holloway, you're with me, documenting search findings. Nora, maintain camp security, monitor radios."

Nora nodded solemnly. "Be careful. That ravine… it has a bad name."

Within minutes, the four of them were moving quickly north, following the creek bed. Boone led the way, his earlier anger channeled into ferocious focus. He moved rapidly but with incredible attention to detail, his eyes scanning the ground, the brush, the trees, reading signs Elise couldn't even see – a freshly broken twig, a scuff mark on a rock, the faintest impression in the moss. He carried a sturdy-looking shotgun now, loaded, held at port arms, his expression grim. Graves followed, armed with a compact, military-style carbine Elise hadn't seen before, his movements economical and tactical. Levi carried his comprehensive medical pack, along with his own sidearm holstered visibly. Elise, armed only with her notebook, camera, and a deep sense of dread, struggled to keep pace while simultaneously scanning the environment through her biologist's lens, trying to note any anomalies.

The terrain grew rougher as they approached the ravine Jules had mentioned. The creek flowed faster here, squeezed between narrowing walls of dark, slick rock covered in moss and ferns. The air grew cooler, damper. A heavy silence descended, reminiscent of the cedar grove, broken only by the rush of water and their own ragged breathing.

"He came through here," Boone said quietly, pointing to faint boot prints in a patch of mud near the creek edge – smaller, commercially lugged soles, definitely Jules'. "Following the GPS track."

They entered the ravine proper. It was deeper and narrower than Elise had imagined, the rock walls rising steeply on either side, blocking out much of the sky. Water dripped constantly, echoing in the enclosed space. Roots snaked down the walls like gnarled fingers. Visibility was limited, the path ahead twisting around corners of rock. It felt like a trap.

"Jules!" Graves called out, his voice sharp, echoing unnaturally. "Jensen, sound off!"

Only the rushing water answered.

Boone held up a hand, signaling a halt. He knelt, examining the ground intently. "Tracks are clear here. Heading upstream. Pace looks… hurried? Stride's longer than it should be on this kind of ground." He touched a small, dark smear on a mossy rock. "What's this?"

Levi knelt beside him, touching the smear cautiously, then sniffing his fingertips. He looked up, his face pale. "Blood," he said grimly. "Fresh. Human."

A collective wave of cold washed over Elise. Blood.

"How much?" Graves demanded, his voice tight.

"Not arterial spray," Levi assessed quickly, scanning the surrounding area. "More like… transfer. From a wound, wiped on the rock. Or maybe from a fall."

"Keep moving," Graves ordered, his grip tightening on his carbine.

They pushed further into the ravine, moving faster now, hope warring with rising panic. Around the next bend, Boone stopped abruptly, his body rigid. He raised his shotgun slightly, scanning the area ahead.

"There," he whispered, pointing.

Scattered across the narrow creek bank and caught in the lower branches of dripping ferns was evidence of a struggle. Clear, undeniable evidence.

Jules's bright blue daypack lay discarded, one strap torn clean through, the contents partially spilled – energy bars, a water bottle, spare batteries. His GPS unit lay nearby, its screen cracked, frozen on the map display showing his last known position right where they stood. A few yards away, snagged on a thorny bush, was a torn piece of technical fabric that matched the lightweight jacket Jules had been wearing.

And there was more blood. Not just smears, but distinct droplets spattered on the rocks and leaves, glistening wetly in the dim light. One larger, darker patch stained the gravel near the creek's edge, already attracting buzzing flies.

But there was no sign of Jules himself. No body. No indication of where he might have gone, or been taken.

"Oh God," Elise breathed, her hand flying to her mouth, the metallic tang of blood thick in the air. Levi immediately went to work, kneeling by the blood patches, his face grimly professional as he assessed the scene from a medical standpoint.

"Significant blood loss indicated here," Levi reported, his voice strained. "Multiple impact points. Signs of dragging evident in the gravel." He pointed to shallow furrows leading from the main blood patch towards the deeper water of the creek, then disappearing on the slick, stony opposite bank. "The pattern suggests... violent removal from the scene."

Boone was examining the ground with microscopic intensity. "His tracks end here," he confirmed, pointing to scuffed impressions near the torn pack. "Mixed with... others." He indicated several partial impressions in the mud nearby, impressions that were chillingly familiar – large, indistinct, but undeniably huge, similar in scale to the tracks found two days prior. "Came up on him fast, looks like. Maybe from that overhang." He glanced up at a shadowed ledge on the ravine wall above them. "Grabbed him. Dragged him across the creek and then... up." He pointed towards the incredibly steep, densely forested slope on the far side of the creek, a near-vertical wall of tangled vegetation and rock.

"Impossible," Graves stated, his eyes scanning the slope. "No human could climb that, let alone dragging someone."

"Maybe not human," Boone replied grimly, his gaze locking with Graves'.

The reality hit Elise with the force of a physical blow. Jules was gone. Taken. The blood, the torn gear, the impossible escape route up the ravine wall, the massive tracks – it all pointed to a violent encounter with the creature whose existence she had so fiercely doubted just days ago. The scientific detachment shattered completely, replaced by raw fear and a sickening sense of loss for the young, overly eager technician.

Panic began to ripple through the remaining team members. Levi looked shaken, his medical assessment confirming the grim reality. Elise felt tears pricking her eyes, her breath coming in ragged gasps. Even Graves' icy composure seemed momentarily fractured, his gaze fixed on the steep slope, a flicker of something – disbelief? Fear? Calculation? – crossing his features.

"We have to find him," Elise pleaded, looking at Graves, then Boone. "He might still be alive! Injured!"

Boone shook his head, his face etched with a terrible certainty that mirrored his own past trauma. "It's too late for that, Doc. Look at the sign. Whatever took him… it wasn't gentle. And it moved fast, straight up that damn cliff face. We can't follow that."

"We have to try!" Elise insisted, desperation clawing at her.

"Boone is right," Graves said, his voice regaining its hard edge, the brief flicker of uncertainty gone, replaced by cold command. "Attempting to scale that slope is tactically impossible and risks further casualties. The subject is highly dangerous, demonstrated clearly here. Jensen is… a confirmed loss."

"A loss?" Elise repeated incredulously, anger surging through her fear. "You're just writing him off? We don't know for sure! We have to search!"

"Our objective is not rescue," Graves stated flatly, his eyes devoid of empathy. "It is reconnaissance and data collection. Jensen understood the risks. Continuing a search in this terrain, knowing the subject is active and hostile in the immediate vicinity, compromises the safety of the remaining team and the mission itself." He turned, already moving back down the ravine. "We retrieve Jensen's damaged equipment for analysis, document the site thoroughly, and return to base camp. Then we reassess our operational parameters and proceed with the primary objective."

"Proceed?" Boone's voice was dangerously low. He took a step towards Graves, shotgun still held ready. "You son of a bitch. You're just gonna leave him? After sending him out here alone? You really don't give a damn, do you? This is just 'data collection' to you, ain't it? People dyin' is just... collateral damage?"

Graves stopped, turned slowly, his hand moving almost casually towards the carbine slung across his chest. "My 'damn', Boone, is ensuring the rest of this team survives and completes the mission we were hired for. Emotional responses won't help us now. Discipline will. We move. Now."

The air crackled with tension, thick enough to taste. Elise held her breath, convinced Boone was going to attack Graves. Levi subtly positioned himself, ready to intervene. But after a long, tense moment where only the roar of the creek filled the silence, Boone slowly lowered his shotgun, his face contorted with helpless rage and disgust. He knew Graves was, in a terrible, pragmatic way, probably right about the futility and danger of a further search up that impossible slope. But the coldness of the decision, the utter lack of regard for Jules, was repellent.

Without another word, Boone turned and began meticulously gathering Jules' scattered belongings – the torn pack, the broken GPS, the piece of ripped jacket. Levi helped, collecting small environmental samples from the bloodstains for later analysis, his movements precise despite the tremor Elise could now see in his hands. Elise took photographs, documenting the grim scene, her hands shaking, the scientific act feeling like a hollow, disrespectful ritual.

They retreated from the ravine in silence, leaving behind the bloodstained rocks and the eerie emptiness where Jules had vanished. The weight of his absence was immense, a physical presence among them. Four remained now, their numbers dwindling, their fears confirmed in the most brutal way possible. The forest felt different now – no longer just watchful, but actively predatory. The sense of isolation intensified, becoming a crushing pressure.

Back at base camp, the news was delivered, and received by Nora with a solemn, unsurprised nod, as if she had expected nothing less from the valley. The fragile cohesion of the team had shattered. Fear was rampant, distrust towards Graves was thick in the air, and the beautiful, imposing wilderness of AO Hollow had transformed into a hunting ground. Graves insisted they were proceeding with the mission, deeper into the valley, but Elise knew, looking at the haunted faces around her, that something had irrevocably broken. They were no longer just searching for answers; they were fighting for survival. And their leader, it seemed, might be the most dangerous variable of all.

Chapter 8: Clashing Views

The return to base camp without Jules cast a pall thicker and more suffocating than the ever-present Olympic Peninsula mist. The space he had occupied – his infectious, sometimes annoying, tech-enthusiasm, his meticulously organized corner of the command tent, his bright blue jacket now lying grimly cataloged in an evidence bag Graves kept locked in a Pelican case – left a tangible void. Grief, raw fear, and simmering resentment created a toxic atmosphere around the flickering campfire that evening.

Dinner was barely touched. No one had the stomach for the bland, salty ration packs. Boone sat sharpening his knife with obsessive, rhythmic strokes, his face a granite mask of fury and sorrow. Nora brewed strong, bitter tea from herbs she'd gathered, offering mugs silently, her eyes holding a deep, weary understanding of the valley's unforgiving nature. Levi methodically checked and re-checked his medical supplies, his movements precise but lacking their usual calm efficiency; Elise saw him pause once, staring blankly into the fire, before shaking his head sharply and returning to his task. Elise herself felt numb, cycling between tearful images of Jules' eager face and chilling replays of the bloody scene in the ravine, unable to reconcile the scientific mission with the brutal reality of their situation.

Graves, predictably, attempted to impose order, or at least the semblance of it. Shortly after their return, he convened a mandatory meeting outside the command tent. The sun was beginning its descent, painting the undersides of the low clouds in streaks of bruised orange and purple, casting long, distorted shadows across the camp clearing.

"Alright," Graves began, his voice clipped, betraying no emotion despite the day's events. "Let's be clear on the situation and the path forward. We have suffered a loss. Jensen's disappearance confirms the presence of an extremely dangerous, large, and unidentified hostile subject within this AO."

He paused, letting the stark confirmation hang in the air. "This necessitates adjustments to our operational posture. Effective immediately: No solo movements, under any circumstances. All personnel will remain armed and maintain Condition Yellow awareness at all times," – he meant alert, aware of surroundings, Elise vaguely recalled from some safety briefing ages ago – "Travel will be in tight formation. Perimeter security will be doubled during night hours – two-person watches, two-hour rotations."

He looked directly at Boone. "While regrettable, Jensen's loss does not negate the mission directive from the Kestrel Foundation. If anything, it increases the urgency of gathering definitive data on the subject responsible. We have visual confirmation," he nodded towards the tent housing the laptop with the trail cam footage, "we have physical track evidence, and now we have undeniable proof of hostile interaction resulting in a casualty. This is critical intelligence."

Boone looked up from his knife, his eyes burning with contempt. "Critical intelligence? Graves, Jules is *gone*. Probably dead! Torn apart by that *thing* you seem so interested in 'documenting'. And you want to push *deeper* into its territory? Are you insane?"

"My objective," Graves stated, his voice hardening, "is to complete the mission safely with the remaining personnel. The subject has demonstrated hostility within Zone Gamma," he indicated the ravine area on a laminated map he held, "but we have no indication it actively patrols the entire valley or that this base camp location is compromised. Our primary survey area lies further south, towards the geological anomalies identified in the initial brief. Retreating now would mean failing the objective and potentially leaving valuable data uncollected."

"Valuable data?" Boone shot back, standing up slowly, knife still in hand though held loosely at his side. "What data is worth another life? Levi's? Elise's? Nora's? Mine? We found those tracks near *our* first camp! That thing was close! It took Jules less than two miles from *here*! You think it doesn't know we're squatting right in its living room? We need to get the hell out of this valley, back the way we came, while we still can!"

"Turning back now might be just as dangerous," Levi interjected quietly, surprisingly siding, in part, with Graves' logic, though his tone lacked Graves' cold detachment. "We don't know the subject's range or patterns. Retreating through territory it's already proven active in – the silent grove, the Zone Gamma ravine – could invite another attack, especially if it perceives us as fleeing. Continuing cautiously on the planned route might be less predictable, statistically safer, assuming we maintain maximum vigilance." He spoke like a man weighing probabilities, trying to find the least terrible option.

Elise felt torn. Boone's visceral desire to escape resonated powerfully with her own fear. Every instinct screamed to get out, back to civilization, away from the creature that had snatched Jules. The scientific curiosity that had initially drawn her felt naive, almost obscene now. But Levi had a point. Would backtracking be safer? Would they be walking back into the creature's preferred hunting grounds? And Graves... his insistence on pushing forward felt dangerously callous, almost suicidal, yet was there a cold, tactical logic to it she couldn't see?

"The Foundation knew the risks involved," Graves continued, ignoring Boone's outburst. "They equipped us to handle contingencies. The mission parameters stand. We continue south tomorrow morning, 0800."

"Like hell we do," Boone snarled. "I ain't leading anyone deeper into this meat grinder. I'm taking Nora, and anyone else with sense enough to come, back out the way we came in. Starting now." He turned towards his tent, clearly intending to pack.

"You will do no such thing," Graves commanded, stepping forward, his hand now resting overtly on the grip of his holstered sidearm. The carbine lay propped against the command tent nearby. "I am mission lead. Failure to follow direct orders constitutes dereliction, Boone. Under the terms of your Kestrel contract, that has significant consequences."

Boone stopped, turned slowly back towards Graves, his own hand drifting towards the shotgun leaning against a log near the fire. "Your contract don't mean shit to me when people are dying, Graves. And your 'authority' ends where my fist meets your jaw if you try and stop me leaving."

The confrontation crackled, raw and dangerous. Elise tensed, bracing for violence. Nora moved slightly, positioning herself subtly behind Boone, a silent statement of solidarity. Levi shifted uncomfortably, looking between the two men, clearly unwilling to take a side but radiating disapproval of the escalating conflict.

"Stand down, Boone," Graves ordered, his voice lethally calm. "Do not make this worse."

"Or what?" Boone challenged, his eyes narrowed. "You gonna shoot me? Add another 'data point' to your report?"

Before the situation could explode entirely, Elise found her voice, surprising herself. "Stop it!" she yelled, stepping between them, hands raised instinctively. "Both of you! This is insane! Fighting each other is exactly what we shouldn't be doing right now! Jules is gone. We're scared. We're trapped. We need to figure this out *together*, not threaten each other!"

Her unexpected outburst seemed to break the spell momentarily. Both men hesitated, looking at her, then back at each other, the immediate tension lowering by a fraction, though the underlying hostility remained thick.

"She's right," Levi said firmly, stepping forward as well. "Internal conflict compromises us further. We need a rational discussion, weigh the options. Boone, Graves, stand down."

Graves slowly removed his hand from his sidearm, though his expression remained flinty. Boone didn't lower his guard completely but took a half-step back from confrontation range.

"Fine," Graves clipped, though his eyes still pinned Boone with suspicion. "We table the route discussion until morning. We follow the doubled watch schedule tonight. No further deviations. Everyone gets what rest they can." He turned abruptly and retreated into the command tent, the flap closing firmly behind him, radiating displeasure.

Boone stared after him for a long moment, then spat into the dirt. He didn't say anything more, just retrieved his shotgun and stalked towards the edge of the firelight, settling onto a log facing the darkest part of the woods, clearly intending to take the first watch himself, trusting no one else, least of all Graves.

The fragile truce held through the evening, but the camp was divided, trust shattered. Elise found herself unwillingly assigned the second watch with Levi. The thought of sitting out there in the profound darkness, armed with only bear spray and a flashlight, listening for sounds that might herald another attack, filled her with icy dread.

Night fell like a lead curtain, absolute and smothering. The fire was kept higher than usual, casting flickering shadows that seemed to writhe and take on monstrous shapes at the edge of vision. The sounds of the forest – amplified by the enclosing valley walls – felt different tonight. Not neutral, not even just watchful, but predatory. Every hoot of an owl sounded like a potential signal. Every rustle in the undergrowth felt like encroaching footsteps. Elise kept remembering the description of the creature in the trail cam footage – massive, fluid, disappearing into shadows. It could be anywhere, watching them right now from the impenetrable blackness just yards away.

When Elise's watch began around midnight, the forest seemed unnervingly quiet again, much like the silent grove. Even the creek seemed to murmur less loudly. The air was still, heavy, carrying the scent of damp earth and decaying leaves. Sitting beside Levi on overturned logs, facing opposite directions to cover the camp perimeter, Elise strained her ears, every nerve ending prickling. The silence was worse than the strange noises. It felt deliberate. Calculated. Like holding one's breath before striking.

Levi, beside her, was a silent, reassuring presence, methodically sweeping his flashlight beam in slow arcs across the near treeline, then clicking it off to preserve night vision. Elise tried to emulate his calmness, tried to control her own shallow breathing, tried to separate imagined threats from real ones.

Then, maybe an hour into their watch, she heard it.

Low. Guttural. Coming from the darkness beyond Boone's tent, uphill slightly. *Hhhhhrrrrrrrrgggggllll*. A wet, heavy sound, like something clearing its throat, or maybe... breathing? It wasn't loud, barely audible over the low crackle of the dying fire, but it was undeniably close.

Elise froze, her heart leaping into her throat. She slowly turned her head towards Levi. He had frozen too, his head cocked, flashlight off, listening intently. He met her wide eyes in the dim firelight and gave a tiny, almost imperceptible shake of his head, signaling silence.

Another sound followed. A soft *thump*, like something heavy shifting its weight on the soft forest floor. Then, silence again. But it was the charged, listening silence from the night before, the silence that felt like scrutiny.

Elise fumbled for the can of bear spray clipped to her belt, her fingers numb with cold and fear. She could feel the hairs on the back of her neck standing on end. Something was out there. Right there. Just beyond the edge of the firelight, hidden by the blackness. Circling. Watching.

They sat paralyzed for what felt like an eternity, straining to hear, to see. The fire popped, sending a shower of sparks into the darkness, momentarily illuminating the first few feet of undergrowth, revealing nothing but damp ferns and dripping branches.

Then, a new sound drifted down from the ridge above the camp, further away now. A low, resonant growl, less aggressive than challenging, a deep rumble that vibrated in Elise's chest. It seemed to echo slightly off the valley walls. After a moment, it faded, replaced once more by the seemingly normal sounds of the night – the creek, a distant owl.

Whatever had been close seemed to have retreated, perhaps responding to the call from the ridge.

Elise let out a breath she hadn't realized she was holding, her body trembling uncontrollably. Levi reached over and briefly squeezed her arm, a gesture of solidarity in the shared terror.

"Did you…?" Elise whispered, her voice shaking.

Levi nodded grimly. "Close," he breathed back. "Very close. Moving parallel to the camp edge, then responded to the call from upslope."

They finished their watch in near-catatonic alertness, every shadow a potential threat, every sound magnified. By the time Boone came to relieve them, looking grim and unrested himself, Elise felt utterly spent, drained by fear and adrenaline. She crawled into her tent, burrowing deep into her sleeping bag, but sleep was a distant memory. The creature wasn't just a myth, wasn't just tracks or blurry footage. It was real, intelligent enough to coordinate, powerful enough to take a man without a trace, and bold enough to circle their camp in the dead of night.

The clash of views between Boone and Graves felt terrifyingly irrelevant now. Whether they retreated or pushed forward, they were trapped in this valley with something ancient and territorial. The fragile sense of safety provided by the camp, the fire, the weapons, felt illusory. They were intruders, vulnerable, and something in the darkness knew it. The forest itself felt like it was holding its breath, waiting for the inevitable confrontation.

Chapter 9: Folklore Fireside

The fragile light of dawn did little to dispel the oppressive weight that had settled over the base camp in AO Hollow. It seeped through the dense canopy not as a promise of warmth or clarity, but as a reluctant dilution of the profound darkness, revealing a scene etched with exhaustion and raw fear. The faces that emerged from the tents were pale, strained, marked by sleeplessness and the lingering terror of the night's close encounter. The subtle sounds Elise and Levi had heard – the breathing, the shifting weight just beyond the firelight, the resonant call from the ridge – had communicated themselves through the thin fabric of the tents or the shared frequency of fear, leaving everyone feeling exposed, vulnerable, and profoundly unwelcome.

Breakfast was a tense, almost silent ritual performed under Graves' watchful, impatient eye. He moved with brisk, deliberate energy, checking equipment, barking orders for water purification and gear consolidation, seemingly determined to maintain a façade of operational normalcy despite the group's near-paralysis. His strategy appeared to be relentless forward momentum, a refusal to acknowledge the depth of their fear or the validity of their dissent.

The unspoken conflict regarding their next move hung heavy in the damp morning air. Boone avoided Graves entirely, his face set in lines of grim resolve. He meticulously cleaned and oiled his shotgun, the metallic clicks and smooth sliding sounds cutting through the quiet, a clear statement of preparedness and defiance. Nora moved with quiet efficiency, breaking down her small section of the camp, her movements economical, her gaze constantly drifting towards the surrounding forest, particularly the steep slopes looming above them. Levi, though clearly shaken by the previous night, forced himself into his routine, checking medical supplies, assisting Elise with stowing the sampling kits they'd used near camp. His professional discipline was a brittle shield against the surrounding dread.

Elise felt adrift. The scientific purpose of the expedition felt like a distant, irrelevant dream. Her world had shrunk to the immediate, terrifying present: surviving the next hour, the next day, in a place inhabited by something powerful and hostile. The clash between Boone's desperate pragmatism – escape at all costs – and Graves' cold, mission-driven insistence on proceeding felt like being trapped between a rockslide and a charging predator. Both options seemed fraught with lethal peril.

Graves brought the simmering conflict to a head as the last of the breakfast rations were being choked down. He unrolled the laminated map across two supply crates, anchoring the corners with rocks.

"Alright," he announced, his voice sharp, cutting through the strained silence. "Route planning. We break camp in sixty minutes. Our trajectory remains south-southeast, following the main creek drainage towards geological Objective Delta." He tapped a point deep within the valley on the map. "Estimated two days' travel, assuming moderate terrain."

Boone stopped oiling his shotgun, placing it carefully across his knees. He didn't look at the map. "You're still set on goin' deeper?" His voice was deceptively calm, dangerously low.

"The mission parameters have not changed, Boone," Graves replied, meeting his gaze coolly. "We have objectives to meet. The recent incidents," he gestured dismissively, encompassing Jules' disappearance and the night's events, "necessitate increased caution, revised security protocols, but not abandonment of the primary goal."

"Primary goal," Boone echoed, a humourless smile twisting his lips. "Right. Document the thing that's pickin' us off one by one. Great plan, Graves. Real genius."

"I'm aware of the risks," Graves clipped. "Kestrel is aware. This is not a recreational hike."

"No kiddin'," Boone shot back. "It's a suicide mission led by a man too damn stubborn or too damn blind to see what's right in front of him. We got proof positive somethin' huge and mean lives here. It took Jules. It circled our camp last night, close enough to smell us. Any sane person would be haulin' ass outta here, not strollin' further into its pantry."

"Panicked retreat through hostile territory is tactically unsound," Graves retorted, repeating the argument that had temporarily held sway the previous day. "Predictable withdrawal invites pursuit. Maintaining our planned southward movement keeps the subject guessing, potentially moves us beyond its core territory."

"Core territory?" Boone scoffed. "Graves, look around! This *is* its core territory! The whole damn valley! Those tracks weren't left by somethin' just passin' through. This is its home. And we ain't welcome."

Elise watched them, her anxiety ratcheting higher. Boone's raw fear felt utterly rational; Graves' cold logic felt increasingly like denial, or worse, deliberate obfuscation. What did Kestrel know? What was Graves' real stake in reaching 'Objective Delta'?

Before the argument could escalate further, potentially into the violence that had simmered the previous evening, Nora spoke. Her voice, though quiet, cut through the tension with surprising authority. She had finished packing her meager belongings and stood near the edge of the clearing, looking not at the arguing men, but towards the silent, mist-shrouded trees.

"You argue about paths," she said, her tone carrying a weight of ancient weariness. "North or South. Retreat or Advance. As if you have a choice."

Both Graves and Boone turned to look at her, momentarily silenced by her unexpected interjection.

"This place," Nora continued, her gaze sweeping across the valley walls, "the Hollow Ground, *snəxʷəlxʷ ləɫ*, it does not care for your maps, your schedules, your weapons. It has its own ways. Its own guardians. You cannot force your will upon it."

Graves frowned, clearly impatient with what he perceived as mystical interruption. "Nora, with respect, we need practical decisions—"

"Practical?" Nora turned her gaze on him, her dark eyes sharp and challenging. "Is it practical to ignore the warnings? Is it practical to march deeper into a place that has already taken one of your own, a place my people have known to avoid for generations beyond counting?"

She looked around at the tense faces – Elise's pale fear, Levi's troubled composure, Boone's raw anger. "You come here with your science, your machines, your soldier's plans," she said, her voice softening slightly, but losing none of its intensity. "You look for a monster, a 'subject'. You do not understand what you have woken."

There was a moment of profound silence, broken only by the gurgle of the creek. Elise found herself holding her breath, captivated by Nora's gravity. This wasn't just local colour; it felt like vital, neglected wisdom.

"Nora," Elise asked quietly, drawn by the conviction in the older woman's voice, seeking something, anything, to anchor her swirling fear and confusion. "You mentioned the Stick-shí'načˇ before. The Forest People. Your elders… what do the stories say? About them? About this place?"

Nora looked at Elise, a flicker of something – perhaps sadness, perhaps appraisal – in her eyes. She hesitated, as if weighing whether these outsiders were capable of understanding, or deserving of the knowledge. Then she gave a slow nod.

"The stories are old," she began, moving closer to the dying embers of the morning fire, as if drawing strength from the connection to tradition. She sat on a log, pulling her worn blanket tighter around her shoulders despite the mild temperature. The others instinctively drew slightly nearer, forming a loose semi-circle. Even Graves lingered nearby, pretending to check his equipment but clearly listening. Boone sat back down, his anger momentarily banked by attentiveness.

"They are not 'stories' like you tell your children," Nora clarified, her gaze sweeping over them. "They are history. They are explanations. They are warnings passed down, breath to breath, generation to generation. They tell us how to live with the power of this land, how to show respect, how to survive."

She paused, gathering her thoughts, her eyes distant. "The Stick-shí'načˇ… that is just one name. Other tribes, other places, have different names. Sasq'ets, the Hairy Man. Our name speaks of their nature – 'Stick-shadows' or 'People who move like shadows among the sticks,' among the trees. They are rarely seen clearly, preferring the deep woods, the twilight hours, the places where mist hangs heavy."

Elise felt a chill despite the damp air. *Shadows among the sticks*. It perfectly described the fleeting glimpse on the trail cam.

"They are ancient," Nora continued, her voice taking on a rhythmic, almost chanting quality. "Older than the first Tall Cedars. Older than the memories of my people. They were here when the mountains were young, when the great rivers carved these valleys. Some stories say they were the first inhabitants, given guardianship over the deepest, most sacred parts of the forest by the Creator."

"Guardians," Elise repeated softly, remembering Nora's earlier words.

Nora nodded. "Guardians. Protectors. Not of us," she clarified, meeting Elise's eyes, "not of humans. They are protectors of the land itself. Of the balance. They keep the boundaries between the worlds – the world of humans, and the older, wilder world that still lives deep in these mountains."

She gestured towards the steep valley walls. "This place, the Hollow Ground, is one of their strongholds. A place where the veil is thin. Where powerful energies gather. Our ancestors knew this. They would come to the edges sometimes, for vision quests, for gathering specific medicines that only grow here. But they never lingered. They never built settlements here. They never hunted deep within its heart. They knew it was not permitted. It belonged to the Stick-shí'nač."

"And what happens," Levi asked quietly, his scientific curiosity apparently piqued despite the danger, "if someone ignores the boundaries? Intrudes?"

Nora's expression grew somber. "The Stick-shí'nač... they are not inherently evil," she said carefully. "They are not monsters seeking blood, not usually. They are like... intense storms, or the avalanche, or the river in flood. A force of nature that demands respect. If you stumble into their path unknowingly, if you are humble, respectful, leave offerings perhaps, they might simply watch you pass. They might make noises to frighten you away – whoops, screams, breaking branches, throwing stones – warnings to turn back."

Elise's mind flashed to the first night, the strange calls, the snapping branch. Warnings. Exactly as Nora described.

"But," Nora continued, her voice dropping lower, "if you are disrespectful? If you make too much noise? If you damage the land, cut the ancient trees, foul the water? If you come with arrogance, with weapons, seeking to dominate or exploit?" Her gaze flickered towards Graves, then away. "Or if you ignore their warnings, push deeper when they have told you to leave?"

She paused, letting the unspoken implication hang in the air. "Then they become enforces. They uphold the ancient laws of the place. Sometimes, they drive intruders mad with fear, haunting their camps, always watching, until they flee in terror. Sometimes... they make them disappear."

Elise thought of Jules, his eagerness to retrieve data overriding Boone's warnings, pushing into the ravine. Ignoring the warnings.

"The stories tell of hunters who became too bold, tracking game too far into forbidden valleys," Nora recounted. "They would vanish. Sometimes their camps were found torn apart, packs shredded, weapons broken – signs of immense strength and anger. Sometimes, like your young man," she nodded towards Graves, her expression softening with empathy despite her earlier challenge, "nothing was found but signs of a struggle, and tracks leading where no human could follow."

Boone shifted on his log, his knuckles white where he gripped the stock of his shotgun. Liam. His brother. Taken after ignoring the weather, pushing further than they should have.

"Do the stories say… what they *are*?" Elise asked, the biologist in her needing some kind of framework, even a folkloric one. "Are they animals? Spirits? People?"

Nora considered the question carefully. "They are… different," she said finally. "Not animals as you understand them. They have intelligence, complex communication. They use tools, some stories say – simple things, wood and stone. They seem to live in family groups. They mourn their dead. They understand territory."

"But they are not human," she added firmly. "They are tied to the wild places in a way humans no longer are. They have strength far beyond ours. Senses far keener. They can move through the thickest forest almost unseen, unheard, when they wish. Some say they can cloud men's minds, make them become lost or walk off cliffs. Some say they have power over the mist, the silence."

The silent grove. Elise shivered. The folklore wasn't just matching events; it was providing chillingly resonant explanations for things she had observed but couldn't scientifically account for.

"Do they… hunt people?" Levi asked, his voice carefully neutral, the medic needing to understand the mechanism of injury, of death.

"Not typically for food, the elders say," Nora replied. "Humans are not their natural prey. The disappearances… they seem more like… removals. Punishments. Territorial enforcements. Taking those who break the rules, who pose a threat, who refuse to leave. Perhaps taken alive, perhaps killed in the struggle… the stories vary. No one taken deep into the Hollow Ground has ever returned to tell."

A heavy silence descended on the group. Nora's words, delivered with quiet conviction and steeped in generations of cultural knowledge, painted a terrifyingly coherent picture. The Stick-shí'nač weren't simply monsters; they were an ancient, powerful, sentient force protecting a sacred domain, operating by rules the outsiders didn't understand and were fatally transgressing.

Elise looked around the small, fragile camp, seeing it suddenly through Nora's lens. They weren't scientists on an expedition; they were intruders in a sacred place, marked by its guardians after ignoring clear warnings. Jules hadn't just disappeared; he'd been 'removed'. The sounds in the night weren't just anomalous bioacoustics; they were communications, threats, assessments by intelligent beings deciding their fate.

The realization was profound, unsettling the very foundations of her scientific worldview. Could this cultural narrative hold more truth about their situation than Graves' mission logs or her own ecological frameworks? The patterns matched too closely to dismiss. The folklore provided context, motive, a terrifying internal logic to the escalating events. It didn't replace science, perhaps, but it offered a desperately needed layer of understanding, a way to interpret the behavior of the creature(s) they faced. Maybe the circling last night wasn't just random intimidation; maybe it was an assessment, a final warning before… what? Another removal? An outright attack?

She looked at Boone. He seemed less angry now, more deeply somber, listening to Nora with an expression of pained recognition. This wasn't just validation for him; it was the articulation of the truth he'd lived with since his brother's disappearance.

Levi appeared deeply thoughtful, perhaps considering the anthropological significance, or perhaps wrestling with the implications for their survival strategy. How do you apply medical logic to wounds inflicted by legendary guardians enforcing ancient laws?

Graves' reaction was the hardest to read. He had listened intently, his usual impatience held in check. Now, he stared towards the southern end of the valley, towards 'Objective Delta', his expression thoughtful, almost brooding. Was Nora's talk of boundaries, arrogance, and enforcement resonating with some hidden knowledge he possessed? Did Kestrel already know about the Stick-shí'nač, perhaps from older, covered-up encounters? Was the 'geological anomaly' they were heading towards somehow connected to the creature's 'sacred ground'? His silence was more unnerving than his earlier dismissals.

"So," Elise said slowly, thinking aloud, trying to bridge the gap between folklore and their predicament. "If these... beings... are guardians, enforcing rules... what happens now? We ignored the warnings. Jules was taken. They circled the camp. What's the next step, according to the stories?"

Nora looked at her, her eyes filled with sorrowful gravity. "The stories say... once blood is spilled, once a deliberate challenge is made and refused... the warnings cease. Patience ends. The Stick-shí'nač may tolerate intrusion for a time, offer chances to retreat. But once that line is crossed..." She paused, letting the fire crackle in the sudden stillness. "Then the guardians actively hunt. Not just to remove, but perhaps to... cleanse. To eliminate the threat entirely."

The implication hung heavy and cold between them. They had crossed the line. The buffer of warnings was gone. They were now, potentially, being actively hunted.

Graves straightened up abruptly, snapping the laminated map shut. "Enough," he commanded, his voice harsh, breaking the spell Nora had woven. "Folklore is informative, Nora, thank you. But it doesn't alter tactical reality. Fear is contagious. We maintain discipline. We proceed south." He refused to acknowledge the shift, refused to validate the fear that Nora's stories had crystallized. "Break camp. Sixty minutes."

He strode back towards the command tent, leaving the others reeling from the weight of Nora's narrative. But this time, his dismissal felt different. Less like ignorance, more like willful denial in the face of something he couldn't, or wouldn't, publicly acknowledge.

Boone watched him go, then looked at Elise, then at Levi. He didn't need to voice the question: *Do we follow him? Deeper into the hunt?*

Elise didn't have an answer. But Nora's words echoed in her mind, intertwining with the scientific data, the missing persons reports, the blurry footage, the bloody scene in the ravine. A terrifying tapestry was forming, woven from threads of science, folklore, and fear. They were caught in the pattern, and pulling free seemed less likely with every passing hour. The valley felt ancient, sentient, and deeply angered. And the path forward, regardless of direction, seemed shrouded in a darkness older and more profound than the forest itself.

Chapter 10: Deep Warning

Despite Boone's simmering resistance and the heavy pall of Nora's folklore fireside revelations, Graves' sheer force of will prevailed. Or perhaps it was the paralyzing fear, the uncertainty of which path held less peril, that ultimately kept the fractured team moving forward under his command. Retreating felt like admitting defeat, like actively running *from* the predator through territory it had already claimed. Pushing south, into the unknown, held a terrifying allure of the unexplored, a sliver of hope – however irrational – that they might move beyond the creature's immediate focus, or that 'Objective Delta', whatever it was, held some key to understanding or escape.

And so, they broke camp under a sky that remained stubbornly overcast, the air thick with unspoken anxieties. Boone packed his gear with a grim, resentful silence, making it clear he was complying under duress, his loyalty now purely functional, devoid of any trust in Graves' leadership. Nora moved with her usual quiet grace, but her eyes held a new depth of sorrowful vigilance. Levi checked everyone's minor cuts and blisters with meticulous care, his professional manner a thin shield over palpable tension. Elise felt numb, operating on autopilot, the weight of her pack negligible compared to the weight of dread pressing down on her spirit. She mechanically checked the memory cards and battery levels on her recovered trail cameras, the scientific routine feeling utterly disconnected from the primal fear coiling in her gut.

Graves set a relentless pace heading south along the main creek, seemingly determined to outrun the tension and doubt consuming his team. He took the lead himself this time, moving with a focused, aggressive energy, his carbine held ready, his eyes constantly scanning the dense woods. Boone fell into the rear guard position, his shotgun a heavy presence, his gaze sweeping back the way they had come as often as it scanned ahead. Levi and Elise were sandwiched between them, Nora slightly ahead of Boone, the five of them forming a tight, wary knot moving through the hostile green vastness.

The valley began to narrow slightly as they progressed south, the creek meandering through groves of enormous, ancient cedars and firs draped in heavy curtains of moss and lichen. The air grew cooler, damper, the silence more profound.

The unsettling absence of normal wildlife sounds that Elise had noted before became pervasive here. No bird song, no chattering squirrels, not even the buzz of insects. Only the sound of the creek, their own heavy breathing, and the swish of their passage through wet ferns disturbed the tomblike stillness. It felt profoundly unnatural, as if the entire ecosystem was holding its breath, aware of their intrusion, aware of the guardians Nora spoke of.

Around midday, as they navigated a particularly dense stand of monolithic cedars whose bases were wider than Elise was tall, Boone called a halt from the rear.

"Hold up," his voice was low, tense. "Somethin' ain't right here."

Graves turned, impatience etched on his face. "What is it, Boone? We need to maintain pace."

"Look at the trees," Boone replied, gesturing around them with his shotgun barrel.

Elise followed his gesture, scanning the massive trunks surrounding them. At first, she saw nothing unusual – just the deeply furrowed, reddish-brown bark characteristic of *Thuja plicata*, coated in thick layers of moss and ferns. Then, her eyes caught it.

Carved into the bark of several of the largest cedars, deliberately placed at eye level or slightly higher, were symbols. They weren't random scratches or natural bark patterns. They were clear, intentional markings.

Some looked incredibly old, the edges of the carvings smoothed by decades, perhaps centuries, of weather and bark growth, almost swallowed by the surrounding moss. These older symbols were abstract, geometric – deep spirals, interconnected triangles, grids of parallel lines. They resonated with a primal, ancient power, reminiscent of petroglyphs Elise had seen in other parts of the world.

But interspersed among these ancient markings were others that looked disturbingly fresh. The cuts were clean, raw wood showing through the darker bark, sap still glistening wetly on the edges in some cases. These newer symbols were cruder, more visceral. Some were simple, bold X's slashed deeply into the wood. Others were jagged, almost violent zig-zag patterns. And on one massive cedar directly facing the path they were taking, there was a large, unmistakable carving that made Elise's blood run cold: a rough outline of a tall, bipedal figure with massive shoulders and a disproportionately large head, standing over a smaller, prone stick-figure shape.

"Sweet merciful..." Levi breathed, stepping closer to examine the carving, his face pale.

"What the hell is this?" Graves demanded, his voice tight, shedding some of his usual control as he took in the gallery of symbols surrounding them.

"Warnings," Nora said softly, stepping forward to stand beside Boone. She reached out and gently touched one of the ancient spiral carvings, her expression filled with a mixture of reverence and fear. "The old symbols... they mark this grove as significant. Sacred ground, perhaps. A place of power for the Stick-shí'nač."

She then pointed to the fresh carvings, her face hardening. "These... these are different. Angrier. They are recent declarations. Territorial markers." She indicated the X's and zig-zags. "Signs of agitation. Warnings to intruders. Put here *for us*, I think." Her gaze rested on the crude depiction of the large figure looming over the smaller one. "And this... this tells a story. A warning of what happens to those who trespass. What happened to your young man, perhaps."

The implication was horrifyingly clear. The creature – or creatures – knew they were coming. It had marked this path, this sacred grove, with fresh warnings, layered over ancient symbols of its dominion, essentially telling them: *This is our place. We are powerful. We know you are here. We have already taken one of yours. Turn back, or face the consequences.*

Elise felt a wave of dizziness wash over her. The intelligence, the communication, the sheer *audacity* of it... leaving symbols carved into trees like some ancient human tribe marking its borders. It shattered any lingering scientific explanations involving simple animal behavior. This was sentient. This was deliberate. This was terrifying. She quickly raised her camera, documenting the symbols, both ancient and new, her hands shaking slightly. This was data, yes, but it felt more like reading a death warrant.

Boone ran a hand over the rough carving of the tall figure, his expression grim. "Marking its territory," he murmured, echoing Elise's thought. "And lettin' us know it knows we're here. This ain't just random. It knew we'd pass this way." How? Had it been tracking them that closely? Observing their route? The level of surveillance implied was deeply unnerving.

Graves stared at the symbols, particularly the fresh ones, his face unreadable but tense. He pulled out his own camera and took several detailed photographs, his movements clipped and efficient, but Elise noticed a slight tremor in his hand as he lowered the camera. He was rattled. Perhaps not by the confirmation of the creature's intelligence – she suspected he already knew or strongly suspected that – but by the immediacy, the freshness, the *directness* of the communication. This wasn't passive evidence like tracks or blurry footage; this was an active message, delivered directly across their path.

He seemed particularly focused on the ancient symbols, comparing them against something on a small, ruggedized device he pulled from his pouch – not the GPS, something else. Did he recognize them? Did Kestrel have archives of such things?

"Dismiss it?" Boone challenged, seeing Graves' mask of control attempt to reassert itself. "Graves, that thing carved a goddamn picture of itself killing someone right on our path! It's talkin' to us! It's tellin' us we're next!"

"It's psychological warfare, Boone," Graves snapped, shoving his device back into its pouch, though his voice lacked its usual unwavering conviction. "Intimidation tactics. Meant to frighten us, make us break ranks, make mistakes."

"And is it working?" Elise asked quietly, looking at the fear etched on Levi's face, feeling the tremor in her own limbs. "Because I'm terrified. If this is its way of warning us off, shouldn't we listen?"

"We listen by increasing caution, not by abandoning the objective," Graves insisted, though his eyes flickered nervously towards the dark woods surrounding the grove. He seemed caught between his programming – follow the mission, achieve the objective – and the undeniable, visceral threat represented by the carvings. Even his military training likely hadn't prepared him for an enemy that communicated through ancient symbols and possibly manipulated the very silence of the forest.

He visibly forced himself back into command mode. "This changes nothing, tactically. It confirms the subject's intelligence and territoriality, which we already inferred. Document the symbols, record the coordinates. We move out in five minutes. Stick tighter together. Eyes open."

He pushed past the largest cedar with the most disturbing carving, deliberately not looking at it again, and continued south along the faint trail, forcing the others to follow or be left behind.

Moving out of the Grove of Symbols felt like leaving a cursed shrine. The air seemed to press down even harder, the silence felt even more profound. Elise couldn't shake the image of the carvings, particularly the fresh, angry ones. The X's felt like targets painted on their backs. The looming figure felt like a promise.

They walked for another hour through the oppressive stillness, the tension ratcheting higher with every step. Every flicker of movement in the peripheral vision, every cracking twig, every strangely shaped shadow seemed like a potential ambush. Elise found herself mimicking Boone and Nora, her head constantly swiveling, scanning the trees, the ground, the ridges above, searching for any sign of movement, any anomaly.

Graves, despite his earlier dismissal, was clearly affected. He moved with a coiled tension, his carbine held at the ready, frequently pausing to listen, to scan the terrain ahead with binoculars. He seemed less like a determined leader now, and more like a man realizing he might have severely underestimated his adversary. The psychological warfare, as he'd termed it, was working.

Late in the afternoon, as the light began to fade rapidly under the perpetually overcast sky, they rounded a bend in the creek and saw something that made them all stop dead in their tracks.

Nestled beneath a dripping overhang of rock, almost hidden by ferns, was what looked like a crude shelter or structure. It wasn't naturally formed. Long, thick branches, some clearly snapped from nearby trees with brute force, were interwoven with smaller limbs, mud, and thick clumps of moss and animal fur, forming a rough, dome-like shape perhaps six feet high and eight feet across. It blended almost perfectly with the surrounding forest debris, camouflaged and organic, yet undeniably constructed. A small opening faced away from the creek, towards the deeper woods.

"What in God's name..." Levi whispered, lowering his pack slowly.

They approached cautiously, weapons ready. Boone circled around the structure, checking the surrounding ground, while Graves and Levi covered the potential approaches. Nora hung back slightly, her expression one of deep disquiet, murmuring something soft under her breath in what Elise guessed was Lushootseed.

"Tracks," Boone reported grimly from the far side. "Same big ones. All around here. Fresh. Whatever made this… it's been here recently."

Elise moved closer, drawn by a morbid, scientific curiosity that momentarily overrode her fear. Peering towards the low opening, she could see the interior was dark, shadowed. A rank, musky odour emanated from within – a mix of damp earth, decaying vegetation, something vaguely mammal-like, and another undefinable, pungent scent that made her nostrils flare. It smelled wild, primal.

Graves motioned for Levi to check the interior, using a powerful flashlight beam to probe the darkness. Levi hesitated for only a second before complying, crouching low and shining the bright beam inside, sweeping it carefully.

"Clear," Levi reported after a moment, his voice tight. "Appears empty. Just… debris inside. Leaves, more fur, some..." he paused, "some bones."

Bones. The word sent another jolt of cold through Elise.

Graves nodded curtly. "Alright. Maintain perimeter. Holloway, document it."

Heart pounding, Elise retrieved her camera and a portable specimen kit. She approached the opening, the musky smell intensifying. Hesitantly, she shone her own headlamp inside.

The interior was rough, essentially a hollow scooped out beneath the interwoven branches. The floor was thickly padded with dried ferns, moss, and large clumps of coarse, dark brown and blackish hair – definitely not bear or deer. And scattered amongst the bedding material were bones. Lots of them. Mostly animal – deer femurs snapped cleanly in half, likely for marrow, elk vertebrae, smaller skeletons of rabbits or marmots. But lying partially buried near the back wall, unmistakably, was a human bone. A tibia, long and slender, looking incongruously delicate amidst the larger animal remains. And beside it, tangled in a clump of the coarse dark hair, glinted something metallic.

Elise reached in carefully with a gloved hand, using forceps from her kit to gently retrieve the object. It was a small, tarnished silver locket, heart-shaped, hinged shut. It looked old, perhaps Victorian or early 20th century.

She held it up, her hand trembling. "Graves... Levi..."

They came closer, peering at the locket in her hand, then into the dark interior at the scattered bones, the human tibia starkly visible now in their combined flashlight beams.

"Analysis?" Graves demanded, his voice strained.

"Definitely human tibia," Levi confirmed grimly. "Adult. Can't tell sex or age without more analysis. The locket... suggests possibly female victim, from decades ago?"

Elise gently pried open the tarnished locket. Inside, miraculously preserved, were two tiny, faded sepia-toned photographs. One showed a young woman with her hair piled high, wearing a high-necked blouse. The other showed a smiling young man in a boater hat. They looked hopeful, happy, caught in a moment from a distant past. Who were they? Hikers? Settlers from a bygone era? Victims who had strayed into this valley long before records were kept, their fate ending here in this primitive den, their memory reduced to a single bone and a forgotten keepsake amidst the leavings of something unimaginable?

The discovery solidified the horror. This wasn't just happening now; it had been happening for a very long time. The creature – the Stick-shí'nač – wasn't a recent phenomenon. It was ancient, its presence woven into the deepest history of this valley, its territory defended, its leavings casually discarded in its den like any other predator, blurring the line between intelligent guardian and monstrous beast.

Graves stared at the locket, then back towards the structure, then at the looming valley walls surrounding them. His face was pale, his jaw working. The confidence, the dismissals, the insistence on mission parameters – it all seemed to crumble in the face of this tangible evidence of the valley's long, dark history of disappearances, laid bare in a primitive nest built by the creature they were supposedly hunting, or perhaps, that was now hunting them.

The Grove of Symbols had been a warning. This den, with its grisly mix of animal and human remains, felt like something else entirely. It felt like confirmation of their fate should they continue to ignore the valley's deepest, oldest law: Turn Back.

Chapter 11: Cut Off

The discovery of the den, the lair, the *nest* – Elise struggled for the right word – cast a chilling pall over the remainder of the day. The stark evidence of the creature's long-term presence and predatory capabilities, the casual mixing of animal and human remains, the tarnished locket hinting at victims lost decades before official records even began – it stripped away any lingering vestiges of scientific detachment or mission focus for everyone except, perhaps, Graves himself, and even he seemed deeply unsettled beneath his rigid composure. They had backtracked hastily from the gruesome site, the musky scent clinging to their clothes and imaginations, the image of the human tibia among the debris burned into their minds.

Fear, cold and sharp, was now a constant companion, tightening its grip with every shadow, every unexplained sound, every mile they ventured deeper into the valley's embrace. The symbols in the grove felt less like warnings now and more like declarations of intent. The nest felt like a promise of their own potential end.

Graves pushed them onward relentlessly, seemingly determined to put distance between them and the disturbing discovery, perhaps hoping that forward momentum would counteract the rising tide of terror and dissent. He abandoned the pretense of following the creek closely, instead choosing a more direct, more arduous route aiming straight for 'Objective Delta,' forcing them up steeper slopes, through denser thickets, across treacherous scree fields where loose rock shifted alarmingly underfoot. The pace was grueling, bordering on reckless, especially as the already weak daylight began its premature fade into the long northern twilight.

Elise stumbled frequently, her legs heavy with fatigue and fear, her mind replaying images from the den. Beside her, Levi moved with his characteristic steadiness, but his face was drawn, his eyes scanning the terrain with an intensity that bespoke deep concern rather than calm assessment. Boone, bringing up the rear, moved with a grim reluctance, his shotgun held perpetually at the ready, his earlier anger replaced by a bleak, fatalistic acceptance, as if he knew they were walking deeper into a trap but felt powerless to stop it. Nora kept pace silently, her connection to the land seemingly allowing her to navigate the difficult terrain with less overt effort, yet her face held the deepest shadows, reflecting an ancestral knowledge of the danger they were courting.

As dusk settled thickly in the valley bottom, painting the world in shades of bruised indigo and charcoal, Graves finally called a halt. He selected a campsite not for comfort or shelter, but for defensibility – a narrow, rocky ledge halfway up the eastern valley slope, offering clear fields of view downward but worryingly exposed from the densely forested slopes rising above them. There was no water source nearby; they would have to rely on the dwindling supplies in their packs until they descended again.

"Camp here," Graves ordered curtly, dropping his pack with a heavy thud. "Set perimeter sensors immediately, Jensen's spares. Double watches start as soon as it's full dark. Cold camp tonight – no fire. Minimal light discipline."

The prospect of a night without a fire, without that small circle of warmth and perceived safety, sent a fresh wave of dread through Elise. A cold camp implied a high threat level, an acknowledgment that any light or smoke could draw unwanted attention. It felt like admitting they were truly being hunted.

Boone said nothing, merely beginning to clear a small patch of ground for his tarp shelter with short, angry movements, positioning himself to face the upward slope, the direction from which an attack seemed most likely. Nora found a shallow indentation in the rock face, pulling her blanket around her, preparing for a long, cold, watchful night.

While Levi administered basic first aid to the various cuts and scrapes accumulated during the day's hard push, Graves and Elise worked to deploy the extra perimeter sensors Jules had packed. These were smaller, simpler seismic and infrared units, lacking the camera capabilities of the main traps but designed to provide early warning of movement near the camp edge. Elise's hands fumbled with the small electronic components, her fingers stiff with cold and trembling slightly.

It was during this process, as full darkness enveloped the ledge, that the first indication of a new, insidious problem arose. Elise switched on one of the seismic sensors, expecting the familiar small green LED indicator light to blink, confirming power and activation. Nothing happened.

"That's odd," she murmured, checking the battery connection. It seemed secure. She tried cycling the power switch again. Still dark. "Maybe the battery's dead?" She pulled a spare from her pouch, tested it quickly on her headlamp (it worked fine), and swapped it into the sensor. Still nothing. The unit remained inert.

"Problem, Holloway?" Graves asked sharply, noticing her pause. He was working on another sensor a few yards away.

"This sensor seems dead," Elise reported, frustration mixing with a new tendril of unease. "Tried a new battery, checked connections. No power light, nothing."

Graves came over, took the sensor from her, and examined it briefly in the red glow of his tactical headlamp. He manipulated the switch, tapped it against his palm. "Faulty unit, probably damaged in transit," he grunted, tossing it back onto the ground dismissively. "Use another."

Elise retrieved a second spare sensor from the case. This one powered up initially, the green light blinking reassuringly for a few seconds. Then, abruptly, it flickered and died, plunging back into darkness.

"What the…?" Elise tapped this one too, wiggled the battery. Nothing. "Graves, this one just died too."

Graves straightened up, frowning, his head tilted as if listening. "My sensor just cut out as well," he said, his voice tight. He shone his light on the small infrared unit he'd been setting up. Its indicator light was also dark. "Check the others."

Quickly, they checked the remaining spare sensors. None of them would power on, or if they did, they flickered out within seconds. It wasn't faulty units; something else was happening.

"Jules' main receivers," Graves ordered, already moving towards the small, protected alcove where they'd stowed the sensitive electronics, including the laptop hub that collected data from the already-deployed camera traps and audio monitors. Elise followed close behind, her heart beginning to pound with a new kind of fear – technological blindness.

Graves unzipped the protective case and pulled out Jules' ruggedized laptop, hitting the power button. The screen remained stubbornly black. He tried again, holding the button down, checking the connection to the external battery pack. Nothing. Dead.

He then grabbed the portable receiver unit linked to the failed perimeter sensors they had just tried to deploy. Also dead. No lights, no response.

"What is going on?" Elise whispered, staring at the inert devices. "A power surge? Some kind of electromagnetic pulse?"

"EMP seems unlikely out here," Graves muttered, his technical mind clearly racing through possibilities, though his expression was tight with concern. "Localized magnetic anomaly? Severe atmospheric interference?" He pulled out his own sophisticated GPS unit, the one he constantly consulted for navigation and scheduling. The screen flickered erratically for a moment, displaying garbled characters and impossible coordinates, then went blank. "My GPS is down too."

Panic, cold and suffocating, began to close in on Elise. No sensors. No laptop to check the deployed cameras or audio monitors. Graves' primary navigation tool was useless. They were electronically blind.

"The sat phone," Levi said, stepping over from where he'd been observing with growing alarm. "Graves, try the satellite phone. The Kestrel prototype. If that works, we can still call for evac, report our situation."

Graves snatched the sleek, experimental satellite phone from its case. He flipped it open, watching the small screen intently. For a moment, it flickered to life, displaying the Kestrel logo, then shifted to a 'Searching for Satellite…' message. The signal strength bar remained stubbornly empty. After a minute of futile searching, the screen displayed a new message: *'COMMUNICATION ERROR: UNABLE TO ESTABLISH UPLINK. CHECK SIGNAL / DEVICE'* – then it too flickered and went dark.

"No," Graves breathed, tapping the phone uselessly. "No, that's impossible. These units are hardened, triple redundancy, designed to penetrate dense canopy, atmospheric interference…" He trailed off, staring at the dead device in his hand, a crack finally appearing in his icy composure.

A wave of true, profound isolation washed over Elise. No perimeter warnings. No access to potential data from their deployed equipment. No GPS navigation beyond basic map and compass. And crucially, no way to call for help. No way to contact the outside world. They were cut off. Utterly, completely adrift in a hostile valley, miles from civilization, hunted by something ancient and powerful.

Boone had overheard the commotion from his position near the ledge edge. He walked over slowly, looking at the collection of dead electronics illuminated by Elise's nervous headlamp beam. He showed no surprise, only a grim, knowing weariness.

"Told you this place wasn't right," he said quietly, his voice heavy. He pulled out his old, reliable Silva compass from a pouch on his belt. The needle spun sluggishly, unwilling to settle decisively on North, swinging back and forth in erratic arcs. He tapped the housing gently. It continued to swing, confused and unreliable.

"Even the damn compass is screwed up," Boone stated flatly, tucking it away. "Magnetic interference? Or maybe..." He looked around at the looming, shadowed slopes, the oppressive darkness. "...Maybe somethin' else."

"What do you mean, 'something else'?" Elise asked, her voice trembling slightly.

Boone met her gaze, his eyes reflecting the ambient gloom. "Nora's people," he said, nodding towards the older woman who watched them impassively from her alcove, "they talk about places like this. Deep places. Places the guardians protect so fiercely... they don't *want* you to leave. Places where the normal rules don't apply. Where the rocks themselves, the air, conspires against intruders. Makes compasses spin, makes machines die, makes trails disappear."

Elise stared at him, horrified. His explanation sounded like pure superstition, a desperate attempt to explain the inexplicable through folklore. Yet... their equipment *was* dead. All of it. From simple sensors to sophisticated satellite technology. Even the basic magnetic compass was malfunctioning. Could there be some bizarre geological phenomenon at play – a massive iron deposit, localized magnetic anomalies far exceeding normal variations? Perhaps. Levi might be able to theorize possibilities.

But Boone's other implication, interwoven with Nora's earlier stories, lingered like a poisonous vapor. What if it wasn't geology? What if the 'guardians', the Stick-shí'nač, possessed abilities beyond mere physical strength? The power to cloud minds, Nora had said. Power over mist... power over silence... power, perhaps, over the very fabric of technology and navigation within their sacred domain? The ability to electronically blind intruders, cut them off, ensure they couldn't call for help or easily find their way out? It sounded impossible, preposterous, straight out of fantasy. Yet, faced with the array of dead devices at their feet, in this valley where the impossible seemed to be rapidly becoming the norm, the line between science fiction and terrifying reality blurred almost completely.

"We're blind," Levi stated, summarizing their predicament starkly. "No early warning systems beyond our own senses. No satellite communication. No reliable GPS. Navigation reverts to map, terrain association, and," he glanced towards Boone and Nora, "instinct."

Graves remained silent for a long moment, staring at the dead sat phone as if willing it back to life. The implications for his meticulously planned operation, his connection to Kestrel, his ability to control the situation, were catastrophic. Finally, he seemed to reach a decision, shoving the phone back into its case, his face hardening back into its default mask of command, though the fear was now visible in the tightness around his eyes, the slight pallor beneath his skin.

"Alright," he said, his voice raspy but regaining its authoritative edge. "Technological setback. Significant, but not insurmountable. We adapt. We revert to traditional navigation methods." He looked at Boone, a grudging acknowledgment in his eyes. "Boone, Nora – your terrain reading is now critical."

He addressed the group, projecting confidence he clearly no longer fully possessed. "Security is paramount. Two-person watches, constant vigilance. We conserve power in essential lights. We maintain tight formation during movement. Our objective remains," he stated, though the words sounded hollow now, "find a location suitable for potential emergency signal fire or clear line-of-sight for conventional radio, if functionality returns intermittently. Failing that, proceed towards Objective Delta, which reconnaissance suggested has features potentially visible from aerial search." It sounded like grasping at straws.

No one argued this time. The catastrophic failure of their technology seemed to have shocked them into a state of numb compliance, or perhaps unified them in the shared terror of their profound isolation. They were truly on their own now, stripped bare of the technological advantages they had relied upon. Their survival depended entirely on their own senses, their wilderness skills, their dwindling supplies, and their ability to navigate a hostile landscape where even the compasses lied, all while being stalked by an ancient power that seemed capable of manipulating their environment in ways they couldn't comprehend.

As Elise settled into her shared, fireless watch rotation later that night, the darkness felt absolute, the silence heavier than ever. The dead electronics felt like anchors dragging them down into despair. Boone's words echoed: *They don't want you to leave.* The chilling possibility lingered. Were they simply lost and facing a natural predator, or had they truly crossed into a place where the laws of nature, physics, and technology were actively being bent against them by an intelligence far older and more powerful than they had ever imagined? The uncertainty was almost as terrifying as the creature itself.

Chapter 12: Something Watches

Survival mode kicked in with the grey, mist-shrouded dawn. The catastrophic failure of their technology, the complete severing of their ties to the outside world, paradoxically forged a tense, fragile unity born of shared peril. The previous day's open conflict between Boone and Graves subsided, replaced by a grim focus on the immediate challenges. There was no more debate about direction; following Graves south towards the vague hope of 'Objective Delta' seemed marginally less suicidal than backtracking through territory now proven to be actively hostile and electronically dead. Navigation fell squarely on Boone and Nora, their expertise now indisputably essential, Graves' GPS unit relegated to useless dead weight in his pack.

Breaking the cold, comfortless camp was done with swift, hushed efficiency. Every movement felt exposed, every sound potentially fatal. They conserved headlamp batteries, operating mostly in the dim twilight filtering through the thick canopy. Without the electronic reassurance of perimeter sensors or the ability to check trail cams, their own senses were stretched taut, straining to interpret the language of the forest – the snap of a distant twig, the flicker of movement in the peripheral vision, the quality of the oppressive silence.

They descended cautiously from the exposed ledge back towards the valley floor, moving in a tight diamond formation: Boone on point, reading the subtle signs of the trail, Nora slightly behind him adding her deeper understanding of the land, Levi and Elise in the middle, Graves taking the rear, his eyes constantly scanning their back trail and the overlooking ridges. Every member was armed – Boone with his shotgun, Graves with his carbine, Levi and Elise now carrying the sidearms Graves had issued from his personal kit (Elise handled the heavy pistol awkwardly, its unfamiliar weight a constant, terrifying reminder of their situation), and Nora preferring her heavy, long-handled belt axe. They were no longer a scientific team; they were a small, heavily armed but deeply vulnerable group of prey trying desperately not to act like it.

The forest seemed to close in around them as they moved south along the creek bed, which widened again here, flowing sluggishly through marshy flats choked with skunk cabbage and alder thickets. The air felt heavy, stagnant, amplifying the eerie silence. The sense of being watched was no longer a vague paranoia; it was a near certainty, a palpable pressure felt on the back of the neck, a prickling awareness of unseen eyes following their progress.

Elise found herself constantly scanning the dense walls of vegetation lining the creek, the tangled roots and shadowed recesses beneath ancient trees, the high ridges looming on either side, half-shrouded in mist. Her scientific training warred with primal fear. Was that darker patch deep within the ferns just shadow, or was it something hiding? Was that slight sway of branches high on the ridge caused by wind, or by movement? Her eyes played tricks on her, conjuring shapes from the interplay of light and shadow, making her jump at perfectly natural occurrences.

Levi seemed to be experiencing the same hyper-alertness, his head constantly swiveling, his hand often resting near the grip of his pistol. Boone and Nora moved with a quieter, more focused intensity, their vigilance honed by experience, less prone to jumpiness but radiating a deep, unwavering awareness of potential threat. Even Graves, despite his forced projection of control, repeatedly swept the overlooking slopes with his binoculars, his movements betraying an underlying tension that contradicted his clipped commands.

It was Boone who saw it first. He froze mid-stride, holding up a hand for the group to halt instantly. He didn't point, didn't make any sudden movements, just tilted his head almost imperceptibly towards the western ridge, high above them.

"Ridge line," he breathed, his voice barely a whisper. "Nine o'clock high. Edge of the scree field."

Elise slowly, carefully, turned her head, following the implied direction of his gaze. Her heart hammered against her ribs. High above the creek, where the dense forest gave way to a steep, unstable slope of broken rock and sparse alpine firs, something moved.

It was tall. Impossibly tall. Standing partially silhouetted against the slightly brighter grey of the mist clinging to the highest peaks. It wasn't rock; it moved. A slow turn of the head, a slight shift of massive shoulders. Dark, indistinct against the grey backdrop, visible for only a few seconds before it stepped deliberately sideways, merging seamlessly into the shadow of a cluster of gnarled, weather-beaten trees growing precariously on the slope. Gone.

"Did you see it?" Levi whispered, his voice tight. Elise nodded mutely, unable to speak, her breath caught in her throat. It hadn't been a trick of the light. It hadn't been an animal. It was large, bipedal, and it had been watching them. Clearly, deliberately watching them from a high vantage point.

Graves had his binoculars up, scanning the spot where the figure had vanished. "Description?" he demanded, his voice low and urgent, but without lowering the binoculars.

"Tall," Elise managed, her voice trembling slightly. "Eight, maybe nine feet? Broad build. Dark colour. Moved deliberately."

"Couldn't make out details," Levi added. "Too far, poor light. But the scale... matched the tracks. And the footage."

Boone lowered his shotgun slightly. "Been pacing us up there for the last hour, I reckon," he murmured. "Just lettin' us see it now. Makin' sure we know it's there."

"Psychological pressure," Graves stated automatically, finally lowering his binoculars, though his face was pale. "Trying to panic us." But his usual dismissal lacked force. Seeing the creature directly, even at a distance, even partially obscured, had clearly shaken him. It validated everything – the tracks, the sounds, the folklore, the disappearance.

"Or," Nora said quietly from beside Boone, her gaze fixed on the empty spot on the ridge, "it is simply showing itself. Asserting its presence. Reminding us this is its domain we are crossing."

They stood frozen for another minute, scanning the ridge line, but the figure did not reappear. The forest seemed to hold its breath around them, the silence amplifying the frantic beating of Elise's heart. Knowing they were being actively watched, stalked from above by something of that size and unknown capability, was infinitely worse than just suspecting it.

"Alright," Graves said finally, his voice strained but determined. "We don't react. We don't show fear. We maintain formation, maintain awareness. Keep moving south. Slowly."

Slowly was an understatement. Every step now felt weighed down by the knowledge of the observer on the ridge. Elise found herself compulsively glancing upwards, scanning the high slopes, expecting to see the tall, dark shape reappear at any moment. The feeling of exposure was intense, vulnerable. They were fish in a barrel, moving along the valley floor while the hunter watched patiently from above.

Over the next hour, they saw movement twice more. Always high on the ridges, always distant, always fleeting. Once, a dark shape moving rapidly between stands of timber on the eastern slope, disappearing before binoculars could be brought to bear. Another time, what looked like two figures, standing motionless for a long moment on a prominent rock outcrop far ahead, silhouetted against the sky, before melting back into the forest. They never got closer, never seemed overtly threatening, yet their intermittent appearances served their purpose perfectly. Nerves frayed. Doubt escalated. The urge to panic, to run blindly, grew stronger.

Graves, perhaps recognizing the devastating effect the sightings were having on morale, or perhaps simply unable to maintain his own composure under the constant surveillance, became increasingly harsh, pushing the team harder despite the known risks.

"Keep moving!" he barked, when Levi paused to help Elise over a particularly treacherous logjam. "Don't bunch up! Maintain intervals! Show no weakness!"

"We show weakness by gettin' someone hurt rushin' on slick logs, Graves!" Boone shot back from the rear, his patience finally snapping again under the strain. "Ease off the pace! Let us move smart!"

"Smart is getting out of this open valley floor and finding defensible ground before full dark!" Graves retorted, refusing to yield. "Move!"

He forged ahead, practically dragging the team behind him through sheer force of will. They splashed through icy creek crossings, scrambled over rocks, pushed through tangled brush, all the while haunted by the knowledge of the watchers on the ridges above. The forest itself seemed to conspire against them, the terrain growing steeper, more broken.

It was mid-afternoon when Elise, stumbling with exhaustion, happened to glance up at the western ridge line at just the right moment. The mist had thinned slightly in that area, offering a pocket of relative clarity against the grey rock face. And there, standing fully exposed on a narrow ledge perhaps three hundred yards above them, was one of the creatures.

This time, it wasn't just a fleeting silhouette. She got a clear, albeit distant, look.

It was massive, significantly larger than any bear, easily eight and a half feet tall, maybe more. Its build was incredibly powerful, thick-limbed, with immensely broad shoulders tapering down to a narrower waist. It was covered in thick, shaggy, dark brown hair, glistening slightly with moisture from the mist. Its head seemed proportionately large for its body, set directly on the shoulders with little visible neck. The face was deeply shadowed, features indistinct at this distance, but the heavy brow ridge was apparent, giving it a brooding, almost simian cast. It stood perfectly still, its long arms hanging loosely at its sides, simply watching them, its posture radiating a calm, patient menace.

Elise stopped dead, frozen, her breath catching in her throat. It wasn't a man in a suit. It wasn't a bear behaving strangely. It wasn't a trick of the light or shadow. It was a real, living creature, utterly unknown to science, watching them with what seemed like quiet calculation from the ridge. The sheer physical presence of it, the raw power hinted at by its build, was overwhelming.

"Graves," she choked out, unable to take her eyes off the figure. "Look. West ridge. Clear view."

The others stopped instantly, following her gaze. A collective gasp went through the group as they saw it. Clear. Unmistakable. Real.

Graves raised his binoculars, his hands visibly shaking this time. He stared through them for a long, silent moment. Boone raised his shotgun instinctively, though the range was far too great for it to be effective. Levi gripped his pistol. Nora murmured something low and urgent under her breath.

The creature on the ledge slowly turned its massive head, its gaze seeming to sweep over each member of the small group huddled by the creek below. Elise felt pinned by that unseen gaze, exposed and insignificant. There was no overt threat in its posture, no aggression, just... assessment. Observation. A silent statement of dominance and presence.

Then, as deliberately as it had appeared, it turned its side to them, took one fluid, surprisingly agile step, and melted back into a shadowed crevice in the rock face, vanishing instantly from view.

The release of tension was explosive. Elise swayed on her feet, feeling dizzy, nausea rising in her throat. Levi let out a long, shuddering breath. Jules's blurry trail cam footage was nothing compared to this. This was undeniable.

"My God," Levi whispered, echoing Elise's shock. "It's real. It's actually real."

Boone lowered his shotgun slowly, his face pale but his eyes burning with a mixture of fear and vindicated certainty. "Told ya," he breathed. "Now do you believe?" He looked directly at Graves.

Graves lowered his binoculars, his face ashen. He seemed momentarily stunned, speechless. The clinical detachment, the mission focus – it had finally shattered against the undeniable reality of the creature standing clearly on the ridge above them. He knew, now, without any doubt, what they were facing. And it wasn't just an 'unconfirmed primate species' or a 'hostile subject'. It was something more. Something ancient, powerful, and utterly alien to his tactical understanding of the world.

"It… it matches the Kestrel profile," Graves stammered, then caught himself, seeming to force the words out through sheer ingrained discipline. "Subject visual confirmation achieved. High degree of certainty." He took a shaky breath, trying to regain control. "Alright. Alright. Maintain positions. Scan for further movement."

But Elise knew, looking at his shocked expression, looking at the shared terror reflected in Levi's and Boone's faces, feeling the cold certainty settling in her own gut, that this clear sighting hadn't just confirmed the creature's existence. It had fundamentally changed the game. They were no longer investigating a mystery; they were unequivocally trespassing in the territory of a known, powerful entity that was actively monitoring their every move. And Graves' insistence on pushing forward now felt less like leadership and more like a suicidal obsession, dragging them all deeper into the lair of the beast they had finally seen, clearly and terrifyingly, with their own eyes. The forest watcher had revealed itself, and the revelation promised only peril.

Chapter 13: The Hollow Trail

The clear sighting of the creature on the ridge precipitated a profound shift within the ragged group. The shared, undeniable visual confirmation vaporized any lingering skepticism and replaced it with a stark, unifying terror. Scientific curiosity, mission objectives, internal conflicts – all receded in the face of the raw, primal fear evoked by the massive, watching figure. They were unequivocally trespassers in the domain of something ancient, powerful, and demonstrably real.

Graves, visibly shaken despite his efforts to maintain military composure, seemed to grasp the futility, or perhaps the sheer suicidal folly, of continuing his rigid southward push towards the hypothetical 'Objective Delta'. The creature wasn't just a rumour or a blurry image; it was a tangible entity capable of traversing sheer rock faces and observing them with chilling patience. His authority, already fractured, crumbled further under the weight of that shared visual evidence. He still radiated tension and a dangerous, unpredictable energy, but the certainty had gone out of his commands.

It was Boone who finally broke the stunned silence that followed the creature's disappearance back into the rock face. He lowered his shotgun, his gaze sweeping across the anxious faces – Elise's wide-eyed shock, Levi's pale intensity, Graves' barely concealed tremor, Nora's somber resignation.

"Alright," Boone said, his voice low but carrying a newfound authority born not of rank, but of grim, validated experience. "Forget Graves' plan. Forget pushin' south. That thing… it's lettin' us see it for a reason. Maybe it's curious. Maybe it's warnin' us off one last time. Or maybe…" he paused, his eyes dark, "maybe it's herdin' us."

The word sent a fresh chill through Elise. Herding. Like livestock. The intermittent appearances, always keeping their distance, always pushing them subtly onward… it fit a terrifying pattern.

"Herdin' us where?" Levi asked, his voice tight.

Boone scanned the surrounding terrain, his gaze moving past the creek, past the immediate slopes, towards a distinctive notch in the western ridge line further south – a deep cleft in the mountain's flank that looked unnaturally shadowed even in the flat, overcast light. "There's a place," he said slowly, reluctantly, as if dredging up a half-buried, unwelcome memory. "An old trail.

Not on any map I've ever seen, not Forest Service, not logging charts. Somethin' older."

He looked towards Nora, a question in his eyes. She nodded slowly, confirming his thought. "The Hollow Trail," she murmured, her voice barely audible. "Our people… we knew of it. Avoided it. Said it led into the heart of *snəxʷəlxʷ tał* – the deepest part of the Hollow Ground. The place where the guardians dwell most strongly."

"My brother…" Boone's voice grew thick with painful memory. "Liam and I… we found the start of it, once. Years ago, before… before he vanished. We were exploring further up this valley than we should've been. Came across this… this path carved into the side of the mountain. Felt… wrong. Old. Like somethin' unnatural had made it." He shook his head. "We got spooked, turned back then. Never went near it again."

He looked back towards the notch in the ridge. "If that thing is herdin' us, if it's tryin' to funnel us somewhere specific… that's where it's pushin' us. Towards the Hollow Trail."

Graves, who had been listening intently, stepped forward. "A trail? Leading where? West? Over the ridge?" Despite his shock, his tactical mind seemed to be re-engaging, grasping for potential escape routes or advantageous positions.

"Don't know where it leads," Boone admitted grimly. "Never followed it. But Nora's right. It felt… different. Like steppin' into another place altogether. The air felt weird. Quiet." He glanced back towards the spot on the ridge where they'd seen the creature. "Maybe that's the way *out*… or maybe it's the way *in*. Deeper in."

"What choice do we have?" Elise asked quietly, voicing the unspoken question hanging heavy in the air. "Backtrack through where Jules was taken? Sit here and wait for it to come down off the ridge? Following this… trail… feels like moving towards *something*, even if we don't know what." It felt like a desperate gamble, choosing the unknown devil over the known one, but paralysis felt like certain doom.

Levi nodded in agreement. "Continuing aimlessly south seems pointless now. And Boone is right – the sightings do feel directive, like controlled exposure. Following this path, if it exists, seems the most logical response to the current situation, however risky."

Graves looked torn. Abandoning his own plan, yielding command to Boone's intuition and Nora's folklore, clearly chafed against his ingrained need for control. But the undeniable reality of the creature, combined with the catastrophic failure of his technology and the growing consensus of his terrified team, left him little choice. His authority was gone; survival instincts were taking over.

"Fine," Graves conceded brusquely, the word tasting like defeat. "Lead the way, Boone. Find this 'Hollow Trail'. But stay alert. This could be exactly what the subject wants – leading us into an ambush zone."

Boone merely nodded, accepting the reluctant mandate. He conferred briefly with Nora in low tones, pointing towards the notch in the ridge, exchanging knowledge passed down through generations and hard-won personal experience. Then, turning away from the main creek, he began leading them westward, angling up the slope towards the shadowed cleft he had indicated.

The ascent was punishing. The terrain became steeper, looser, the footing treacherous on damp moss covering unstable rocks. They climbed out of the marshy valley bottom, pushing through dense thickets of vine maple and rhododendron that clawed at their clothes and skin. The silence persisted, thick and expectant. The feeling of being watched intensified, becoming almost a physical pressure. Elise kept glancing back, expecting to see the tall figure reappear on the opposite ridge, but there was nothing. Just the brooding, mist-shrouded mountains and the vast, indifferent forest.

After nearly an hour of strenuous climbing, the forest began to change subtly. The trees grew larger, older again, spaced further apart. Immense Douglas firs and western hemlocks soared towards the hidden sky, their trunks thick and weathered. The ground underfoot became strangely smoother, covered in a deep, springy carpet of rust-colored needles that muffled their footsteps almost completely.

And then they saw it. Emerging from the gloom, hugging the steep contour of the mountainside, was the trail.

It wasn't a natural game trail, worn down by migrating elk or deer. This path was deliberately constructed, though clearly ages ago. It was about four feet wide, carved directly into the side of the mountain, a narrow shelf cut from the rock and soil. In some places, large, flat stones had been set into the earth like crude paving, mostly obscured now by centuries of needlefall and moss. In others, retaining walls built from carefully stacked rocks, now leaning and tumbledown, held back the unstable slope above. The sheer labor involved in its creation, especially given the primitive tools likely available, spoke of immense effort and purpose. But who – or what – had built it? And why?

The trail led directly towards the shadowed notch in the ridge, disappearing into a deeper darkness between towering rock buttresses. Standing at the threshold, peering along the ancient path, Elise felt a profound sense of unease wash over her, stronger than anything she had felt before. The air here *did* feel different, just as Boone had described. It felt thin, static, carrying a faint, almost undetectable vibration, like the hum of electricity before a lightning strike. The silence was absolute, not even the whisper of wind penetrated this high cleft. It felt… sequestered. Separate from the rest of the valley.

"This is it," Boone said quietly, his voice hushed, reverent and fearful. "The Hollow Trail." He hesitated at the entrance, peering into the gloom, his hand tightening on his shotgun.

Nora stood beside him, chanting softly under her breath, her eyes closed for a moment before she opened them, her expression grimly determined. "This path leads to the heart," she whispered. "Respect is needed now, more than ever."

Graves pushed forward impatiently, eager to see where it led. "Is it stable? Can we make better time on this?"

"Feels stable enough," Boone replied, testing the ground with his boot. "But I wouldn't rush. Feels… fragile. Like the whole place is holding its breath."

Cautiously, Boone stepped onto the trail, followed by Nora, then Elise, Levi, and finally Graves. The moment they moved onto the path proper, the feeling of entering somewhere distinct intensified. It was like stepping through an invisible veil. The muffled silence deepened further. The air grew colder, carrying a strange, metallic tang Elise couldn't identify. The light seemed dimmer here, absorbed by the dark rock and the immense trees leaning over the path.

They moved along the Hollow Trail in single file, the silence broken only by the crunch of their own boots on the thick layer of needles. The path contoured along the mountainside, sometimes offering dizzying views down the steep slope towards the valley floor far below, other times plunging into shadowed recesses where ancient trees formed a near-solid roof overhead.

Elise found herself scanning the surroundings with heightened intensity. It wasn't just the feeling of being watched anymore; it felt like the trail itself, the very rocks and trees, were aware of their passage. She noticed strange anomalies in the vegetation lining the path. Trees with bizarrely twisted trunks, growing in unnatural spirals. Patches where the moss grew in unusually thick, almost sculpted patterns. And markings, different from the ones in the grove below.

Here, scratched onto rock faces or carved into tree bark flanking the trail, were symbols that looked less like warnings and more like... something else. Complex, interwoven patterns, almost like knotwork. Some resembled stylized representations of eyes, staring out from the rock. Others were intricate, labyrinthine designs that seemed to pull the eye inward. They looked incredibly ancient, weathered by countless seasons, yet undeniably deliberate. Were they warding signs? Way markers? Or depictions of the guardians themselves, their presence embedded into the fabric of the trail?

"Look at this," she murmured, stopping beside a large hemlock where a particularly intricate symbol, resembling a figure with multiple limbs radiating from a central point, was deeply etched into the bark, covered now by a thin layer of translucent green moss. She carefully photographed it, along with others they passed. The symbols felt less overtly threatening than the fresh carvings below, but carried a deeper, more ancient and unsettling power.

Boone nodded grimly. "Seen these before. Faint traces, down near where Liam... near where we camped back then. Didn't know what they meant." He ran a gloved finger over the mossy carving. "Feels like... ownership. Like signposts in their language."

They pressed on, the trail leading them steadily deeper into the mountain's flank, towards the shadowed notch. The sense of isolation grew profound. They were now walking a path likely unseen by human eyes for centuries, possibly millennia, heading into a place local folklore deemed the sacred, forbidden heart of the valley.

As they rounded a sharp bend, the trail opened slightly into a small, bowl-shaped depression tucked against the mountainside. And here, the silence reached its apex. It wasn't just the absence of sound; it felt like a *presence* of silence, heavy and absolute. No bird call, no insect buzz, no wind rustle, not even the sound of their own breathing seemed to carry more than a few inches. It pressed in on Elise's ears, creating a disorienting, underwater sensation.

This, she realized with a certainty that chilled her to the bone, must be the 'Hollow' itself – the specific place within the Hollow Ground that gave the area its name. A dead zone. A pocket of profound, unnatural stillness.

The small depression was sparsely vegetated, the ground covered only by the thick carpet of reddish needles. A few stunted, twisted fir trees clung to the edges, their branches reaching like skeletal arms. The air felt heavy, stagnant, and strangely cold. It felt like a place where life struggled to persist, overshadowed by some immense, invisible weight.

"We camp here," Boone decided abruptly, his voice sounding oddly muffled in the oppressive quiet. He glanced at the sky, where the grey light was rapidly failing. "Can't risk movin' on this trail in the dark. And somethin' tells me… this is as far as we're meant to get easily."

No one argued. The feeling in the Hollow was profoundly unnerving, but attempting to navigate the precarious trail in darkness felt infinitely worse. And the sense of having reached a significant threshold, a potential terminus or transition point, was palpable.

They set up another cold camp, huddling together for warmth and perceived security in the center of the silent depression. Tents felt flimsy, inadequate against the crushing stillness. Conversation was minimal, conducted in hushed whispers that seemed to be swallowed instantly by the heavy air. Eating felt difficult, swallowing past the lump of fear in their throats.

Elise sat wrapped in her sleeping bag, leaning against her pack, trying to make notes in her journal by the dim red light of her headlamp. *"Entered 'Hollow Trail' region approx. 15:00 hrs. Path displays evidence ancient construction, significant age. Unusual symbolic markings noted on trees, rocks – distinct from Zone Beta grove symbols. Proceeded approx. 2km WSW along trail to reach depression designated 'The Hollow.' Extreme auditory suppression effect noted within Hollow – near total absence ambient sound, muffled close-proximity sounds. Air temperature depressed, subjective feeling 'static charge' or pressure. Cause unknown – geological? Atmospheric? Other?"* The word 'Other' felt woefully inadequate.

As full darkness claimed the Hollow, the silence became almost unbearable. It wasn't peaceful; it was menacing. It felt like listening intently for a sound that never came, stretching nerves to the breaking point. Elise found herself straining her ears, desperate for any noise – an owl, the wind, anything – to break the oppressive spell, but there was nothing. Just the frantic pounding of her own heart and the shallow whisper of her breath in the cold air.

They took watches again, huddled together, back-to-back, peering into the impenetrable blackness surrounding their tiny island of fragile humanity. The silence played tricks on the mind, magnifying inner anxieties, conjuring imagined sounds – whispers, footsteps, breathing – just at the edge of hearing. Was something out there, moving silently through the deadened air, watching them from inches away? Or was it just the sound of their own fear echoing in the vacuum?

Trapped on an ancient trail, surrounded by cryptic symbols, camped in a pocket of profound and unnatural silence, deep within the territory of a creature whose existence was now terrifyingly confirmed, Elise felt stripped bare. Science offered no explanation for the dead electronics, the spinning compass, the oppressive quiet, the ancient trail itself. Folklore provided a narrative, but one steeped in terror and the promise of retribution. Their leader was compromised, their technology useless, their path forward uncertain and likely perilous. They had followed the whispers and tracks, endured the folklore fireside, survived the disappearance and the confrontation. Now, led by instinct and dread onto the Hollow Trail, they had arrived in the dead heart of the valley, and the silence felt like the deepest warning yet. It felt like the stillness before the storm, the quiet breath held before the final, devastating strike.

Chapter 14: Bones and Remains

Sleep in the Hollow was less a state of rest and more a shallow, twitchy suspension of consciousness, punctuated by phantom sounds conjured from the oppressive silence and the ever-present thrum of adrenaline. Elise woke repeatedly, heart pounding, convinced she'd heard movement just beyond the thin tent wall, only to find the absolute stillness mocking her frayed nerves. When the first hints of grey light finally began to dilute the impenetrable blackness, it brought not relief, but merely the continuation of dread in a visible spectrum.

Breaking camp was a grim, silent affair performed with economical movements born of fear and exhaustion. No one spoke more than necessary, the muffling effect of the Hollow making conversation feel strained and pointless anyway. Every rustle of gear, every zip of a pack, sounded unnaturally loud in the immediate vicinity before being swallowed by the surrounding vacuum. Elise forced down a cold energy bar, the processed food tasting like cardboard and ash in her dry mouth. The stagnant, metallic-tinged air of the Hollow felt heavy in her lungs, thick with unseen pressures.

Boone and Nora conferred in low whispers near the edge of the small depression, their gaze fixed on the continuation of the Hollow Trail as it climbed subtly out of the bowl and disappeared around another rocky bend. What lay beyond this pocket of unnatural stillness? Did the silence extend, or was this a localized phenomenon, a specific nexus point within the larger valley? And more importantly, were *they* still out there, the guardians, the Stick-shí'nač, watching, waiting for them to emerge from this strange sanctuary?

Graves seemed impatient to move, pacing the small campsite like a caged animal, his eyes scanning the silent trees, his hand never straying far from the carbine now perpetually slung across his chest. The shock of the clear sighting and the technological failure seemed to have resolved into a kind of fatalistic determination. His objective remained, nebulous and increasingly suspect though it was, and reaching it seemed the only path he could conceive, regardless of the cost or the accumulating evidence that they were marching deeper into mortal danger. He offered no input on navigation, tacitly ceding that role to Boone and Nora, but his tense energy pushed the group forward by sheer inertia.

As they shouldered their packs, the weight feeling heavier in the strange atmosphere of the Hollow, Nora paused, facing the center of the depression. She reached into a small pouch at her belt and produced a pinch of something dry and dark – tobacco, Elise guessed, a traditional offering. Murmuring words Elise couldn't understand, words that felt both respectful and supplicating, Nora scattered the offering onto the needle-covered ground. It was a small gesture, steeped in ancient tradition, acknowledging the power of the place, asking for safe passage perhaps. Graves watched with barely concealed impatience, but Boone and Levi waited respectfully until she was finished. The ritual felt necessary, a fragile appeal to forces far beyond their control or comprehension.

Then, led by Boone's cautious steps, they left the unnatural silence of the Hollow behind, stepping back onto the ancient trail. As they moved beyond the rim of the depression, the oppressive silence lessened slightly, though the normal forest sounds did not immediately return. The air still felt thin and charged, the quiet still profound, but it lacked the near-total auditory void of the Hollow itself. It was like moving from a soundproof chamber into a heavily muffled room.

The trail continued its contour along the steep mountainside, leading them steadily higher and deeper into the western range. The ancient paving stones became more frequent underfoot, hinting that this section might have been more significant, more heavily traversed by whatever beings constructed it ages ago. The strange, interwoven symbols carved into rocks and trees also seemed more numerous here, their complexity deepening, some incorporating shapes that disturbingly resembled the massive footprints they had found.

The sense of being watched returned with full force, a prickling awareness that seemed to emanate from the very trees and rocks around them. Elise found herself scanning every shadow, every thicket, half-expecting to see the towering dark figure step out onto the path ahead. The tension was palpable, a physical tightness in her chest, a constant state of readiness that was utterly exhausting.

They had been walking for perhaps an hour after leaving the Hollow, the trail now switchbacking up a particularly steep section towards the jagged ridgeline visible intermittently through breaks in the canopy, when Boone suddenly stopped again, holding up a hand, his head cocked, listening intently.

The others froze instantly, straining their ears in the heavy silence. At first, Elise heard nothing but her own ragged breathing and the frantic drumming of her heart. Then, faintly, carried on a sudden, brief eddy of wind that rustled the high branches, she caught it – a rhythmic *chonk... chonk... chonk*. A dull, percussive sound, like wood striking wood, or perhaps stone striking wood. It was distant, seeming to come from somewhere further up the trail, closer to the ridge.

Chonk... chonk... chonk. It stopped. Silence rushed back in, amplifying the residual echo in Elise's ears.

"Wood-knocks," Boone breathed, his voice tight. "Like Nora said. Signals."

"How far?" Graves asked urgently, peering up the trail.

"Hard to tell," Boone admitted. "Sound plays tricks up here. Quarter mile, maybe? Up near the crest."

"A warning?" Levi questioned quietly.

"Or a lure," Graves countered, his eyes narrowed. "Trying to draw us into prepared ground."

Nora shook her head slowly. "Not a lure," she stated with quiet certainty. "A statement. They know our path. They are ahead."

The thought of the creatures deliberately making noise, signaling their presence ahead of them, was deeply unnerving. It suggested confidence, control. They weren't just reacting; they were dictating the encounter, controlling the flow of information, playing a psychological game with terrifying expertise.

"Proceed with extreme caution," Graves ordered, redundancy thick in his voice as caution was their only operating mode now. "Boone, take it slow. Scan constantly."

They advanced up the trail at a crawl, every sense hyper-alert. The rhythmic knocking did not resume. The silence felt even more charged now, pregnant with anticipation. The trail became steeper, narrower, clinging precariously to the mountainside. The trees thinned slightly as they gained elevation, replaced by stunted subalpine firs and patches of low-growing juniper clinging to rock faces. The air grew noticeably colder.

Rounding a sharp, exposed corner where the trail skirted a sheer drop-off, Boone stopped dead again, his body rigid. He slowly raised his shotgun, pointing not ahead, but slightly off the trail, downslope into a dense cluster of strangely contorted fir trees and rhododendron thickets.

"There," Boone whispered, his voice rough. "Smell that?"

Elise inhaled cautiously. Underneath the cold, clean scent of pine needles and damp rock, another odour tainted the air – the same rank, musky, vaguely mammalian scent they had encountered near the den, but stronger here, fresher. And mingled with it was something else… the faint, coppery tang of decay.

Graves moved up beside Boone, peering into the thicket. "See anything?"

"No," Boone replied. "But somethin's in there. Or *was*, damn recently. Smell's strong. And look…" He pointed towards the base of the thicket, where the dense undergrowth met the rocky ground just below the trail edge.

Following his gesture, Elise saw it. Partially hidden beneath overlapping ferns and fallen branches, something pale gleamed dully against the dark earth. It looked… organic. Curved.

Graves motioned for Levi and Elise to investigate, while he and Boone maintained watch, scanning the trail ahead and the slopes above and below. Carefully, Elise and Levi edged off the main trail, pushing through the wet, resistant branches of the rhododendrons towards the pale object. The musky, decaying smell intensified as they got closer, thick and nauseating.

Reaching the spot Boone had indicated, Levi used a sturdy branch to push aside the concealing ferns. Elise stifled a gasp, bile rising in her throat.

It wasn't just one object. It was a nest.

Similar in construction to the den they'd found further down, but larger, cruder perhaps, more exposed. A massive jumble of snapped branches, some thick as a man's thigh, interwoven with bark strips, moss, ferns, and huge clumps of the same coarse, dark hair they'd seen before. It formed a wide, shallow bowl pressed into the earth, partially sheltered by the overhanging firs.

And scattered within and around the nest, like grotesque decorations, were bones.

Deer skulls with antlers still attached, spinal columns of elk picked clean, jawbones of what might have been cougar or bear. But sickeningly prominent, mixed haphazardly amongst the animal remains, were human bones. A rib cage, bleached white but mostly intact, lay canted against the side of the nest. A scattering of vertebrae. A shattered pelvis. And skulls. At least three human skulls, nested among the debris, their empty sockets staring sightlessly towards the grey sky. One skull had a clear, circular hole punched through the temple, suggesting a violent end long before being brought here. Another was cracked, fragments missing.

Near the center of the nest, half-buried beneath a pile of hair and rotting vegetation, was something that made Elise's stomach heave violently. The desiccated, leathery remains of a human hand and forearm, skin stretched taut over bone like dark parchment, fingers curled slightly as if grasping for something in its final moments.

"Oh, God... oh, dear God," Levi choked out, stumbling back a step, his face ashen. Even his medical training hadn't prepared him for this grotesque charnel house.

Elise felt rooted to the spot, morbid fascination warring with utter revulsion. Her scientific mind tried to process the scene – evidence of long-term occupation, varied diet, tool use implied by the snapped branches and possibly the hole in the skull, potential multi-generational use given the weathering on some bones versus others. But the human horror overwhelmed the scientific impulse. These weren't just specimens; they were victims. Hikers, hunters, perhaps Nora's Tallsalt ancestors, individuals who had met a terrifying end in this valley, their remains becoming part of the creature's nest, trophies or mere leftovers.

Fighting back nausea, she raised her camera, forcing herself to document the scene. Every click of the shutter felt like a desecration. She photographed the overall nest structure, the jumble of bones, close-ups of the human skulls, the mummified hand, the surrounding hair clumps, trying to capture details that might provide clues – age of remains, potential tool marks on bones, anything.

While she worked, Levi cautiously probed the edges of the nest with a stick, uncovering more fragments – broken femurs, smaller bones, and then, something that glinted dully. He carefully worked it free. It was a rusted metal D-ring carabiner attached to a frayed, rotten piece of brightly coloured climbing webbing. Near it, half-stuffed into a crevice between branches forming the nest wall, was a tattered, mud-stained piece of waterproof material – part of a backpack, perhaps, or outerwear. And attached to it, miraculously intact, was an identification tag encased in plastic.

Levi picked it up with trembling, gloved fingers, wiping away the grime. He read the faded print aloud, his voice hollow. "David Chen. University of Washington Geology Department. Student ID…" He trailed off, lowering the tag, his face grim.

David Chen. The geology student Graves had listed in the briefing. Missing since 2018. Presumed lost to exposure or a fall. The official story. The convenient lie. The reality lay here, in this horrifying nest, amidst the bones of countless other victims stretching back through unknown years. He hadn't fallen. He had been taken. Hunted. Brought here. His final resting place a grotesque jumble of remains in the lair of the creature that ruled this valley.

The discovery was irrefutable, devastating confirmation. It answered the question of the disappearances with brutal finality. The creature didn't just remove intruders; it collected them, their bones becoming part of its home, a testament to its dominance.

"Graves! Boone!" Levi called out, his voice strained. "You need to see this. We found Chen. Or what's left of him."

Graves and Boone scrambled down from the trail cautiously, their weapons held ready, their faces hardening as they took in the gruesome scene. Graves stared at the skulls, the scattered bones, the mummified hand, his face pale but his eyes narrowed in intense, almost clinical observation. He knelt beside Levi, examining the recovered ID tag and climbing gear without a word. This wasn't folklore; this was hard evidence, linking a specific missing person directly to the creature's nest.

Boone scanned the nest, his gaze lingering on the human skulls, his expression a mixture of horror and grim understanding. This, perhaps, was the fate his brother Liam had met twenty-two years ago. His body never found, possibly brought to a similar nest somewhere else in this vast, unforgiving wilderness. The muscle in his jaw worked, his grief and anger palpable but contained.

"So much for 'lost to exposure'," Boone bit out, his voice thick with sarcasm and disgust, directed squarely at Graves. "This look like exposure to you, Graves? Kestrel know about this? They know what this thing *does* to people?"

Graves ignored him, his focus absolute as he took his own series of detailed photographs, meticulously documenting the ID tag, the climbing gear, the human remains in situ. He seemed less interested in the horror and more in the implications. Confirmation of the subject's predatory behavior towards humans? Validation of Kestrel's classified data? Evidence to justify... what? What was the ultimate goal here?

Elise finished her own photographic documentation, feeling profoundly shaken, dirty, complicit just by witnessing this horror. She collected small samples where possible – strands of the coarse hair, scrapings from tool marks she thought she saw on a large animal femur, a soil sample from beneath the mummified hand – bagging and tagging them with numb precision, the scientific act feeling increasingly hollow. What good was data when faced with such raw, ancient brutality?

They retreated from the nest site quickly, scrambling back up to the relative safety of the Hollow Trail, leaving the grisly tableau undisturbed but forever etched in their minds. No one spoke for a long time as they continued their climb towards the ridge, the rank smell seeming to follow them, clinging to the damp air.

The reality had settled in, heavy and suffocating. They weren't just intruders; they were potential additions to the collection. The Stick-shí'nač, the guardian, the ancient protector, was also a killer, a collector of bones, its motives inscrutable, its methods brutal. The lines blurred – was it defending territory, punishing transgression, or simply hunting? Perhaps all three.

David Chen's ID tag felt like a concrete anchor dragging them down into the abyss of their situation. They were following an ancient, mysterious trail into the heart of a forbidden valley, actively hunted or herded by a creature of immense power and unknown intelligence, a creature that built nests from the remains of its victims. Their technology was dead. Their escape route was uncertain. Their leader seemed driven by motives far removed from their survival. The forest watched, the silence pressed in, and the bones in the nest served as a grim prophecy of their own possible fate. The Hollow Ground had revealed another of its terrible secrets, and the weight of that knowledge threatened to crush what little hope remained.

Chapter 15: Night Terror

The gruesome discovery of the nest and David Chen's remains irrevocably poisoned the remaining shreds of hope or deniability within the group. The creature wasn't just a myth, a shadow, or a watcher on the ridge; it was a tangible predator with a history, a creature capable of brutal violence and methodical collection. The Hollow Trail no longer felt like a potential path to understanding or escape, but like a deliberate route deeper into the abattoir. Every shadow seemed to harbor menace, every snap of a twig sent jolts of adrenaline through exhausted bodies. The weight of the human remains back in that horrifying nest pressed down on them, a silent testament to the valley's lethal nature.

They reached the top of the ridge just as the last vestiges of grey light bled from the sky, plunging the high country into a profound and chilling darkness. The wind swept colder here, unimpeded by the dense forest below, whistling mournfully through stunted, wind-blasted firs and across exposed rock faces. The view, intermittent through swirling mist, was terrifyingly vast – endless waves of dark, convoluted mountains stretching into the gloom, emphasizing their utter isolation.

There was no debate about camping. Continuing along the exposed ridgeline in the dark, especially after the day's discoveries and the clear signs of being watched or herded, felt suicidal. They found a slightly sheltered depression just below the main crest, surrounded by a ragged cluster of rocks and gnarled krummholz trees that offered meager protection from the wind and observation. It felt terribly exposed, but it was the best they could do.

Another cold camp. The absence of fire felt more acute here in the biting wind, the darkness more absolute. They huddled together for shared warmth and the illusion of safety, chewing grimly on tasteless energy bars, sipping cold water from their dwindling supplies. Conversation was nonexistent, replaced by the howling wind, the occasional clatter of dislodged pebbles somewhere on the slopes below, and the frantic drumming of their own hearts.

Graves, perhaps finally grasping the extremity of their peril or maybe just recognizing the tactical vulnerability of their position, seemed to deploy every remaining non-electronic security measure in their possession. He supervised the placement of tripwires rigged with chemical light sticks around the cramped perimeter – designed not to stop anything, but to provide a visual alert if something crossed the boundary. He designated overlapping fields of observation for the mandatory two-person watches, his instructions clipped and precise, the military planner reasserting control through procedure even as the situation spiraled far beyond any conventional tactical scenario.

Elise found herself on the first watch rotation again, paired this time with Boone. Huddled behind a low cluster of rocks, wrapped in every layer of clothing she possessed, she peered out into the swirling blackness, the wind tearing at her hood, chilling her to the bone. Boone sat beside her, shotgun across his lap, motionless as stone, his senses seemingly merging with the wild night. The silence of the Hollow was gone, replaced by the roar of the wind, which paradoxically felt both more natural and more terrifying, potentially masking the sound of approach.

Hours crawled by, each minute stretched taut with anticipation. The wind shrieked like a banshee, rattling the stunted trees, throwing sudden flurries of icy rain or sleet against their faces. Elise's eyes strained, trying to penetrate the gloom, mistaking wind-whipped branches for moving figures, seeing menace in every shifting shadow cast by the thin, occluded moonlight that occasionally broke through the racing clouds.

Suddenly, Boone tensed beside her, his head snapping up, listening intently over the howl of the wind. "You hear that?" he breathed, his voice barely audible.

Elise strained her ears. At first, she heard only the wind. Then, beneath the roar, a deeper sound – a low, guttural *huffing*, like a large animal exerting itself, coming from downslope, closer than it should be. And another sound – the distinct clatter of rocks dislodged, rolling down the steep incline below their perch.

Something was climbing towards them. Something big and heavy.

Boone slowly, silently raised his shotgun, thumbing the safety off. Elise fumbled for her own pistol, its unfamiliar weight cold and terrifying in her trembling hand, whilst simultaneously unsheathing the large canister of bear spray.

The huffing sound grew louder, closer. A large rock suddenly tumbled past their position, crashing down the slope just yards away. Whatever was climbing was doing so with

124

incredible power and speed, undeterred by the steep, unstable terrain and the darkness.

"Contact!" Boone yelled, his voice carrying sharply over the wind. "Downslope! Closing fast!"

Instantly, the camp exploded into tense action. Graves, Levi, and Nora scrambled from their tents, weapons appearing in their hands as if by magic. Headlamps flared on, beams cutting wildly through the darkness, searching for the source of the sound.

Then it burst over the lip of the ledge directly below them, less than twenty feet away, momentarily silhouetted against the turbulent sky.

It was enormous. Easily nine feet tall, maybe taller, with a build that dwarfed even the largest grizzly bear. Its massive shoulders hunched against the wind, thick, shaggy dark hair plastered down by the wet, its head lowered slightly, revealing the heavy brow ridge Elise had glimpsed on the ridge earlier. It moved with shocking speed and agility despite its bulk, planting huge, splayed feet onto the rocky ground, long arms held slightly out for balance. Its eyes, reflecting dimly in the beams of their headlamps, seemed small, deep-set, glinting with a terrifyingly alien intelligence. A low growl rumbled in its chest, vibrating through the rock.

For a frozen second, nobody moved, paralyzed by the sheer scale and proximity of the creature. It felt like a force of nature materialized before them, ancient, powerful, and undeniably real.

Then, with a deafening roar that seemed to shake the very mountain, it charged.

Not towards Boone and Elise, but directly towards the center of the camp, towards the tents, towards Levi who stood momentarily frozen between Graves and Nora.

"Scatter!" Graves screamed, finally reacting, raising his carbine. "Fire! Warning shots! Deterrents!"

Chaos erupted. Levi, jolted into action, raised his pistol and fired – the crack of the gunshot shockingly loud, echoing flatly against the roar of the creature and the wind. The shot went wide, impacting harmlessly on the rocks beyond.

The creature barely seemed to notice the gunshot. It covered the distance to the tents in two immense strides, its long arms reaching out. With horrifying ease, it swiped one massive forearm through Levi's tent, shredding the nylon and carbon-fiber poles like tissue paper. It lunged towards Levi, who desperately tried to sidestep, firing again, the muzzle flash illuminating the creature's terrifyingly close, grimacing face – bared teeth, flat nose, deeply furrowed brow.

"Levi!" Nora screamed, lunging forward with her axe held high, a fearless, desperate attempt to distract the beast.

Graves opened fire with his carbine, short controlled bursts aimed not at the creature itself, but towards the rocks near its feet, trying to deter, to turn it, adhering perhaps even now to some Kestrel protocol about lethal force only as a last resort, or perhaps fearing he couldn't actually stop it.

Boone fired his shotgun into the air, the booming blast momentarily competing with the creature's roar, adding to the cacophony and confusion. Elise, fumbling in terror, finally thumbed the safety off the bear spray and unleashed a long, desperate cloud of blinding orange mist towards the creature's head.

The combination of noise, gunfire, and the acrid cloud of capsaicin seemed to have an effect. The creature recoiled slightly, shaking its massive head, letting out another bellowing roar, this one sounding less aggressive and more frustrated, perhaps pained by the spray. It swiped blindly, its huge hand catching Levi a glancing blow across the chest, sending him tumbling backwards with a cry of pain, his pistol flying from his grasp.

The creature hesitated for a fraction of a second, disoriented by the spray and the multiple points of attack. It seemed to decide the fight wasn't worth the cost, or perhaps its objective was simply disruption and terror, not annihilation – not yet. With incredible speed, it turned, scooped up a large supply pack that had been lying near the shredded tent – containing vital food and fuel – and bounded back towards the ledge edge.

"It's getting away!" Graves yelled, firing another burst near its retreating form.

Boone fired his shotgun again, this time aiming low, towards its legs, the buckshot peppering the rocks harmlessly as the creature launched itself back down the dark, precipitous slope with the same shocking agility it had displayed coming up. Rocks clattered, the heavy huffing faded rapidly, and then there was only the sound of the howling wind and their own panicked gasps for air.

It was over as quickly as it had begun, leaving behind devastation and terror.

"Levi!" Elise scrambled towards where he lay groaning on the rocky ground, Nora already kneeling beside him. Graves and Boone rushed over, weapons still scanning the darkness below the ledge, adrenaline keeping them hyper-alert.

Levi clutched his chest, his face pale and contorted in pain, but he was conscious. "Ribs," he gasped. "Might be… broken. Hurts… to breathe."

Nora carefully helped him sit up slightly, while Elise shone her headlamp on his chest. His outer jacket was torn, and angry red welts were already forming where the creature's massive hand had impacted. It was a glancing blow, yes, but the sheer force behind it had been enough to potentially cause serious injury.

"Easy, Levi, easy," Elise murmured, trying to keep her voice calm despite the shaking in her hands. She assessed him quickly – conscious, airway clear, breathing shallow but present, no obvious external bleeding beyond scrapes. "We need to check for flail chest, pneumothorax." She looked up at Graves, her earlier fear replaced by urgent, professional focus. "He needs proper assessment, pain management, support for his breathing. How bad is the med kit stocked?"

Graves nodded curtly, already directing Boone. "Boone, maintain watch below. Signal any movement. Nora, help Holloway. I'll secure the perimeter, check remaining gear." He seemed to function better now that there was immediate, tangible damage to manage, a crisis to contain.

While Elise and Nora carefully cut away Levi's outer layers to assess the damage – confirming significant bruising and likely multiple fractured ribs, but thankfully no apparent paradoxical movement suggesting flail chest yet – Graves conducted a quick, grim inventory of the damage.

Levi's tent was obliterated. A second tent, Elise and Nora's, was partially collapsed, ripped by the creature's passage. Crucially, the supply pack the creature had taken contained nearly half their remaining food rations and their primary cooking fuel canister. Their already precarious situation had just become significantly worse. Limited food, damaged shelter, a seriously injured team member, and confirmation that the creature was not only real and intelligent, but overwhelmingly powerful and willing to directly attack their camp.

Elise finally allowed herself to fully acknowledge the truth she had been resisting. The creature wasn't a myth, wasn't a misidentification, wasn't even just an unknown primate. It was a force of nature, terrifyingly strong, surprisingly agile, intelligent enough to employ tactics, and demonstrably dangerous. The brief, chaotic, violent encounter had shattered the last remnants of scientific objectivity, replacing it with the cold, hard certainty of survival against a monstrous adversary.

They worked through the remainder of the howling night, tending to Levi, splinting his injured side with SAM splints and elastic bandages from the thankfully well-stocked med kit, administering potent painkillers that left him groggy but breathing slightly easier. They salvaged what they could from the damaged tents, huddling together in the one remaining intact shelter – Graves' small one-person tent now crammed with four frightened people while Boone stoically maintained watch outside.

The mood was bleak. The attack had proven their vulnerability, stripped them of vital supplies, and injured one of their own. They were high on an exposed ridge, cut off from the world, with dwindling resources and a powerful predator actively engaging them. The mission, whatever its original clandestine purpose, was irrelevant now. Survival was the only objective. And looking at Levi's pain-etched face, at the shredded remains of the tents, at the empty space where their food pack had been, survival felt like a rapidly dwindling possibility. The night terror had passed, but the dawn promised only more fear and uncertainty in the heart of the Hollow Ground.

Chapter 16: Choke Point

Dawn arrived not with hope, but with the harsh clarity of desperation. The wind still howled across the exposed ridge, tearing at the tattered remains of their camp, whipping icy mist into their faces. The attack had left them physically and psychologically battered. Levi, dosed with painkillers, drifted in and out of consciousness, his breathing shallow and laboured despite the tight compression bandages supporting his fractured ribs. Every pained inhalation was a stark reminder of their vulnerability, of the immense power they had faced. The shredded tents, the missing food pack – these were tangible symbols of their dwindling resources and violated security. The memory of the creature's roar, its terrifying speed, the glint of intelligence in its eyes – this haunted the weary silence between gusts of wind.

There was no question of staying on the ridge. It was a death trap – exposed, indefensible, offering no shelter from the elements or the creature that now knew exactly where they were and how vulnerable they had become. The immediate priority, overriding even Graves' fractured sense of mission, was to get Levi to a more sheltered location, preferably somewhere defensible, where they could regroup, assess their rapidly diminishing options, and simply try to survive the next hours.

Packing the remnants of their camp was a grim, hurried affair conducted under Boone's watchful eye. He scanned the surrounding slopes constantly, shotgun held ready, convinced the creature, or perhaps others, might still be observing them, assessing their weakness after the night's attack. Elise and Nora worked together, carefully assisting Levi, supporting his injured side, minimizing jarring movements. Even walking a few steps elicited sharp groans of pain from him, despite the heavy dose of medication. Moving him any significant distance, especially downhill on treacherous terrain, was going to be incredibly difficult and slow. Graves, strangely subdued after the attack, seemed to focus his energy on consolidating their remaining supplies, his face a mask of grim calculation as he assessed their dwindling rations and lack of fuel. The bravado, the insistence on protocol, had been stripped away, leaving behind a man grappling with the catastrophic failure of his plan and the raw reality of their fight for survival.

"Down," Boone decided, pointing towards a steep, narrow canyon cutting sharply into the eastern slope below them, its mouth barely visible through the swirling mist. "Not back the way we came. Follow this ridge north a ways, then drop into that cut. Looks tight. Might offer some cover, maybe water down low. Better than sittin' up here like targets."

Nora nodded agreement. "That canyon… the elders called it *x̲ə́čátəd* – the place where the walls lean in. Dangerous in heavy rain, flash floods. But sheltered. And," she added ominously, "difficult for large things to maneuver easily within, perhaps."

It sounded like their best, perhaps only, option. Graves offered no argument, merely nodding curtly, accepting Boone's leadership by default now. Getting Levi down the steep, unstable slope towards the canyon mouth was torturous. They fashioned a makeshift sling for him using spare tent fabric and trekking poles, allowing Elise and Nora to support most of his weight while Boone cleared the path ahead and Graves covered their rear, constantly scanning the back trail. Progress was agonizingly slow. Every step risked dislodging loose rock; every patch of wet moss threatened a slip. Levi, despite the painkillers, frequently cried out as unavoidable jolts sent waves of agony through his injured chest. The wind howled around them, seeming to mock their slow, painful descent. The sense of being watched persisted, unseen eyes potentially tracking their labored retreat from the high ridges.

It took them nearly three exhausting, nerve-wracking hours to reach the mouth of the canyon Boone had indicated. It was indeed narrow, a deep slash in the mountainside carved by millennia of water runoff. The rock walls rose sheer and damp on either sides, perhaps only thirty feet apart at the entrance, leaning inwards slightly as Nora's name for it suggested, blocking out much of the sky and significantly muffling the roar of the wind. A small, intermittent stream trickled down the center over smooth, water-worn stones. The air inside felt immediately stiller, colder, heavy with the scent of damp rock, moss, and stagnant water.

They collapsed just inside the entrance, muscles trembling with exertion, lungs burning from the cold air and stress. Levi groaned, slumping against the canyon wall, his face pale and beaded with sweat despite the chill. Elise immediately checked his vitals, relieved to find his breathing hadn't worsened significantly during the descent, though the pain was clearly intensifying as the initial dose of medication wore off. She administered another, smaller dose, knowing they had to conserve their limited supply.

"We rest here," Boone declared, slumping down himself, though his eyes never stopped scanning the canyon entrance and the slopes visible above the narrow slit of sky. "Need to let Levi recover a bit. Need to figure out what the hell we do next."

The canyon offered a deceptive sense of security. The towering rock walls felt like ramparts, protecting them from the wind and offering limited avenues of approach for whatever lurked outside. But the confinement also brought a new kind of fear – claustrophobia, the feeling of being trapped. The leaning walls seemed to press inwards, the narrow strip of sky infinitely distant. Sounds echoed strangely within the confined space – the drip of water, the trickle of the stream, their own ragged breaths – making it difficult to discern distant noises.

Graves, after ensuring Levi was as stable as possible, began exploring slightly deeper into the canyon, carbine held at the ready. He returned after ten minutes, his expression grim.

"It narrows further in," he reported. "Maybe fifteen feet across in places. Some tight turns, a few small rockfalls creating partial blockages. Didn't see an obvious exit at the lower end within a few hundred yards – seems to just peter out into dense ravine choked with deadfall. Might be passable, might not. Water source is just seepage further up, this stream seems to originate from higher snowmelt." He looked around the confined space. "Defensible? Yes, against a direct assault from below or above. But it's also a bottleneck. A kill box, if something decides to trap us in here."

His words hung heavy in the cold, still air. They had traded the exposure of the ridge for the confinement of a potential trap.

While Levi rested, drifting into a pained, shallow sleep, the others held a hushed, tense council of war. Options were bleak. Remaining in the canyon indefinitely wasn't feasible – limited water, dwindling food, Levi's condition likely to worsen without proper medical care. Attempting to climb back out onto the exposed slopes felt like suicide, especially with an injured man. Pushing deeper into the canyon, hoping for an exit at the bottom, was a gamble – they could become trapped in an impassable dead end. Backtracking along the Hollow Trail, past the nest, past the Grove of Symbols, through the dead zone… that seemed equally unthinkable, inviting confrontation in territory the creature had clearly marked and defended.

"There's got to be another way," Elise insisted, tracing lines on her basic topographical map – one of the few pieces of non-electronic gear still functioning, though its accuracy in this uncharted region was questionable. "Maybe traverse north along the slope? Try to bypass the Hollow Trail section entirely? Aim back towards the logging roads eventually?"

Boone shook his head. "Traversing these slopes laterally? With Levi? In this terrain? We'd be lucky to make half a mile a day. Exposed the whole time. Nah. Our best bet," he said reluctantly, "might be goin' *down* this canyon. See if it opens up lower down, connects to another drainage system that leads outta here eventually. It's a risk, might be a dead end like Graves said. But sittin' here, waitin'… that ain't an option."

Nora listened silently, her gaze fixed on the damp canyon walls. When Boone finished, she spoke softly. "This place… xə́čátəd… the stories say it echoes. That sounds carry strangely. And that the guardians sometimes used places like this… to funnel prey. To trap things."

Another wave of dread washed over Elise. *Funnel prey.* Herding. Had they been deliberately maneuvered here? Driven off the ridge by the attack, guided towards this specific canyon by fear and desperation, only to find themselves cornered?

Graves seemed to latch onto the tactical implication. "If they're trying to trap us, what's the blocking move? Entrance or exit?"

"Or maybe just… containment?" Levi murmured, awake now, his voice weak. "Keep us pinned down here while… while what? It decides what to do next?"

The uncertainty was agonizing. Were they safer inside the canyon's confining walls, or more vulnerable? Was it a temporary refuge, or the final stage of a sophisticated trap set by an ancient intelligence?

They spent the rest of the short day huddled just inside the canyon mouth, taking turns watching the entrance and the narrow strip of sky above. The enforced inactivity frayed nerves further. Every shadow seemed to deepen with menace. Every drip of water sounded like a stealthy footstep. The silence from outside the canyon felt unnerving – had the creature simply moved on, or was it patiently waiting, observing from the rim above?

As twilight began to creep into the deep gorge, extinguishing the already limited light, Boone, posted near the entrance, suddenly went rigid. He slowly lowered himself behind a jagged outcrop of rock, signaling frantically for silence.

Elise's heart leaped into her throat. She strained her ears, listening over the trickle of the stream. At first, she heard nothing. Then, faint but distinct, came the sound of something moving on the rocks high above the canyon rim, directly overhead. Not the random clatter of dislodged stones, but rhythmic, deliberate sounds. *Scrape... pause... scrape...* Like claws on rock? Or heavy feet finding purchase?

Then, a low sound drifted down, distorted by the canyon acoustics but unmistakable – the same deep, guttural *huffing* they'd heard before the attack on the ridge.

It was above them. Pacing. Trapped on the rim.

A shower of small pebbles suddenly cascaded down the near vertical canyon wall, clattering onto the stony floor near where Levi lay huddled. It wasn't an accidental rockfall. It felt deliberate. A probe? A reminder?

"It knows we're here," Graves whispered unnecessarily, his face pale in the deepening gloom, carbine clutched tightly. "It's patrolling the rim."

They were pinned down. Whatever slim chance they might have had of climbing back out was gone. The creature was directly above them, controlling the high ground. Leaving the canyon now would mean walking directly into its path.

Nora's words echoed with chilling prescience: *Funnel prey. Trap things.*

They spent the night huddled deeper within the canyon's embrace, seeking refuge beneath a slight overhang perhaps fifty yards in from the entrance. The darkness was absolute, the confinement oppressive. Sleep was impossible. Every hour or so, they would hear it – the scrape of movement on the rim above, the occasional dislodged pebble skittering down the walls, the low, resonant huffing breathing drifting down into their rocky prison.

It wasn't attacking. Not yet. It seemed content to simply… wait. To let them know it was there. To let the fear, the confinement, the dwindling supplies, do their work. It was a terrifyingly patient predator, employing psychological tactics as effectively as physical force.

Trapped between leaning walls of ancient rock, injured, running low on food, with a seemingly supernatural predator pacing patiently above them, the group felt despair closing in like the damp, cold walls of the canyon itself. Boone's earlier speculation returned to haunt Elise with chilling force: *Maybe it's herdin' us.* Herded off the ridge, herded into this canyon… herded towards what final destination? The choke point felt less like a refuge now and more like a deliberately chosen cage, the bars formed by sheer rock and the pacing menace above. They were caught, contained, and utterly at the mercy of the ancient guardian whose territory they had so foolishly invaded. The silence from above was the most terrifying sound of all, pregnant with the promise of imminent, unavoidable confrontation.

Chapter 17: Betrayal

Trapped. The word echoed in the cold, damp confines of the canyon – *x̂əčátəd*, the place where the walls lean in. It resonated in the shallow, pained breaths Levi took as he huddled beneath a meagre overhang, drifting in and out of a feverish state induced by pain, medication, and possibly the beginnings of infection. It whispered in the howl of the wind that funneled sporadically down from the rim high above, carrying the chilling reminder of the entity that paced there, patient and predatory. It screamed in the silence between those gusts, a silence thick with fear, dwindling hope, and the corrosive acid of suspicion.

Forty-eight hours they had been pinned down in the choke point. Two full rotations of the earth, marked only by the subtle shifts in the quality of the grey light filtering down from the narrow strip of sky. Their rations were dangerously low, carefully portioned out by Nora into near-starvation amounts. The trickle of water from the seepage further up the canyon required constant, laborious filtering and provided barely enough to stave off dehydration. Levi's condition was deteriorating; his breathing grew slightly more ragged, his skin felt clammy, and his intermittent moans held a sharper edge of agony. Without proper medical attention, without rescue, his chances dwindled with each passing hour.

The creature above remained a constant, terrifying presence. They rarely saw it now, perhaps glimpsing a fleeting shadow against the sky if they risked peering up at the wrong moment. But they heard it. The occasional scrape of movement on rock. The chillingly close, deep *huff-huff-huff* breathing that seemed to drift down on the cold air currents, especially during the dead stillness of the night. The deliberate, terrifying *clack* of rock against rock, seemingly designed purely to remind them of its presence, to keep their nerves perpetually frayed. It wasn't attacking, not directly. It didn't need to. It was besieged them with patience, letting the canyon, the hunger, the fear, and Levi's slow decline do its work. Psychological warfare, as Graves had initially dismissed it, conducted with chilling expertise by something not human.

The confinement and the constant, low-level terror worked like acid on the already fractured bonds of the team. Graves maintained a façade of command, organizing watches, rationing duties, demanding situational reports, but his authority was a hollow shell. The technological failure, the clear sighting of the creature, the disastrous attack on the ridge camp, and the undeniable evidence in the nest had exposed the flaws in his planning and the potential deception underlying the mission. He spent hours staring at his dead satellite phone, tinkering uselessly with the inert GPS, or poring over the paper topographical maps, his face drawn and grim, radiating a frustrated, impotent energy. He seemed trapped not just by the canyon, but by the collapse of his control.

Boone was a coiled spring of resentment and watchful tension. He obeyed Graves' direct orders regarding watches and basic duties, but volunteered nothing, offering no counsel, his interactions clipped and bordering on insubordinate. Most of his time was spent near the canyon mouth, concealed behind rocks, shotgun always ready, eyes scanning the limited view outwards, every sense strained for any change in the environment, any sign of approach. He exuded a grim readiness for confrontation, whether with the creature above or with the man who had led them into this nightmare.

Nora seemed to draw inward, her resilience manifesting as a deep, quiet stoicism. She tended to Levi with gentle efficiency, conserved resources with innate wisdom, and often sat gazing at the ancient canyon walls, her lips occasionally moving in silent prayer or chant. She represented a connection to a deeper understanding of the place, a wisdom Graves had dismissed and Boone had only begun to truly appreciate in the face of their shared peril. Her presence was grounding, yet also served as a constant reminder of the ancient forces they had provoked.

Elise felt trapped in a fugue state of fear, exhaustion, and burgeoning, gnawing suspicion. The scientist in her desperately sought rational explanations, clung to shreds of observation, but the overwhelming evidence pointed towards something far outside the known parameters of biology or ecology. Nora's folklore, Boone's tragic history, the creature's calculated behavior, the nest's gruesome contents – it all wove together into a narrative that felt terrifyingly coherent. And at the center of it, increasingly, felt like Graves and the mysterious Kestrel Foundation he represented.

His lack of surprise at certain discoveries, his insistence on pushing forward despite mounting evidence of extreme danger, his cryptic references to 'profiles' and 'suppressed evidence'... it didn't add up. The mission felt less like discovery and more like... something else. Verification? Recovery? Containment? What had Kestrel *really* known before sending them in here? What was Graves' personal stake? His behavior after the attack, his focus on consolidating gear while Levi lay injured, his almost clinical documentation of the nest... it felt wrong, detached in a way that went beyond military training.

The suspicion festered during the long, terrifying watches, huddled in the cold dampness, listening to the creature pace above. It gnawed at her during the meager meals, watching Graves isolate himself, consulting his maps with an intensity that seemed focused on more than just escape routes. It grew as she tended to Levi, seeing the life drain slowly from him, a casualty of a mission whose true objectives felt deliberately obscured.

On the third night in the canyon, the suspicion coalesced into resolve. Fear warred with a desperate need for answers, for truth, for anything that might give them leverage or understanding in their fight for survival. She found herself on watch with Graves during the pre-dawn hours, the darkest and coldest part of the night. Levi was fitfully asleep under Nora's watchful eye near the overhang. Boone was taking his own brief, exhausted rest further back in the canyon. The only sounds were the drip of water, the low moan of wind at the canyon mouth, and the occasional, chilling scrape from the rim above.

Graves sat propped against the canyon wall, carbine across his lap, staring out towards the entrance, though little was visible beyond the first few yards of rock. He looked utterly spent, the mask of command slipping in the isolating darkness, revealing the weary, perhaps frightened, man beneath. His breathing was steady, but there was a tension in his posture that spoke of sleeplessness.

His main pack lay beside him. He hadn't stowed it further back with the others' gear, keeping it close, as always. Elise had noticed before he seemed almost obsessively protective of it, rarely letting it out of his sight. Inside, she knew, were his personal effects, spare ammunition, more maps, and perhaps... something else. The files. The hidden directives. The truth.

The thought of searching his pack felt like a profound violation, a betrayal of even the tattered remnants of team structure. But looking towards the overhang where Levi lay suffering, thinking of Jules vanished into the forest, remembering the horrors of the nest, the feeling grew that knowing the truth, whatever it was, might be their only remaining weapon, or at least provide clarity in their impending doom. Hesitantly, fueled by a desperate blend of fear and conviction, she decided.

Making sure Graves was focused outwards, seemingly lost in thought or listening intently to the sounds from above, Elise shifted slightly, positioning herself between him and the pack. Her heart hammered against her ribs so hard she was convinced he must hear it. With excruciatingly slow, cautious movements, praying the gentle trickle of water or a sudden gust of wind would cover any small sound, she reached towards the pack's main flap.

It was secured by heavy-duty plastic buckles. Her fingers, numb with cold and trembling, fumbled with the first one. It clicked open with a sound that seemed deafeningly loud in the strained silence. Graves shifted slightly, turning his head fractionally towards her. Elise froze instantly, holding her breath, convinced she was caught. But he merely scanned the immediate area around them with his red-filtered headlamp, then turned back towards the canyon mouth, apparently having heard nothing amiss.

Exhaling silently, Elise tackled the second buckle. Click. She gently lifted the main flap. Inside, visible in the faint ambient light filtering down from the sky, were neatly organized stuff sacks, spare clothing, ammunition clips… and tucked deep along the internal frame, almost hidden, was a slim, hard-sided document case she hadn't seen before. It wasn't standard military issue; it looked expensive, waterproof, probably secured.

Her stomach tightened. This had to be it. Taking another deep breath, she carefully slid her hand into the pack, her fingers brushing against cold metal clips and nylon. She worked the document case free from its tight position, the movement agonizingly slow. It was heavier than it looked. As she drew it out, she saw it wasn't locked with a key or combination, but with two small, recessed latches that required specific pressure points to open – designed for quick access by someone who knew how, but otherwise unobtrusive.

Holding the case low, shielded by her own body and the darkness, she manipulated the latches as quietly as she could. They sprang open with soft clicks. She lifted the lid just enough to peer inside, using the faintest possible setting on her own headlamp, angled carefully away from Graves.

Her breath caught. It wasn't filled with mission papers or personal documents. It was filled with data drives, high-capacity memory cards, and incredibly, several thin folders containing printed documents and glossy photographs.

Heart pounding, hands shaking almost uncontrollably now, she carefully slid out the top folder. The label, printed in stark, block capitals, read: **PROJECT CHIMERA – AO HOLLOW – PRELIMINARY ASSESSMENT & CONTAINMENT DIRECTIVES (EYES ONLY: KESTREL LEVEL 7 CLEARANCE).**

Project Chimera? Containment Directives?

She opened the folder carefully, the crisp paper rustling faintly. The first page was a highly detailed satellite image of the valley system, far more granular than the maps they'd been shown. But this image wasn't just topographical. It was overlaid with thermal imaging data. And clearly visible, clustered primarily in the southern reaches of the valley – near Graves' 'Objective Delta' – were multiple large, distinct thermal signatures corresponding to no known wildlife patterns. There were dozens of them, some moving, some stationary. The valley wasn't just home to *one* creature; it was teeming with them.

Her blood ran cold. Kestrel knew. They knew the valley was populated.

She flipped the page. A classified geological survey report, heavily redacted, but mentioning 'anomalous subterranean resonance patterns' and 'uncharted cavern systems' primarily located beneath the southern basin. Was *that* Objective Delta? Access to caves? A denning site?

Next, a series of blurry, black-and-white aerial reconnaissance photos, dated from the late 1970s, showing similar large figures moving through clear-cut areas bordering the AO. Attached was a scanned internal memo, referencing a joint Forest Service / US Army report (Project Code: BACKWOODS), recommending the area be designated restricted access due to 'persistent, unexplained large predator encounters' and 'significant personnel risk'. The memo concluded with a recommendation for 'passive observation and information suppression'. The government knew. Decades ago. And covered

139

it up. The ranger's journal back in Bluffs End, if it existed, likely contained corroborating accounts.

Elise's nausea intensified. This wasn't exploration; it was intrusion into a known, dangerous habitat deliberately kept secret.

Then she saw the next folder, labelled simply: **SUBJECT 'GOLIATH' – POST-MORTEM FINDINGS – DR. ARIS THORNE (KESTREL PATHOLOGY).**

Post-mortem? They had recovered a body? Or… captured one alive that later died?

With trembling fingers, she opened it. Inside were glossy, high-resolution photographs that made her want to retch. A massive, hairy humanoid body lay strapped to a stainless-steel autopsy table in what looked like a sterile, windowless facility. Its scale was immense, easily nine feet long even lying down. The creature was powerfully built, covered in thick, dark hair matted with what looked like dried blood and mud. Its face, Slack in death, held the same heavy brow ridge, flat nose, and simian cast she had glimpsed on the ridge. This was one of them.

Accompanying the horrific photos was a detailed, clinical autopsy report. Elise, with her biology background, skimmed the technical jargon, her mind reeling:

- *Subject: Adult Male, estimated age 40-50 years based on dentition and osteological analysis.*
- *Height: 2.8 meters (approx. 9' 2"). Estimated weight: 350 kg (approx. 770 lbs).*
- *Physiology: Anomalous blend pongid and hominid characteristics. Extreme muscle density. Skeletal structure exhibits unique adaptations for bipedal locomotion over uneven terrain AND significant arboreal capability (hyper-flexible shoulder joints, elongated phalanges).*
- *Cranial Capacity: Estimated 1800cc (significantly larger than Homo sapiens, exceeding Neanderthal range). Complex neural pathways indicated in preliminary brain tissue histology.* (Indicating high intelligence).
- *Sensory Organs: Enlarged olfactory bulb. Evidence suggests advanced low-light visual acuity. Unique inner ear structure potentially capable detecting infrasound.* (Explaining their ability to sense intruders, navigate in darkness, and perhaps cause the unsettling feelings?)
- *Genetics: Preliminary DNA sequencing incomplete/unstable. Indicates distinct species, non-human primate*

lineage, possible relict hominoid divergent from known evolutionary trees. (A unique species, exactly as the euphemism suggested).

• *Cause of Death: Massive internal hemorrhaging secondary to multiple high-caliber projectile wounds. Evidence suggests capture trauma involving tranquilizer agents and explosive netting.* (Captured, not found dead. Wounded in the process).

• *Notable Anomalies: Unusual resilience to standard chemical tranquilizers. Rapid tissue regeneration observed post-capture but prior to death. Presence of metallic trace elements (lead, depleted uranium?) embedded in older scar tissue, suggesting prior hostile encounters, likely military/undisclosed.* (Prior attempts? Military involvement?)

Elise felt sick. They had captured one, likely after a violent struggle, maybe years ago, related to 'Project Backwoods'? Studied it. Dissected it. The clinical report detailed the violation, the cold reduction of this incredible, sentient being into tissue samples and data points. The term 'Goliath' felt obscene.

Beneath the autopsy report was a final memo from this Dr. Aris Thorne to Kestrel Command. *"Subject 'Goliath' exhibits physiology and implied intelligence far exceeding initial projections. Extreme territoriality and social bonding behavior observed pre-capture (subject died attempting to protect juvenile). Recommend immediate cessation of active recovery protocols. Containment breach or sustained hostile engagement in AO Hollow risks unacceptable casualties and potential wider exposure. Area should be quarantined under guise of seismic instability/viral outbreak. Further engagement is strongly discouraged."*

A recommendation for quarantine, not further engagement. A warning from their own scientist. A warning Graves and Kestrel had clearly ignored.

Finally, tucked at the bottom of the document case, was the current mission directive Elise hadn't seen before. Title: **PROJECT CHIMERA – PHASE 2: HABITAT VERIFICATION & ASSET RECOVERY.** The text was brief, chillingly direct: *Primary Objective: Locate and confirm Subject Primary Denning Site (Ref: Geo Target Delta). Secondary Objective: Deploy deep-penetration seismic/imaging probes. Tertiary Objective (Contingent): Secure high-value biological samples (living subject tissue if feasible/necessary – see Protocol 7: Live Capture).* There was no mention of an 'ecological assessment'. No mention of investigating disappearances except as indicators of subject activity. And Protocol 7... Live Capture? They were equipped, or expected, to potentially *capture* one of these beings? After the 'Goliath' incident? It was insane.

And then, the final line, underscored: *Absolute operational secrecy paramount. Witness contamination (local populace, SAR, unaffiliated researchers) unacceptable. Neutralization authorized under extreme compromise conditions.*

Neutralization authorized. Not of the creature. Of *witnesses.*

Elise's blood turned to ice water. This wasn't just a cover-up; it was ruthless. Kestrel wasn't just studying these creatures; they were treating them like assets or threats to be managed, contained, or recovered, and they were willing to silence anyone who got in the way. Jules wasn't just a casualty of the creature; his disappearance potentially served Kestrel's secrecy objective. Maybe Graves wasn't meant to save him. Maybe their own survival wasn't guaranteed if they became inconvenient 'witnesses'.

She carefully, silently slid the folders back into the case, her mind numb with horror and the sickening weight of the betrayal. Graves wasn't just a cold, mission-driven leader; he was knowingly leading them into the den of creatures Kestrel had previously captured and studied, creatures their own expert had warned against engaging. He was operating under directives that prioritized secrecy and 'asset recovery' over their lives. The mission was a lie from start to finish.

Just as she eased the document case back into Graves' pack, a hand clamped down hard on her shoulder. Elise gasped, spinning around, heart leaping into her throat.

Graves stood over her, his face inches from hers, illuminated by the dim red glow of his headlamp. His eyes, no longer weary, were chips of ice, narrowed with cold fury and suspicion. He hadn't been asleep or lost in thought; he had been watching her.

"Looking for something, Dr. Holloway?" he hissed, his voice dangerously low, his grip tightening on her shoulder, pinning her against the rock wall.

Before Elise could stammer out a reply, another figure moved swiftly out of the deeper shadows of the canyon. Boone. He hadn't been asleep either. He must have seen Elise approach Graves' pack, seen Graves grab her.

"Get your damn hands off her, Graves," Boone growled, stepping between them, shotgun held loosely but ready.

Graves released Elise abruptly, turning to face Boone, his own hand instinctively going to the sidearm on his hip. "Stay out of this, Boone. The doctor was compromising sensitive mission materials."

"Sensitive?" Boone spat the word. "You mean the truth you been lyin' about since we got here? The truth about what Kestrel really wants? The truth about what happened to that 'Goliath' thing?"

Graves froze, his face paling. "How do you…?" He looked back sharply at Elise, understanding dawning. "You read the files." It wasn't a question.

"Damn right she did," Boone confirmed, taking another step closer, his knuckles white on the shotgun. "And I heard enough. 'Containment directives'. 'Asset recovery'. 'Neutralization authorized'. You lyin' son of a bitch. You knew what was out here. You knew Kestrel poked the nest before. You knew people got killed, got dissected. And you marched us right into the middle of it anyway! For what? Rocks? Tissue samples?"

"You don't understand the strategic importance," Graves began, trying to regain control, falling back on jargon. "The subject represents an unprecedented biological discovery, a potential threat—"

"Threat?" Boone roared, shoving Graves hard in the chest, sending him stumbling back against the canyon wall. "We weren't a threat till *you* brought us here! They were defendin' their home! From people like you! People like Kestrel! What happened to 'Goliath'? Did you kill it? Did Kestrel kill it?"

"It was a necessary action," Graves ground out, regaining his footing, anger flushing his face. "The creature was incredibly dangerous—"

"It was defendin' its kid!" Boone yelled, pointing towards Elise, who still held the horrific knowledge from the autopsy memo. "Your own damn doctor said so! Said to leave 'em alone! But Kestrel wouldn't listen, would they? And neither did you! You just followed orders, brought more people here to die!"

Driven by years of suppressed grief for his brother, by the fresh horror of Jules' disappearance, by the confirmation of Graves' calculated deceit, Boone lunged. He didn't swing the shotgun, but dropped it aside, throwing a wild, powerful right hook that connected solidly with Graves' jaw.

Graves staggered, surprise and pain registering on his face. He reacted instantly, years of military training kicking in. He deflected Boone's next swing, driving a hard knee into Boone's midsection, followed by a chopping blow to the side of his neck.

Boone grunted, stumbling back but not falling, his wilderness-toughness absorbing the impact. He lowered his head and charged, tackling Graves around the waist, driving him hard against the rocky canyon wall.

The two men grappled fiercely in the dim light, crashing against the rocks, their harsh breathing echoing in the confined space. It wasn't a skilled fight; it was raw, desperate rage against cold, trained efficiency. Fists flew, landing with sickening thuds. They spun apart, circled each other, Boone bleeding from a cut above his eye, Graves breathing heavily, favouring the side where Boone's first punch landed.

"Stop it!" Elise screamed again, though her voice was lost in the fury. Levi groaned from the overhang, weakly trying to push himself up. Nora stood frozen, watching the primal conflict unfold, perhaps seeing it as the inevitable outcome of the lies and intrusion.

High above, on the canyon rim, the scraping sound returned, louder now, more insistent. A low growl drifted down. The creature was aware of the conflict below. Attracted by the noise, the violence.

Boone landed another heavy blow to Graves' ribs. Graves retaliated with a quick, brutal jab to Boone's throat, making him gasp and stagger back. Graves seized the momentary advantage, lunging forward, attempting to pin Boone against the wall again.

But Boone, fueled by righteous fury, twisted away, grabbed Graves' arm, and used his momentum to send Graves crashing face-first into the unforgiving rock. Graves cried out, slumping to the ground, momentarily stunned.

Boone stood over him, chest heaving, blood dripping onto the dusty ground, poised to strike again.

"Boone! Enough!" Elise cried, finally finding her voice, grabbing his arm. "He's down! Stop! Listen!" She pointed upwards frantically. "It heard us! It's right above us!"

Boone froze, his rage momentarily checked by the immediate, external threat. He listened, hearing the unmistakable scrape and huff from the rim. He looked down at the dazed, bleeding Graves, then back towards Elise and the others, the fury in his eyes slowly being replaced by the grim understanding of their renewed peril.

The betrayal was complete. The team was irrevocably broken. Graves' secrets were out, revealing a mission far darker and more callous than any of them had imagined. But their internal conflict had likely just sounded a dinner bell for the patient predator waiting above, drawn by the sounds of violence, ready perhaps, to finally descend into the trap it had sprung.

Chapter 18: Escape Attempt

The echoes of the brutal confrontation hung heavy in the cold, thin air of the canyon, mingling with the scent of damp rock, fear, and fresh blood. Boone stood breathing heavily, blood trickling from the cut above his eye, staring down at Graves who was slowly, painfully pushing himself up from the dusty ground, spitting out a mouthful of blood and grit. Graves' face was already beginning to swell where Boone's fists had connected, his lip was split, and he favoured his ribs, likely cracked from the impact against the wall. The violence had been raw, cathartic for Boone perhaps, but ultimately futile, achieving nothing but alerting the creature above to their distress and further fracturing their already precarious unity.

"It heard us," Elise repeated urgently, her voice tight with panic, gesturing frantically towards the canyon rim where the scraping sounds persisted, closer now, more deliberate. "Boone, Graves, for God's sake, stop! It's right there!"

The immediate, shared threat seemed to penetrate the haze of rage and pain. Graves staggered to his feet, instinctively reaching for his carbine lying nearby, his eyes flicking upwards, acknowledging the peril. Boone, his fury momentarily spent, retrieved his shotgun, his gaze also fixed on the unseen rim, the reality of their situation crashing back in. The betrayal, the anger – it still simmered, unresolved, but survival instinct temporarily trumped internal conflict.

"We have to get out of here," Levi gasped from his position near the overhang, struggling to sit up straighter despite the pain radiating from his ribs. "Now. While it's just... watching. Before it decides to come down."

"Out where?" Graves countered raggedly, wiping blood from his split lip. "We're boxed in. It controls the rim."

"Maybe not all of it," Boone said, his eyes scanning the towering rock walls, his tracker's mind already working, searching for possibilities. He pointed further up the canyon, away from the entrance where they'd heard the most recent sounds. "That ridge line... it curves. Canyon twists. Maybe further up, there's a break? A ledge? Somewhere high enough we might get a signal out?"

It was a desperate long shot. Their sophisticated satellite phone was dead, along with all the other electronics. But maybe, just maybe, a standard emergency radio, or even a basic signal mirror if the sun ever broke through, might have a chance from a high, exposed point further away from whatever localized interference plagued the valley floor and this specific canyon. Hope was a flimsy reed, but it was all they had left.

"Too risky," Graves started to object, falling back into cautious tactical assessment. "Moving deeper into the canyon might be walking further into the trap. We don't know what's up there."

"Sitting here waitin' to get picked off ain't risky, it's suicide!" Boone retorted, his anger flaring again. "We gotta try somethin', Graves! Unless you got a better idea? Or maybe another Kestrel secret that'll save us?" The sarcasm was biting.

Graves glared at Boone but offered no alternative. His authority was gone, his secrets exposed. He was just another trapped victim now, albeit one burdened with the terrible knowledge of *why* they were trapped.

Nora, who had remained a silent, watchful presence throughout the fight, now spoke, her voice calm but firm. "Boone is right. Waiting here invites death. The high ground is our only chance, however small. If there is a path upwards, further in, we must take it."

With Nora adding her weight to Boone's desperate gamble, Graves seemed to accept the inevitable. He gave a curt, pained nod. "Alright. We move. Up-canyon. Look for any ascent route. Levi, can you make it?"

Levi grimaced, pushing himself carefully to his feet with Nora's help. "Have to," he ground out between clenched teeth. "Slowly."

Gathering their meagre remaining supplies was done with frantic haste. Every scrape of a pack buckle, every clink of a water bottle, seemed amplified, potentially attracting further attention from above. They moved out quickly, heading deeper into the narrowing canyon, away from the entrance where the sounds from the rim had been most prominent.

The canyon floor became rougher, choked with larger boulders and debris from past rockfalls. The trickle of water disappeared underground, leaving only damp, slippery stones. The walls leaned in closer, amplifying the feeling of claustrophobia. They moved in near total darkness, relying on the dimmest settings of their headlamps, pointed downwards to minimize visibility from above. Elise stayed close to Levi, supporting him, her ears straining for any sound from the rim behind or ahead of them. Had the creature followed? Or was it waiting, anticipating their move?

After maybe two hundred yards of slow, painstaking progress, battling the uneven terrain and Levi's hindered pace, Boone stopped. Ahead, the main canyon appeared to narrow into an impassable V-shape, choked with massive, wedged boulders. A dead end, just as Graves had feared.

"Damn it," Boone breathed, scanning the towering walls in the faint light.

But then Nora pointed upwards, towards the left-hand wall. "There," she whispered. "Look."

Following her gesture, Elise saw it – a faint, almost invisible diagonal fissure cutting across the rock face, leading steeply upwards. It wasn't a ledge, barely even a crack, more like a series of tiny, eroded footholds and handholds ascending the near-vertical wall, partially hidden by hanging curtains of moss and scraggly, tenacious ferns. It looked impossibly steep, terrifyingly exposed.

"Is that… climbable?" Elise asked, her voice filled with doubt.

Boone peered up, assessing it with a critical eye. "Maybe. For someone light, experienced. Looks like an old water seepage line, maybe slightly widened by frost wedging. Holds are probably slick, maybe loose." He shook his head. "No way Levi makes that. Hell, I don't know if *I* can make that with a pack on."

"But it's high," Graves stated, his tactical mind latching onto the key feature. He shone his light beam briefly upwards, estimating the height. "That fissure seems to lead towards a small notch or platform near the rim, maybe eighty, ninety feet up. If anywhere offers line-of-sight..." His voice trailed off, the desperation evident.

A grim realization settled over the group. Reaching that potential signaling point was a one-person job, maybe two at most, traveling light and fast. A climber's route, not a team escape path. And someone would have to risk the terrifyingly exposed ascent, potentially under the watchful eyes of the creature.

"I'll go," Graves said immediately, surprising Elise. Perhaps seeing his authority crumble, his mission in tatters, he felt a need to reclaim purpose, to take the risk himself. "Give me the emergency beacon, any lightweight signal gear we still have. I have climbing training. I can make that ascent."

Boone looked skeptical. "You sure, Graves? That ain't no rappel tower."

"I'm the best equipped," Graves stated curtly, shedding his main pack, pulling out a small, basic emergency locator beacon (PLB – Personal Locator Beacon, relying on a different satellite network than the dead sat phone, offering a tiny sliver of hope), a signal mirror, and a high-intensity strobe light from his survival kit. He clipped them securely to his harness. "The rest of you find cover back down the canyon, near that overhang. Maintain watch. Give me… ninety minutes. If you don't hear from the beacon, or see a signal… assume the attempt failed. Then," he hesitated, the implication hanging heavy, "your best bet is probably trying to push through that deadfall at the lower end after all. Try to find another way out."

The plan felt suicidally thin, relying on unknown signal propagation, minimal gear, and a treacherous climb under potential hostile observation. But it was the only plan they had.

"Be careful, Graves," Elise found herself saying, a strange mix of residual distrust and genuine fear for him welling up.

Graves gave a curt nod, his face set in hard lines. He checked the action on his carbine one last time, slung it securely across his back, then approached the base of the fissure. Taking a deep breath, he found the first handhold, tested it, and began to climb.

The ascent was agonizingly slow, terrifyingly exposed. Graves moved with economical precision, testing each hold before committing his weight, his dark shape stark against the grey rock face in the faint pre-dawn light that was just beginning to filter down. He climbed steadily, disappearing at times behind curtains of dripping moss or rock bulges, then reappearing higher up. The rest of the team watched from the canyon floor below, hearts pounding, hardly daring to breathe, scanning the rim above for any sign of the creature.

He was perhaps two-thirds of the way up, maybe sixty feet off the canyon floor, reaching for a handhold just below the target notch, when it happened.

A shadow detached itself from the deeper blackness of the canyon rim directly above the fissure. Not subtly, not stealthily, but with terrifying speed. It wasn't the creature itself, initially. It was a rock. A large one, easily the size of a microwave oven, deliberately dislodged from the rim.

"Graves! Look out!" Boone roared from below.

Graves heard the warning, glanced up, saw the plummeting rock, and instinctively flattened himself against the fissure, trying to make himself as small a target as possible. The rock crashed down past him, missing him by inches, exploding against the canyon wall further below with a deafening boom that echoed like cannon fire through the confined space, showering the team on the floor with smaller fragments and dust.

Graves clung precariously to the rock face, clearly shaken, dust raining down around him. But before he could recover, before he could resume his climb or attempt a retreat, a second, darker shadow appeared on the rim above.

This one *was* the creature.

It moved with terrifying agility to the very edge of the canyon rim, peering down directly at Graves' exposed position. Even from the floor, Elise could see its massive silhouette, the powerful shoulders, the large head. It didn't throw another rock. It did something worse.

With a low growl rumbling in its chest, it reached down. Not with its hand, but with something long, flexible, almost prehensile – a thick, sturdy vine or perhaps a section of incredibly tough root it must have carried or ripped from the ground nearby. In a horrifyingly fluid motion, it looped this vine down towards Graves.

Graves saw it coming, tried to scramble sideways, tried to unlimber his carbine, but he was too exposed, his grip too precarious. The loop snaked around his ankle with uncanny precision. Before Graves could even cry out, the creature *pulled*.

The force was immense, irresistible. Graves was plucked from the rock face like an insect, his hands scrabbling uselessly for purchase. He yelled then, a choked cry of terror and surprise, as he was hauled bodily upwards, dangling helplessly from the vine.

The team below could only watch in horror, powerless. Boone raised his shotgun, firing upwards in a futile gesture, the pellets spanging harmlessly off the rock face far below the rim. Levi cried out Graves' name. Nora covered her face, whispering frantic prayers.

The creature hauled Graves effortlessly up over the rim, his struggles abruptly silenced as he disappeared from view. For a moment, there was silence, save for the wind and their own ragged breathing. Then, a single, chilling sound drifted down – a heavy, wet *crunch*, followed by utter silence from the rim above.

Graves was gone. Taken. Eliminated with brutal efficiency, his desperate escape attempt turned into a horrifying execution. The creature hadn't just prevented him from signaling; it had actively intervened, using tools, strategy, and overwhelming force.

The hope, fragile as it was, died with Graves. The escape attempt had failed catastrophically. They were trapped, leaderless (though Graves' leadership had been suspect at best), with dwindling supplies, a severely injured man, and the knowledge that the creature was not just watching, but actively, intelligently, and lethally preventing any attempt to summon help or flee its domain.

Elise stared up at the empty rim where Graves had vanished, her body trembling violently, a cold, abyssal despair opening within her. They were well and truly caught in the beast's jaws now. Four remained: Boone, the haunted tracker; Nora, the repository of ancient, terrifying wisdom; Levi, gravely injured and weakening; and herself, the biologist forced to confront a reality far stranger and more deadly than any textbook could contain. The canyon, their supposed refuge, now felt unequivocally like a tomb. And the silence from the rim above was the sound of the lid closing.

Chapter 19: Myth Made Flesh

Despair, cold and absolute, settled over the four remaining survivors in the wake of Graves' horrific demise. The creature's deliberate, calculated act – using a tool, intervening specifically to stop the escape attempt, the chilling finality of the sound from the rim – obliterated any remaining hope of rescue or strategic maneuvering. They were utterly trapped, at the mercy of an intelligence that was both ancient and terrifyingly adaptive. The canyon felt less like a choke point now and more like a designated holding pen, its rock walls echoing with the ghosts of Graves' final moments and the silent, patient menace of the guardian pacing above.

They huddled together near the overhang where Levi lay, the shock rendering them almost mute. Boone, his face grim and etched with a new layer of weary horror, kept watch on the rim, shotgun held ready, though the gesture felt futile against the creature's demonstrated power and cunning. Nora tended to Levi, her expression unreadable but radiating a profound sorrow, occasionally murmuring quiet words in Lushootseed, perhaps prayers for the departed, perhaps pleas for the living. Elise felt numb, disconnected, her mind struggling to process the cascade of horrors – Jules vanished, the nest of bones, Graves plucked from the rock face. The scientific framework she had clung to felt shattered beyond repair, leaving only raw fear and a sickening awareness of their insignificance in the face of the valley's ancient power.

Levi, mercifully, had lapsed back into a painkiller-induced stupor and seemed largely unaware of Graves' end, though his shallow breathing and feverish skin spoke of his own precarious state. Conserving the remaining medication was critical, but letting him suffer wasn't an option. Elise checked his bandages, noted the increased heat radiating from his injured side – infection was clearly setting in, adding another layer to their desperate predicament.

As the grim reality solidified, a stark choice presented itself. They could stay in the canyon, wait for the creature to decide their fate, likely succumbing to starvation, infection, or direct attack. Or they could try to move, make a desperate break, despite the seeming hopelessness. But where? Back down the canyon, towards the potentially blocked lower end Graves had mentioned? Back along the Hollow Trail, past the nest and the

Grove of Symbols, risking another encounter in territory already proven deadly? Neither option seemed viable.

It was Boone, hours later, as the weak midday light filtered down, who voiced the unthinkable. "We stay here, we die," he stated flatly, his voice raspy. He hadn't moved from his vigil near the canyon mouth, but his gaze shifted towards the inner canyon, towards the dead end Graves had feared, but also the direction from which they hadn't yet heard movement from the rim. "Goin' back... that feels like walkin' into its jaws. Maybe... maybe that dead end Graves saw ain't the whole story. Maybe there's another way through. A crawlspace. Another fissure. Somethin'."

It was the barest sliver of possibility, born more from desperation than logic. But sitting and waiting felt like accepting death. "Levi can't travel far," Elise pointed out quietly, gesturing towards his still form.

"We carry him," Boone said grimly. "Slow, yeah. Dangerous, yeah. But maybe... maybe it won't expect us to push *deeper* into the dead end. Maybe it's focusin' its attention on the entrance, waitin' for us to bolt back out."

It was a thin strategic hope, relying on predicting the actions of an alien intelligence, but it was better than nothing. Nora nodded slowly. "If there is a hidden way, it will be in the deepest part. Sometimes places that seem closed... open, if approached with respect. Or desperation."

And so, the decision was made. Harnessing Levi into the makeshift sling again, Boone took point, moving slowly, testing the unstable ground, scanning ahead into the deepening shadows of the inner canyon. Elise and Nora supported Levi between them, his groans muffled by clenched teeth and medication, his weight a terrible burden. Their progress was excruciatingly slow, perhaps only a few dozen yards every fifteen minutes.

The canyon did indeed narrow, the walls pressing in, casting the path in perpetual twilight. They navigated around massive boulders that seemed deliberately placed, squeezing through tight gaps, the rock cold and damp against their skin. The sense of confinement intensified, becoming almost suffocating. There was still no sign of the creature from the rim directly above this deeper section, but the feeling of being watched persisted, a constant pressure. Was it allowing them to move deeper into the trap?

After what felt like an eternity of slow, painful progress, they reached the apparent end of the canyon. A jumbled mass of enormous boulders, some the size of small cars, formed a seemingly impenetrable wall, choking the passage completely. Rainwater and seepage trickled down through the cracks, pooling slightly at the base before disappearing into the jumble. It looked exactly like the dead end Graves had described. Despair washed over Elise anew. They had gambled, moved deeper, and found only a final wall to their prison.

"Damn it," Boone breathed, slumping against a rock, defeat heavy in his voice. "Graves was right. Boxed in."

Nora, however, moved forward, towards the base of the rockfall. She didn't try to climb, but instead ran her hands gently over the surface of the largest boulder, seemingly listening, feeling. She knelt, examining the smaller gaps between the massive stones near the floor, where the water seeped away.

"Wait," Nora murmured, her voice hushed with discovery. "Here. Air moves." She pointed to a narrow gap between two colossal boulders, almost completely hidden by ferns and debris. A faint but discernible current of cooler air flowed outwards from the darkness beyond. "And… there are markings. Old ones."

Elise and Boone hurried over. Pushing aside the wet ferns, Elise shone her light into the gap. It was narrow, maybe only three feet high and two feet wide, a tight squeeze. But beyond the initial constriction, it seemed to open slightly into pitch blackness. And on the surface of the rock just inside the opening, barely visible under centuries of grime and mineral deposit, were faint scratches – the same ancient, interwoven spiral patterns they had seen on the Hollow Trail.

"A passage?" Elise whispered, incredulous. "Hidden behind the rockfall?"

"Looks like it," Boone said, hope flickering faintly in his eyes. "Maybe part of the original trail system? Blocked by this slide ages ago, but maybe still goes through?"

It was another gamble. Squeezing into that dark, unknown passage felt terrifying. What if it narrowed further? What if it collapsed? What if something was waiting inside? But the alternative was staying trapped in the canyon under the creature's patient watch.

The decision was immediate, unspoken. Boone went first, stripping off his pack and shotgun, pushing them ahead of him as he wriggled through the tight opening. After a moment, his muffled voice came back, "It opens up! Tunnel, maybe? Smooth floor. Can't see far, but feels… stable. Big enough to stand inside."

Next came Levi. Getting him through the opening was a nightmare. Weakened, groaning with pain, barely conscious, he had to be carefully maneuvered, pushed and pulled by Nora and Elise from behind while Boone guided him from within the passage. It took twenty agonizing minutes, every movement potentially aggravating his injuries, the enclosed space amplifying his pained sounds.

Finally, he was through, collapsing just inside the entrance. Nora squeezed through next, then Elise, pushing their packs ahead. The transition was abrupt. One moment they were in the cold, damp canyon; the next, they were in absolute darkness, the air still, cool, and carrying the scent of dry dust and deep earth.

Their headlamps cut beams through the blackness, revealing they were inside a natural tunnel or perhaps an artificially widened lava tube. The walls were smooth, water-worn in places, arching overhead maybe ten feet high. The floor was mostly level, covered in fine dust and small pebbles. It felt ancient, untouched.

"Which way?" Elise asked, her voice echoing slightly in the confined space. The passage seemed to slope gently downwards, disappearing into darkness ahead.

Before Boone could answer, a low sound echoed from *behind* them, from the canyon they had just vacated. A deep, resonant rumble, followed by the unmistakable sound of shifting rock.

They froze, exchanging terrified glances. Had the creature heard them? Was it investigating the rockfall? Or worse, was it coming *through*?

"Go!" Boone urged, grabbing his shotgun and pack. "Deeper in! Now!"

There was no time for debate. They plunged into the darkness of the tunnel, half-carrying, half-dragging the barely conscious Levi, Nora guiding the way, Boone bringing up the rear, constantly glancing back towards the entrance. The tunnel twisted, turned, sloped downwards. Their headlamp beams bounced off the dark, damp walls, revealing nothing but more tunnel ahead. The silence was profound, broken only by their ragged breathing, Levi's moans, and the frantic pounding of their own hearts. They felt like worms burrowing desperately into the earth, fleeing a monstrous predator.

After perhaps fifty yards, the tunnel opened abruptly into a larger space. Their headlamp beams swept across a natural cavern, maybe thirty feet across, the ceiling lost in darkness high above. Stalactites hung like stone icicles, dripping water that echoed loudly in the stillness. The air here felt slightly warmer, less stagnant.

"Hold up," Boone breathed, leaning against the cavern wall, catching his breath. Elise and Nora gently lowered Levi to the relatively dry floor.

It was in that moment of pause, in the relative quiet of the cavern, bathed in the unsteady beams of their headlamps, that they became aware they were no longer alone.

From the darkness at the far side of the cavern, where another passage presumably led deeper into the earth, came a soft shuffling sound. Then, a low guttural cough, instantly recognizable, chillingly close.

Weapons came up instantly. Boone leveled his shotgun. Elise fumbled with her pistol, aiming towards the sound. Nora stood protectively over Levi, axe held ready. Their beams converged on the dark opening.

Slowly, deliberately, a figure emerged from the blackness.

It was one of them. Massive, nine feet tall, covered in shaggy dark hair, moving with that unsettling fluid grace. It stepped into the center of the cavern, blinking slowly in the sudden glare of their headlamps. Its face, seen clearly now at a distance of less than thirty feet, was deeply furrowed, the brow heavy, the nose broad and flat, the jaw powerful. Its eyes, dark and deep-set, seemed to hold an ancient, weary intelligence. They showed no aggression, no overt hostility, just… calm observation.

Before they could fully react, paralyzed by shock and terror, another figure emerged from the darkness behind the first. Slightly smaller, perhaps eight feet tall, its build leaner, its movements quicker, more tentative. It stayed close to the larger one, peering at the humans with what looked like cautious curiosity. A younger one, perhaps? An adolescent or sub-adult?

And then, a third figure stepped out, flanking the first on the other side. This one was colossal. Taller than the first by at least a foot, broader across the shoulders, its hair tinged with grey streaks around the muzzle and temples. It moved with immense presence, an aura of authority and power radiating from it. Its gaze, when it settled on the terrified humans, felt heavy, ancient, filled with an intelligence that seemed to encompass centuries of lonely guardianship. The alpha. The elder. The patriarch of this hidden clan?

Three of them. Standing there in the cavern's stillness, bathed in the panicked beams of their lights. Myth made flesh. Not just one lone monster, but a family, a social unit.

They did not attack. They did not roar or charge. They simply stood, watching the intruders who had stumbled into their subterranean refuge. The large male in the center tilted its massive head slightly, regarding Levi's injured form with apparent interest. Then, it raised its head and let out a sound unlike anything Elise had heard before – not a roar, not a whoop, but a deep, resonant call, almost like a Tibetan singing bowl, a hum that vibrated through the rock, through the air, through Elise's very bones. It wasn't threatening; it felt… questioning? Or perhaps communicative, a signal to others deeper within, or even a message directed at the humans themselves?

The younger one echoed the sound, a slightly higher pitched, hesitant hum. The giant elder remained silent, its dark eyes fixed on Elise, holding her gaze with an unnerving intensity. In those ancient eyes, she saw not mindless savagery, but awareness. Consciousness. Intelligence. A profound, non-human sentience that existed entirely outside her scientific understanding.

They weren't just monsters. They weren't just animals. They were *beings*. Survivors from another age, hidden in the earth, guardians of a sacred valley, and now, finally, encountered face-to-face in the heart of their hidden world. The terror remained, cold and profound, but mingled with it now was something else: awe. Awe at the impossible made real, awe at the confirmation of something ancient and utterly unknown dwelling alongside humanity, hidden just beyond the edges of the mapped world. The encounter shifted everything, turning fear into a complex maelstrom of dread, wonder, and the terrifying uncertainty of what came next.

Chapter 20: The Silent Grove

Time seemed to fracture in the cavern's echoing stillness, stretching into an unbearable elasticity. Bathed in the trembling beams of their headlamps, the four humans remained frozen, weapons half-raised, hearts hammering against ribs like trapped birds. Across the cavern floor, the three immense figures stood motionless, their dark eyes absorbing the light, reflecting back an unnerving, ancient intelligence. The deep, resonant hums faded, leaving a silence more profound than any they had yet experienced, a silence that seemed to thrum with unspoken meaning, with the sheer weight of this impossible encounter.

Elise couldn't tear her gaze away from the largest one, the elder. Its sheer physical presence was overwhelming – the power coiled in its massive frame, the wisdom suggested by the streaks of grey in its dark, shaggy pelt, the intensity of its dark, deep-set eyes that seemed to penetrate her very soul. This was no rampaging beast driven by instinct alone. This was a patriarch, a leader, possessing an awareness that felt ancient and deliberate. Seeing it, seeing the smaller family unit – the likely adult male, the curious, more slightly built adolescent – shattered the monolithic 'monster' narrative that fear had constructed. These were beings with social structure, with relationships, beings who likely felt loss, loyalty, territoriality, perhaps even curiosity. The 'Goliath' autopsy report flashed through Elise's mind – *social bonding behavior observed... subject died attempting to protect juvenile.* Had 'Goliath' been this elder's mate? Or another clan member? The thought added another layer of tragedy and potential motive to their current predicament.

Beside Elise, Boone was rigid, shotgun held ready but seemingly forgotten, his knuckles white. His face, pale beneath the grime and dried blood, was a mask of conflicting emotions: terror, certainly, but also a strange, awestruck disbelief, perhaps even a glimmer of horrified recognition. Was this the face of the thing that had haunted his nightmares for twenty-two years, the being that had stolen his brother? Seeing it now, not as a fleeting shadow in a snowstorm but as a family unit in repose, seemed to both validate his trauma and complicate it beyond measure.

Nora stood stock-still, her axe held loosely, her lips moving in a silent prayer or incantation. Her expression was one of profound, almost fearful reverence. She wasn't seeing monsters; she was seeing the Stick-shí'nač made manifest, the ancient guardians of her people's stories, stepping out of legend and into the trembling beams of their lights. For her, this was less a discovery and more a confirmation of the sacred, dangerous power inhabiting this valley.

Levi, propped against the cavern wall, seemed barely conscious, his eyes half-lidded, though whether from pain, medication, or the shock of the encounter was impossible to tell. Perhaps mercifully, he seemed only partially aware of the giants standing just yards away.

How long they stood locked in that silent tableau, Elise couldn't guess. Seconds stretched into minutes. No one moved, no one spoke. The only sounds were their own ragged breathing, the slow drip of water from unseen stalactites high above, and the faint, pained whimpers escaping Levi's lips. The creatures, too, remained largely motionless, observing, assessing, their immense patience a terrifying counterpoint to the humans' frantic internal states.

Then, the largest one, the elder, slowly raised one massive, long-fingered hand – not in a threatening gesture, but in a calming one, palm facing slightly outwards. It let out another low, soft hum, deeper this time, almost a subsonic vibration that Elise felt more than heard. It took a single, deliberate step *backwards*, further into the darkness of the passage from which they had emerged.

The other two followed suit immediately, the adult male giving one last, long look towards Levi before turning, the adolescent casting a final, quick, almost shy glance towards Elise before melting back into the shadows. Within seconds, they were gone, swallowed by the darkness as silently as they had appeared.

The release of tension was so abrupt, so profound, that Elise nearly collapsed. Her legs trembled violently, threatening to buckle. Boone let out a long, shuddering breath, lowering his shotgun, his hands shaking. Nora sank slowly to her knees, tears finally tracing paths through the grime on her cheeks – tears of fear, relief, or reverence, Elise couldn't tell.

"They... they left?" Elise stammered, her voice barely a whisper, disbelief warring with overwhelming relief. "They didn't attack?"

"No," Boone said, his voice hoarse. He wiped a hand across his face, smearing blood and sweat. "They just... looked.

Showed themselves. Then backed off." He sounded utterly bewildered. "Why?"

"Perhaps," Nora murmured, looking towards the dark passage where the beings had vanished, "they were leading us."

"Leading us?" Graves would have scoffed at the idea, Elise thought, a brief pang of something unidentifiable – not grief, perhaps just the acknowledgment of his absence – hitting her. But standing here, after that encounter, the idea didn't seem entirely preposterous. The deliberate sighting on the ridge, the non-fatal attack, the herding into the canyon, the discovery of the hidden passage... what if it wasn't all just random hostility? What if there was a purpose behind it?

"They could have killed us easily," Levi whispered weakly from the floor, his eyes open now, clearer than before, suggesting he had witnessed more than they realized. "That big one... just stood there. Had us dead to rights."

"So why didn't they?" Elise asked, voicing the question hanging heavy in the subterranean air. "What do they want?"

"Maybe," Boone said slowly, thoughtfully, looking around the cavern, then back towards the dark passage ahead, "maybe they wanted us to *come* here. Through the tunnel. To... wherever this leads." He frowned, suspicion warring with a nascent, terrifying sense of wonder. "But why?"

The answer, or perhaps just the next stage of the mystery, lay deeper within the earth. Shaken but propelled by a desperate need to understand, or simply to escape the suffocating darkness of the tunnel, they decided to press on. After checking Levi again, ensuring he was stable enough to move, they reconfigured, Boone taking point, shining his headlamp beam into the darkness of the unexplored passage.

This passage was different from the tunnel they'd arrived through. It felt less natural, more deliberately smoothed, the walls showing faint vertical striations that might have been tool marks, impossibly ancient. It sloped gently upwards now, and after only twenty or thirty yards, Elise saw a faint lightening ahead. Not daylight, but a softer, greener, diffused luminescence.

As they approached the source of the light, the passage opened out abruptly, not into another cavern, but into a place unlike anything Elise could have ever imagined.

They stepped out onto a wide ledge overlooking a vast, circular depression, almost perfectly round, sunk deep into the heart of the mountain. It was perhaps half a mile across, maybe more, its floor lost in shadow far below. But it wasn't the scale that took Elise's breath away; it was the *light*.

The entire depression glowed with a soft, ethereal, blue-green light. It didn't seem to emanate from a single source, but rather to suffuse the very air, originating perhaps from the rocks themselves, or from vast banks of phosphorescent moss and fungi clinging to the unseen floor and lower walls. The light was cool, gentle, bathing everything in an otherworldly luminescence that felt both beautiful and deeply unnerving.

And within this softly glowing Grotto, spread across the shadowed floor below, were structures.

Dozens of them. Tall, conical shapes resembling immense termite mounds or primitive teepees, constructed from interwoven branches, mud, bone, and what looked like slabs of slate-like rock. They varied in size, some towering thirty feet high, others smaller, clustered together in what seemed like distinct family or clan groupings. Faint trails, worn smooth by the passage of immense feet over countless generations, connected the structures, converging towards the center of the depression where a larger, flatter area seemed to serve as a communal space.

Thin tendrils of smoke or steam rose lazily from vents near the tops of several of the larger structures, suggesting internal heat sources – geothermal activity? Controlled fires? The air here, while still cool, lacked the biting chill of the higher elevations or the stagnant dampness of the tunnel. It felt… protected. Sheltered. Alive.

But most striking were the other constructions scattered amongst the conical dwellings. Immense totemic figures carved from massive tree trunks or assembled from colossal stones, depicting stylized representations of the creatures themselves, often intertwined with spirals, eyes, and other symbols Elise recognized from the Hollow Trail. There were also intricate standing stones arranged in circles and lines, reminiscent of megalithic sites like Stonehenge or Carnac, hinting at astronomical observation or complex rituals. And everywhere, integrated into the structures, leaning against walls, piled in designated areas, were bones – vast quantities of animal bones, primarily elk and deer, but also bear, cougar, and other mountain fauna, cleaned and stacked with an almost ritualistic neatness that contrasted sharply with the horrifying jumble of the hunting nest they had discovered earlier. Here, the bones felt less like trophies and more like... resources? Or perhaps tributes?

This wasn't just a denning site; it was a *settlement*. A hidden, subterranean village inhabited by a species unknown to the outside world, a place of obvious social complexity, artistry, and perhaps even spiritual significance, existing for millennia in utter secrecy beneath the Hollow Ground.

The four humans stood frozen on the ledge, gazing down at the incredible scene, speechless with awe and a fear deeper than any they had felt before. This was the heart of the mystery. This was the reason the valley was guarded so fiercely. This was the secret the Stick-shí'nač had protected for generations uncounted.

"Sweet Mother of God," Boone breathed, his voice filled with pure wonder, the shotgun hanging forgotten at his side. "It's... it's a city."

"Not a city," Nora corrected softly, her voice trembling with reverence. "A sanctuary. *The* Sanctuary. The place the stories whispered about but no living person had ever seen. The home of the First People."

Elise felt her scientific mind struggling to categorize, to comprehend. This defied everything she knew about primate behavior, hominid evolution, North American megafauna. A subterranean, tool-using, art-creating, potentially ritualistic society of giant undiscovered primates, hidden beneath the Olympic mountains? It was impossible. Yet, it lay spread out before her eyes, bathed in ethereal light. The implications were staggering, rewriting not just biology books, but potentially the entire history of life on the continent.

Intriguingly, as they watched from the ledge, they realized something else. The creatures they had encountered in the cavern were not here. The glowing settlement below appeared deserted, though the faint smoke tendrils suggested recent occupation. Where were they? Had the three they encountered deliberately led them here, then retreated elsewhere? Why show them this sacred, hidden place?

And perhaps most significantly, the intense feeling of being watched, the oppressive psychic pressure they had felt constantly since entering the Hollow Trail, had vanished. Here, on the ledge overlooking the glowing sanctuary, the air felt calm, neutral. Still silent, yes – the strange luminescence seemed to absorb sound – but lacking the active menace, the charged expectancy, of the outer valley. It felt… permitted. As if they had finally reached a place where the guardians did not perceive them as an immediate threat, or perhaps a place the guardians themselves held in such reverence that violence was forbidden within its bounds.

"They… they didn't follow us," Levi murmured weakly, confirming Elise's thought. "It feels… calm here."

"We've reached the heart," Nora whispered, awe transforming her features. "They brought us here. They wouldn't follow us in. This place is… theirs. Hallowed ground."

Why? Elise wondered desperately. Why reveal their greatest secret to intruders they had previously hunted and attacked? Was it a test? An offering? A warning of a different kind? Or was there some deeper purpose she couldn't yet fathom?

She looked down at the incredible scene again – the glowing moss, the bone-adorned structures, the megalithic arrangements, the faint smoke rising in the still air. It was a place of profound mystery, terrifying beauty, and overwhelming ancient power. They had survived the terror, the chase, the betrayal, and had stumbled, perhaps deliberately led, into the most impossible discovery imaginable. They were standing on the threshold of a lost world, the Silent Grove revealed, and the questions far outweighed the answers. What secrets did this place hold? And what would the guardians, the Stick-shí'nač, the First People, do next?

Chapter 21: Communication

The transition from the claustrophobic darkness of the tunnel to the luminous expanse of the hidden sanctuary felt like stepping onto another planet. The four survivors stood huddled on the rock ledge, blinking, their senses struggling to process the impossible vista spread below. The soft, ethereal blue-green light, source unknown, cast strange, elongated shadows from the immense, bone-adorned structures dotting the depression floor. The air felt cool, clean, carrying the faint scent of damp earth, moss, and something else – a dry, dusty aroma like ancient stone. Most profound was the silence, not the oppressive, unnatural void of the Hollow, but a deep, hallowed stillness, as if the very air reverently muffled sound within these hidden walls.

Elise felt stripped bare, caught between the terror of their situation and the overwhelming, almost religious awe evoked by the scene. Before her lay the culmination of every whispered legend, every blurry photograph, every dismissed track – not a monster, but a civilization. Primitive, perhaps, by human technological standards, but undeniably complex, ancient, and possessing an artistry and intelligence that defied every established scientific paradigm. Her mind, trained to observe, categorize, and analyze, felt utterly overwhelmed, yet simultaneously ignited by the sheer magnitude of the discovery. This was the ultimate unknown, the greatest biological mystery on Earth, unveiled not in a fossil bed or a laboratory slide, but as a living, breathing, hidden world.

Beside her, Boone remained frozen, his shotgun held loosely now, his gaze sweeping across the silent village below. The hardened lines of fear and anger on his face had softened into something akin to stunned disbelief. This hidden world, the home of the beings that had haunted his life and taken his brother, was not the simple monstrous lair he might have imagined. It possessed a structure, a purpose, a *beauty* even, that complicated his grief and terror in ways he couldn't yet process. The clarity of his hate seemed muddied by the undeniable evidence of sophisticated sentience spread before him.

Nora stood with her head bowed slightly, hands clasped, murmuring softly in Lushootseed. Tears still tracked pathways on her weathered cheeks, but her expression held more reverence than fear now. This was the heart of the legends, the sacred ground her ancestors had only ever whispered about, a place imbued with the power of the First People, the Stick-shí'nač. To stand here, overlooking their hidden home, felt like sacrilege and apotheosis rolled into one. She was witnessing the truth behind the oldest stories, a truth far grander and more complex than perhaps even the elders had fully grasped.

Levi stirred weakly from his position on the dusty cavern floor just behind them, his pained groans momentarily silencing their thoughts. Elise knelt beside him quickly, checking his pulse, assessing his breathing. He was conscious, his eyes fluttering open, unfocused.

"Where…?" he rasped, his voice thin and dry. "So… bright…"

"Easy, Levi," Elise murmured, offering him a small sip of water from her canteen. "We're… somewhere else now. Somewhere safe, maybe." The word felt absurd even as she said it, yet the immediate threat seemed to have receded here, replaced by an atmosphere of profound stillness.

Looking down at Levi's pale, feverish face, the reality of their situation crashed back through Elise's awe. They couldn't stay on this ledge indefinitely. Levi needed better shelter, more consistent care than they could provide huddled in the open. Their food was nearly gone. Despite the seeming tranquility of the sanctuary, they were still trapped, injured, and desperately vulnerable. And the creatures… where had they gone? Why lead them here only to disappear? Were they being tested? Observed from unseen vantage points within the glowing grotto?

"We need to get down there," Elise said finally, her voice hushed but firm, forcing practicality over paralysis. "We need shelter for Levi. Water, if there's a source beyond seepage. And… we need to understand why they brought us here."

Boone turned sharply, his eyes wide with renewed alarm. "Down *there*? Doc, are you crazy? Into the middle of their… their village? After everything? After Graves? They could be waiting for us!"

"They could have killed us in the cavern, Boone," Elise argued gently but insistently. "They could have killed us on the ridge. They chose not to. They showed themselves, then led us through that tunnel. It feels… deliberate. Not like an ambush." She looked towards Nora for support.

Nora hesitated, her gaze sweeping across the glowing structures below. "This ground is sacred to them," she said slowly.

"Perhaps violence is not permitted within these walls, for them as well as for us. Perhaps... perhaps they see us differently now that we are here. Not just as intruders to be driven off, but as... something else." She looked uncertain, grasping for understanding within the framework of her ancestral knowledge. "The stories sometimes spoke of the Stick-shí'nač testing those who accidentally strayed close. Judging their hearts. Their intentions."

"Judging our hearts?" Boone scoffed, though the sound lacked its usual force. "We came here armed, secretive, led by a man working for God knows who, wantin' God knows what! We blundered into their territory, ignored their warnings! Jules is gone, Graves is gone! How the hell do they judge *that*?"

"Maybe," Elise ventured, thinking of the creature's focus on the injured Levi in the cavern, "they see past Graves' intentions. Maybe they see *our* fear, our desperation. Levi's injury." She looked down at the settlement again, her scientific mind wrestling with the seemingly impossible empathy implied. "Primatology shows complex social animals often react differently to injured or non-threatening individuals. Could they possess that level of discernment?"

It was a wild leap, bordering on anthropomorphism, yet the creatures' actions defied simple predatory logic. The restraint shown in the cavern felt significant.

"It's a hell of a gamble, Doc," Boone said grimly. "Betting our lives on the goodwill of nine-foot-tall monsters that collect human bones."

"Staying here is a gamble too," Elise countered quietly. "A losing one, for Levi at least. Down there," she gestured towards the depression, "there might be shelter. Water. Maybe even... a chance." A chance for what, she wasn't sure. Understanding? A truce? Escape?

The argument hung in the still, luminous air. Finally, Boone sighed, running a hand through his matted hair. The exhaustion, the fear, the sheer weight of their impossible situation seemed to settle on him. "Alright," he conceded reluctantly. "Alright. We try it. But we stick together. Weapons ready. One wrong move, one sign of aggression from them... we react. Understand?" His gaze was hard, fixed on Elise. He trusted her instincts less than his own ingrained fear.

"Understood," Elise agreed readily. "Cautiously. Respectfully," she added, glancing at Nora.

Finding a way down from the ledge proved surprisingly easy, reinforcing the feeling that their arrival here was not entirely accidental. A narrow, winding path, almost like a natural ramp formed by erosion or deliberately smoothed, led down from the tunnel exit along the inner wall of the depression towards the valley floor. It was steep but manageable, even with the difficult task of supporting Levi.

As they descended, the details of the hidden sanctuary became clearer, more overwhelming. The scale was immense. The conical structures towered above them, intricately woven from massive branches, mud, and stone slabs, adorned with unsettling patterns made from carefully placed animal bones – vertebrae tracing spiral patterns, femurs radiating outwards like sunbursts, skulls positioned near entrances like silent sentinels. The air hummed faintly with the blue-green luminescence, which seemed strongest emanating from vast carpets of thick, velvety moss clinging to the lower walls and the ground between structures. The moss itself pulsed with a faint, cool light, casting everything in an otherworldly glow.

The silence persisted, broken only by their own hushed movements and the ever-present drip of water from unseen sources high above, echoing strangely in the vast space. There was still no sign of the creatures themselves. The village felt simultaneously ancient and recently occupied – the structures maintained, the pathways clear, the faint scent of woodsmoke lingering near some dwellings – yet eerily empty, like a stage waiting for its actors to appear.

They reached the floor of the depression, finding themselves standing amidst the towering structures, feeling dwarfed, insignificant, acutely aware of their intrusion. They found a relatively sheltered spot near the edge of the settlement, nestled between two of the smaller conical dwellings, partially hidden from the central clearing but offering a vantage point. Here, they carefully settled Levi, making him as comfortable as possible on a bed of scavenged dry moss and spare clothing.

While Nora stayed with Levi, murmuring comforting words, Boone scouted the immediate perimeter, shotgun held ready, every sense on high alert, suspicious of the silence, expecting an ambush at any moment. Elise took the opportunity to examine their surroundings more closely, her scientific curiosity overriding her fear now that the immediate threat seemed less pressing.

She approached one of the nearby structures, running a hand over the rough, interwoven branches. The construction was incredibly robust, clearly designed to withstand considerable weight and perhaps the passage of ages. The integration of bone wasn't haphazard; it was artistic, symbolic. She recognized patterns echoing the symbols from the Hollow Trail, suggesting a consistent visual language, a culture expressing itself through architecture and art. Peering cautiously towards the low, arched entrance, she saw only darkness within, but the same faint, musky scent lingered, confirming these were indeed their dwellings.

She noticed tools, or what seemed like tools, leaning against the structure wall – large, heavy sticks stripped of bark and sharpened to a crude point at one end, almost like primitive spears or digging implements. Nearby lay several large, smooth river stones, showing signs of being used for grinding or pounding. Evidence of technology, simple yet effective, adapted to their immense strength and specific needs.

The central clearing drew her attention. Dominated by a ring of massive standing stones, taller than any human, arranged with apparent astronomical significance, it felt undeniably like a place of ceremony or communal gathering. Intricate carvings covered the stones – more spirals, eyes, interconnected lines, and striking depictions of the creatures interacting with the environment, hunting immense prehistoric-looking elk, gathering plants, even seemingly looking up at star patterns. A history etched in stone, telling the story of a species hidden from time.

Elise felt a dizzying sense of vertigo, the scale of the discovery threatening to overwhelm her. This wasn't just a new species; it was a non-human culture, ancient, complex, thriving in secret. The urge to document everything, to understand, was powerful. But fear remained a cold counterpoint. Where were they? Why had they allowed them in here?

Returning to the sheltered spot where Levi rested, she found Boone still scanning the silent village, his expression tight with suspicion. "See anything?" she asked quietly.

Boone shook his head. "Nothin'. Too quiet. Feels wrong." He distrusted the calm, seeing it as the lull before the storm.

It was then that Elise made a decision, driven by a desperate hope that understanding might be their only path to survival. Conflict had led to death and despair. Perhaps, just perhaps, a different approach might yield a different result.

"Boone," she said, keeping her voice low but firm. "I'm going to try something."

Boone looked at her sharply. "Try what? Doc, don't do anything stupid."

"We need to show them we aren't a threat," Elise argued. "Constantly aiming weapons, hiding… maybe that confirms their suspicions. Maybe we need to make a peaceful gesture."

"A peaceful gesture?" Boone repeated incredulously. "Like waving a white flag at a grizzly bear? They're nine-foot-tall predators, Doc! They understand strength and threat, not 'peaceful gestures'!"

"We don't know that," Elise insisted. "They showed restraint in the cavern. They possess high intelligence – the structures, the symbols prove that. Maybe they *can* understand intent. It's a risk, I know. But what other option do we have?"

Nora looked up from tending Levi, her eyes meeting Elise's. After a moment's hesitation, she nodded slowly. "Respect," she murmured. "An offering. It is the old way. Show you mean no harm. That you acknowledge their power, their ownership of this place."

Boone looked torn, his instincts screaming against it, but the desperation of their situation, and perhaps Nora's quiet endorsement, made him hesitate. "What kind of offering?" he asked grudgingly.

Elise thought quickly. What did they have? Weapons were out – that signaled threat. Their remaining food was too precious, needed for Levi. Their equipment was mostly dead or essential. She looked down at her own gear. Her binoculars? Useful, but potentially perceived as spying. Her camera? Too complex, maybe threatening. Then her eyes fell on something simple in her side pouch – a small, brightly polished piece of quartz crystal she carried as a geology fieldwork keepsake, a token from a less terrifying expedition. Smooth, non-threatening, naturally occurring but visually distinct.

"This," she said, holding up the crystal. "Natural. Not a weapon. Something… simple."

She also remembered the sounds they'd heard in the cavern – the deep, resonant hums. "And maybe... the sound. The call they made."

"You gonna *hum* at 'em?" Boone asked, disbelief warring with grudging curiosity. "What if they take it wrong? Think you're mockin' 'em? Or challengin' 'em?"

"It's a risk," Elise admitted again. "But maybe mimicking their own sound shows we're paying attention, that we're trying to understand, not just intrude blindly."

Taking a deep breath, steeling herself against the paralyzing fear, Elise decided. She looked towards the silent central clearing, then towards the shadowy passages leading out of the sanctuary. "Stay here. Keep Levi safe. Cover me, but," she locked eyes with Boone, "do *not* fire unless they attack first, aggressively. Give this a chance. Please."

Boone hesitated, clearly hating the idea, but finally gave a stiff, reluctant nod. "Five minutes, Doc. If anything looks sideways, I'm reactin'. And you get your ass back here, fast."

Nodding gratefully, Elise took the quartz crystal in her hand and slowly, deliberately, stepped out from their sheltered spot, walking towards the edge of the central clearing. Every step felt immense, each footfall unnaturally loud in her own ears despite the muffling silence. She felt terribly exposed, vulnerable, expecting a roar, a charge, an attack from any direction at any second.

Reaching the edge of the large circle of standing stones, she stopped. Holding her breath, she forced herself to emulate the sound she remembered from the cavern – a low, resonant hum, starting deep in her chest. It felt foolish, inadequate, a tiny human sound in this vast, ancient space. She held the hum for several seconds, then let it fade into the profound quiet.

Silence. Nothing happened. No response. No movement from the shadows.

Heart pounding, she tried again, louder this time, concentrating, trying to imbue the sound with respect, with non-aggression. *Hmmmmmmmmmmmmmm.*

Still nothing. Disappointment mingled with a surge of relief. Maybe they weren't even nearby? Maybe the gamble was pointless?

Then, she tried the offering. Placing the polished quartz crystal carefully on the flat top of a low, moss-covered stone near the path, where it would be clearly visible, she took several steps back, keeping her hands open and visible at her sides, trying to project calmness she definitely didn't feel.

She waited. The silence stretched, thick and expectant. Boone and Nora watched intently from the shadows, weapons ready. Levi remained oblivious.

Just as she was about to give up, convinced it was useless, a flicker of movement caught her eye. From behind one of the largest conical structures near the far side of the clearing, a figure emerged cautiously.

It was the adolescent. The smaller, leaner one they had seen in the cavern. It moved with hesitant steps, staying close to the shadow of the structure, its large dark eyes fixed on Elise, then flicking towards the gleaming crystal on the stone, then back to Elise. It seemed wary, curious, but not immediately hostile.

Elise held her breath, remaining perfectly still.

The adolescent creature took another tentative step forward, then paused, tilting its head, studying her. It let out a soft, questioning sound, a higher-pitched version of the hum Elise had attempted. *Hmm?*

Hope surged through Elise, fragile but fierce. It had heard her. It seemed to recognize the sound, perhaps the intent. Slowly, carefully, trying not to make any sudden movements, Elise responded, humming again, softer this time, mirroring its questioning tone. *Hmmmm?*

The adolescent watched her, unmoving, for a long moment. Then, it did something extraordinary. It glanced down at the quartz crystal gleaming on the stone. It looked back at Elise. Then, it slowly raised one of its long-fingered hands, mirroring the gesture Elise had made, palm facing slightly outwards. It held the gesture for a second, then lowered its hand. It took another hesitant step towards the stone with the crystal, its eyes never leaving Elise.

A connection. Fragile, tentative, fraught with potential misunderstanding, but undeniable. A moment of interspecies communication, however basic, occurring in a place that defied science, steeped in folklore and fear.

But as Elise felt a cautious elation begin to bubble within her, she saw Boone shift from the corner of her eye. He had raised his shotgun slightly, tracking the adolescent's movement towards the crystal, his stance tense, ready. His fear, his ingrained distrust, threatened to shatter this incredibly delicate, potentially vital moment of understanding. The truce, if it could even be called that, hung by the thinnest of threads, vulnerable to the slightest misstep, the slightest sign of perceived aggression from either side.

Chapter 22: Hunter Becomes Hunted

The cavern held its breath. The soft, ethereal blue-green light seemed to pulse faintly around the two figures poised at the edge of the central clearing – Elise, small and fragile, holding perfectly still, her heart hammering; and the adolescent Stick-shí'nač, immense yet hesitant, taking tentative steps towards the glittering quartz crystal she had left as an offering. Behind Elise, Boone remained a tense silhouette in the shadows, shotgun half-raised, his distrust a palpable force threatening to derail this improbable moment of connection. Nora watched with wide, tear-filled eyes, her hands clasped tightly, witnessing legend unfold with a mixture of awe and terror.

The adolescent creature reached the low stone. It stopped, its large, dark eyes flicking from the crystal, to Elise, then towards the shadows where Boone lurked, sensing his tension perhaps. It seemed to hesitate, considering. Then, slowly, deliberately, it extended one long-fingered hand, the digits surprisingly deft, and picked up the smooth quartz crystal. It turned the crystal over in its massive palm, examining it closely, tilting its head as if assessing its texture, its weight, the way the strange light refracted within it.

It looked back at Elise, holding the crystal. It made the soft, questioning hum again. *Hmm?* Was it asking what it was? Why she had left it? Elise could only guess, but the act felt significant – acceptance of the offering, a reciprocal curiosity.

Hope surged wildly in Elise's chest. This was it. Proof of concept. They could communicate, however crudely. They could potentially de-escalate, show peaceful intent, perhaps even bargain for their passage or Levi's safety. Forcing herself to remain calm, suppressing the tremor in her limbs, Elise took a tiny, slow step forward, keeping her hands visible, open.

"We mean no harm," she whispered, the words feeling foolishly inadequate, knowing the creature likely didn't understand the language, but hoping the tone conveyed her intent. "We are... lost. Trapped. One of us," she gestured slightly back towards Levi's resting place, "is injured. We need help. Or safe passage."

The adolescent tilted its head again, its dark eyes seeming to hold hers. It couldn't understand the words, surely, but did it grasp the meaning? The desperation? The plea? It clutched the crystal slightly tighter, then made another soft humming sound, longer this time, less questioning, perhaps acknowledging.

It felt like a breakthrough, a moment pregnant with possibility. Maybe, just maybe, they could find a way out of this nightmare that didn't involve more violence, more death.

But the moment, fragile as a soap bubble, was shattered by a sudden, violent intrusion.

"Get… away… from her… beast!"

The voice was weak, slurred, but filled with a delirious combination of fear and aggression. It came from behind Elise, from the sheltered spot where Levi lay.

Elise spun around, horrified. Levi had somehow, despite his injuries and the heavy painkillers, pushed himself partly upright against the dwelling wall. His face was flushed with fever, his eyes wide and unfocused, glittering with delirium. In his hand, shaking uncontrollably, was his pistol – the one he had dropped during the attack on the ridge, which Boone must have recovered and placed near him. He was aiming it, waveringly but unmistakably, towards the adolescent creature standing near the offering stone.

"Levi, no!" Elise screamed, lunging towards him. "Don't shoot! It's okay!"

But Levi wasn't listening. His mind, clouded by pain, fever, and possibly infection setting in, saw only the giant, terrifying figure that had attacked their camp, injured him, killed Graves. He saw a monster, not a potential communicator. Fear and disorientation had overridden reason.

"Stay back!" he yelled again, his voice cracking, as Elise desperately tried to reach him, to knock the weapon aside.

Boone reacted instantly from the shadows, realizing the catastrophic potential. "Levi, put it down! Now!" he roared, starting to move towards them.

But it was too late. Driven by delirium and terror, Levi squeezed the trigger.

CRACK!

The gunshot exploded in the confined sanctuary, deafeningly loud, echoing viciously off the unseen cavern ceiling and the surrounding structures. The bullet went wide, ricocheting harmlessly off one of the massive standing stones in the central clearing with a sharp *ping*. But the act itself, the sudden violence, the shattering of the stillness, the unmistakable aggression – it irrevocably broke the tentative truce.

The adolescent creature flinched violently at the sound, dropping the quartz crystal. It let out a high-pitched shriek, a sound of pure terror and surprise, utterly unlike the resonant hums it had made before. It stumbled backwards, scrambling away from the offering stone, its eyes wide with panic, looking wildly from Levi to Elise to the shadows where Boone was emerging.

And from the darkness beyond the central clearing, from deeper within the sanctuary, came an answering sound. Not a shriek, but a deafening, earth-shattering roar of pure, unadulterated rage. It was the sound of the elder. The patriarch. The guardian whose trust, whose sanctuary, had just been violated by gunfire.

"NO!" Elise screamed, realizing instantly what Levi had done, the catastrophic consequences of his fevered action. "It was a mistake! He's delirious! He didn't mean—"

But her words were drowned out by the thunderous roar echoing through the cavern. The peaceful, hallowed atmosphere vanished in an instant, replaced by naked, terrifying hostility.

The adolescent, recovering from its initial shock, turned and fled, scrambling back towards the passage it had emerged from, disappearing into the darkness with surprising speed.

And then, from multiple passages leading into the sanctuary, figures began to emerge. Not just the elder or the adult male they had seen in the first cavern encounter, but others. Four, five, six massive, dark shapes converging on the central clearing, drawn by the gunshot and the adolescent's distress call. They moved with terrifying speed and purpose now, their earlier calm observation replaced by bristling aggression. Their deep-set eyes glowed dimly with reflected light, fixing on the humans huddled near the dwellings. Low, rumbling growls emanated from their chests, vibrating through the floor.

The elder strode into the center of the clearing, towering over the others, its grey-streaked muzzle pulled back in a fearsome snarl, revealing immense, yellowed canines. It let out another deafening roar, directed squarely at the intruders, a sound that promised imminent, devastating violence.

"Run!" Boone yelled, grabbing Elise's arm and pulling her back towards the relative cover of the dwellings. He scooped up

Levi, who had collapsed again after firing the shot, semiconscious now, seemingly unaware of the chaos he had unleashed, and half-dragged, half-carried him deeper into the shadows. Nora was already there, axe held ready, her face a mask of horrified despair.

The truce was over. The fragile moment of communication, the slim hope of understanding, had been shattered by a single, panicked shot. They weren't guests anymore, not test subjects, not even just intruders. They were attackers. They had brought violence into the sanctuary. And the guardians, the Stick-shí'nač, roused to fury, were closing in.

The shift was terrifyingly abrupt. One moment, Elise had felt a glimmer of hope, a connection across an impossible species divide. The next, they were plunged back into the nightmare, facing the concentrated wrath of multiple enraged giants in the heart of their hidden world. Levi's delirium hadn't just broken the truce; it had likely sealed their fate. The hunters, who had briefly become the observed, the communicators, were now undeniably, terrifyingly, the hunted once more. And this time, escape seemed utterly impossible. The Silent Grove was about to erupt in violence.

Chapter 23: Wrath of the Forest

Chaos erupted in the heart of the Silent Grove. The air, moments before filled with a tentative, hopeful stillness, now vibrated with the low, guttural growls of multiple enraged Stickshí'nač converging on the central clearing. The ethereal blue-green light reflecting off their dark, bristling fur and fearsome, snarling faces transformed the sanctuary from a place of wonder into a nightmarish arena. The elder, a titan of muscle and fury, stood silhouetted against the luminescent moss, its roar echoing off the cavern walls like thunder, a primal declaration of war against the intruders who had desecrated their sacred space with gunfire.

"Back! Get back!" Boone yelled, shoving Elise and Nora deeper into the narrow space between two of the conical dwellings. He propped the barely conscious Levi against the cold, hard wall made of interwoven branches and stone, then spun around, leveling his shotgun towards the encroaching figures in the clearing. His face was grim, etched with the certainty of a final, desperate stand. The brief hope he might have allowed himself to feel after witnessing the creature's intelligence and the potential for communication had vanished, replaced by the cold, hard reality of survival against overwhelming odds.

"They ain't gonna listen now, Doc!" he shouted over the cacophony of growls. "We fight, or we die!"

Elise fumbled with her pistol again, her hands slick with sweat, her mind reeling from the whiplash transition from potential peace broker to cornered prey. Levi's single, delirious shot had undone everything. They had violated the sanctuary, proven themselves unpredictable, dangerous. The time for offerings and tentative hums was over.

The creatures didn't immediately charge. They spread out, forming a loose semicircle around the central clearing, their movements deliberate, coordinated. It wasn't a mindless frenzy; it was tactical. They used the massive standing stones and the larger dwelling structures for cover, melting into the deep shadows between the eerie glowing patches of moss, their immense forms appearing and disappearing as they repositioned, cutting off potential escape routes. The adult male Elise recognized from the cavern encounter circled wide to the left, while two others, slightly smaller but equally menacing, moved to block the passage leading back towards the tunnel they had arrived through. The elder remained in the center, radiating command, its burning gaze fixed on the small group of humans huddled between the dwellings.

"They're... they're flanking us," Graves would have said, Elise thought with a detached flicker of irrelevant memory. They were being systematically surrounded, penned in.

Nora clutched her axe, her eyes wide with terror but also with a strange, fatalistic understanding. "The guardians protect their own," she murmured, almost to herself. "We brought violence here. Now... now comes the cleansing."

One of the creatures on the right flank suddenly let out a short, sharp bark, seemingly a signal. Immediately, another creature, hidden amongst the shadows near the cave wall far behind them, responded. From that direction came a deep, booming *thump*. And then another. *THUMP*.

Elise spun around, heart lurching. One of the creatures, using its immense strength, was systematically smashing the entrance to the tunnel they had used to enter the sanctuary. Great slabs of rock were being torn from the cavern wall and hurled against the opening, sealing it off, blocking their only known retreat path. The sounds echoed horribly in the enclosed space – the grinding of stone, the shattering impacts, the low grunts of effort from the creature doing the work.

Trapped. The realization hit with physical force. Even if they somehow survived an immediate attack, their way out was being deliberately, methodically destroyed.

"See?" Boone growled, his gaze flicking between the encroaching figures in the clearing and the sounds of destruction behind them. "They ain't lettin' us leave. This is it."

The elder took a step forward, then another, moving out from behind the standing stones into the full luminescence of the moss fields. It stopped, perhaps thirty yards away, and fixed its gaze upon them. It didn't roar this time. Instead, it lowered its massive head slightly and let out a series of deep, guttural clicks and pops, sounds utterly alien yet clearly communicative, directed towards its companions.

Responding instantly, two of the other creatures began moving, not directly towards the humans, but towards the conical dwellings flanking their position. They moved with terrifying purpose, immense hands reaching out towards the intricately woven structures.

"What are they doing?" Elise breathed, watching in horrified fascination.

With startling ease, the creatures began to *push*. Bracing their massive shoulders against the dwellings, groaning with effort, they started to destabilize the ancient structures. Branches snapped, mud crumbled, stones dislodged. The towering cones began to lean inwards, slowly at first, then with gathering momentum.

"They're trying to crush us!" Boone yelled, realization dawning. "Trying to bury us under our own cover! Move! Out into the open!"

There was nowhere else to go. Staying put meant being crushed by the collapsing dwellings. Scrambling back towards the sealed tunnel was pointless. Their only option was to move forward, out from between the structures, into the central clearing, directly exposing themselves to the waiting semicircle of enraged giants.

Boone fired his shotgun into the air again, hoping the blast might deter them, buy them a precious second. The creatures flinched at the sound but didn't stop pushing. The dwellings leaned further, ominous cracking sounds echoing through the cavern.

"Go! Go!" Boone shoved Elise forward. Nora grabbed Levi, hauling him upright despite his pained protests, half-carrying, half-dragging him out into the eerie green light of the central clearing.

They stumbled into the open space just as the two dwellings behind them gave way entirely, collapsing inwards with a tremendous roar of snapping branches, crumbling mud, and showering debris, kicking up clouds of ancient dust that momentarily obscured the view. The place where they had been huddled just seconds before was now a ruinous pile.

Now they were completely exposed. Standing in the center of the glowing moss field, Levi sagging between Elise and Nora, Boone pivoting desperately, shotgun ready, facing the tightening semicircle of silent, watching giants. The elder stood directly before them, perhaps twenty yards away now, flanked by the adult male and two others. Their eyes seemed to burn in the dim light, fixed on their cornered prey. The tension was unbearable, the air thick with menace.

This felt like the end. Surrounded, outnumbered, outmatched in strength and knowledge of the terrain. Elise closed her eyes for a fleeting second, picturing her lab back home, the familiar clutter, the scent of old books and formaldehyde – a world away, impossibly distant now. She fumbled with the safety on her pistol, though the weapon felt laughably inadequate against these titans.

Then the attack came, but not in the way she expected. It wasn't a direct charge. It was coordinated, strategic, exploiting the environment itself.

The elder let out another series of clicks. Instantly, the two creatures flanking them darted towards the massive standing stones that formed the ceremonial circle. With horrifying grunts of effort, they began to push against the bases of the ancient megaliths.

"What now?" Boone muttered, aiming his shotgun towards one of the straining creatures.

The purpose became terrifyingly clear as the first massive standing stone, likely weighing several tons, began to tilt precariously on its base. It leaned, balanced for a heart-stopping second, then crashed downwards with devastating force, impacting the mossy ground exactly where the humans had been standing moments before, sending shockwaves through the floor. Another followed suit on the other side, creating a pincer movement of falling rock.

"Move back!" Boone yelled, pulling Elise and Nora further towards the center of the circle as more stones began to tilt and fall, targeted with chilling precision, designed to crush, confuse, and separate them. Dust filled the air, mingled with the eerie green luminescence. The sounds of impacting stone were deafening, adding to the terror.

Through the dust and chaos, Elise saw the adult male creature seize its opportunity. While the others focused on bringing down the stones, it charged, not directly at them, but towards Levi, who had stumbled and fallen during the panicked retreat.

"Levi!" Nora screamed, trying to reach him, but another falling stone blocked her path.

The creature reached Levi in two immense strides. It didn't strike him, didn't seem interested in finishing him off. Instead, with startling gentleness amidst the violence, it scooped him up, cradling his injured body almost protectively in one massive arm, then turned and began retreating rapidly towards the darker edges of the clearing, back towards one of the dwelling structures that remained standing.

"It's taking Levi!" Elise cried out, bewildered by the action. Why take him alive? Why protect him after the attack?

"Boone! Stop it!" she yelled, seeing Boone raise his shotgun, aiming at the retreating figure carrying Levi.

"He's bait! Or food! Can't let it take him!" Boone roared back, torn between the urge to rescue and the instinct to fight.

But before Boone could fire, the elder intervened again. It let out a short, sharp bark, and simultaneously charged towards Boone, not with killing intent, it seemed, but to intercept, to block his shot. It moved with incredible speed, closing the distance in seconds.

Boone, seeing the patriarch bearing down on him, had no choice but to abandon his aim at the figure carrying Levi and focus on the immediate, overwhelming threat. He fired the shotgun directly at the elder's massive chest.

The impact, at such close range, was tremendous. The buckshot slammed into the creature's thick fur and dense muscle, staggering it. The elder roared, a sound of pain and fury this time, clutching at its chest where dark blood began to well through the matted hair. It stumbled back a step, momentarily halted.

But it wasn't down. Its eyes, blazing with pain and rage, fixed on Boone. It lowered its head and charged again, heedless of the injury.

"Boone! Get out!" Elise screamed, firing her pistol wildly towards the charging giant, the bullets likely having little effect on its thick hide and muscle.

Nora, seeing Boone in imminent danger, acted with desperate courage. She hurled her axe, end over end, towards the elder's head. The heavy blade struck glanced off the creature's thick skull with a sickening thud, embedding slightly near its temple. Not a killing blow, but enough to cause a fresh wave of pain and disorientation.

The elder roared again, momentarily distracted, swiping at the axe handle protruding from its head. This gave Boone the precious second he needed. Instead of standing his ground to reload, knowing it was futile, he turned and sprinted, not back towards Elise and Nora, but sideways, towards a narrow, shadowed fissure leading out of the main clearing, a different passage from the one they'd used to enter or the one being sealed. It was a desperate gamble, trying to draw the elder's wrath away from the others, hoping to find another escape route, or perhaps simply accepting his fate while buying time for Elise and Nora.

"Boone! Don't!" Elise shrieked, watching him run.

The elder, recovering quickly, saw Boone fleeing. Ignoring Elise and Nora, ignoring the axe still embedded near its temple, it changed direction, its rage now entirely focused on the human who had wounded it. With terrifying speed, it lumbered after Boone, crashing through the remaining standing stones, disappearing into the same shadowed fissure Boone had taken refuge in.

Sounds of a violent struggle echoed briefly from the passage – Boone's defiant yell, the creature's enraged roars, the heavy thud of bodies colliding with rock – then, abruptly, silence. A profound, chilling silence that spoke more eloquently than any scream.

Elise stared at the empty fissure, her mind refusing to accept what had just happened. Boone… he had drawn the elder away. He had sacrificed himself. Tears streamed down her face, hot against her cold skin. First Jules, then Graves, now Boone… taken by the valley, by its guardians.

She turned towards Nora, who stood trembling, axe forgotten, her face pale with shock and grief. The creature carrying Levi had vanished into the shadows. The other creatures had seemingly melted back as well, the immediate, furious assault seemingly paused now that the primary aggressor (Boone) had been dealt with and the injured human (Levi) secured. The central clearing was a wreck of fallen stones and debris, illuminated by the pulsing green light, utterly silent except for their own ragged sobs.

They were alone again. Two women, deep beneath the earth in a hidden sanctuary turned battlefield, their guide and protector gone, their injured companion captured, their escape routes blocked or unknown. The wrath of the forest had descended, swift and brutal, leaving devastation in its wake. Hope felt like a distant, extinguished star. Only survival remained, a desperate flicker in the overwhelming darkness. And even that seemed impossible now.

Chapter 24: The Buried Files

The silence that descended upon the ruined ceremonial clearing after Boone's disappearance into the fissure, after the elder's enraged pursuit and the subsequent abrupt cessation of struggle, was profound and terrifying. It wasn't the hallowed stillness they had first encountered upon entering the sanctuary, nor the watchful quiet of the Hollow Trail. This was the silence of aftermath, thick with the echoes of violence, loss, and unspoken menace. Elise stood trembling, tears streaming unnoticed down her grimy cheeks, staring at the dark, narrow opening that had swallowed Boone whole. He was gone. The raw, pragmatic, deeply wounded man who had guided them, fought for them, and ultimately sacrificed himself for them, was gone. The finality of it felt like a physical blow, leaving her gasping for air in the cool, subterranean atmosphere.

Nora sagged against one of the few remaining standing stones, her face buried in her hands, her shoulders shaking with silent sobs. The stoic strength she had maintained throughout their ordeal seemed finally broken by the loss of Boone, a fellow traveler who, despite being an outsider, had come to understand and respect the power of this place, albeit through tragic personal experience. The legends of her people, the stories of the Stick-shí'nač, had proven devastatingly true, and the cost of that truth was accumulating in blood and disappearances.

Even Levi, semi-conscious nearby where the creature had inexplicably left him after taking him from the chaos – perhaps discarding him as less important once Boone became the primary target, or perhaps intending to retrieve him later? – seemed to sense the shift, moaning softly, his brow furrowed in pain and confusion. His single, delirious shot had precipitated this catastrophe, but blaming him felt pointless, cruel. He was as much a victim of this place, and perhaps of Graves' and Kestrel's manipulations, as any of them.

Elise forced herself to move, functioning on autopilot, driven by a clinical instinct honed by years of fieldwork in challenging conditions, even though the biologist in her felt utterly irrelevant now. She knelt beside Levi, checking his breathing, his pulse. Both were thready, weak. His skin was hotter now, the infection clearly worsening without antibiotics. His injured side looked severely bruised, purpling beneath the makeshift bandages. He needed real medical attention, warmth, fluids – things utterly unavailable in this subterranean crypt. Keeping him alive felt like prolonging the inevitable, yet abandoning him was unthinkable.

"We... we have to help him," Elise whispered, her voice cracking, looking helplessly at Nora.

Nora wiped her eyes, forcing herself upright, her inherent resilience reasserting itself, though her face remained etched with grief. "Water," she said hoarsely. "And shelter from the damp. That... that passage..." She nodded towards the fissure where Boone and the elder had vanished. "If it leads somewhere... maybe there's cover."

The thought of entering the passage where Boone had met his end was terrifying, but staying exposed in the ruined clearing felt equally perilous. The other creatures – the adult male, the two that had pushed the dwellings, the one who had sealed the tunnel entrance – where were they? Had they retreated deeper into the sanctuary? Or were they still nearby, watching, waiting? And the adolescent, the one who had shown tentative curiosity... where was it? The dynamics of the Stick-shí'nač 'clan' remained utterly opaque, their motives inscrutable.

Summoning reserves of strength neither knew they possessed, Elise and Nora managed to get Levi partially upright, supporting his weight between them. Driven by desperation, they began moving slowly towards the shadowed fissure, casting fearful glances around the eerily silent, glowing grotto. Every fallen stone, every dark dwelling entrance, seemed to hold potential menace.

The fissure Boone had fled into was narrow, barely shoulder-width apart, its walls slick with moisture and coated in patches of the ubiquitous phosphorescent moss, casting the immediate interior in a dim, pulsing green light. It seemed less a natural passage and more like a fracture in the rock, possibly widened over time. There was no immediate sign of struggle, no bloodstains readily visible in the dim light – the silence that had fallen after Boone's final cry remained chillingly unexplained. Had the elder simply dragged him deeper within? Or had something else happened?

Hesitantly, pushing Levi ahead of them, they squeezed into the narrow opening. The air inside was cold, damp, smelling strongly of wet rock and decaying vegetation. The passage twisted sharply after only a few feet, blocking any view back into the main sanctuary chamber. It continued deeper into the rock, sloping slightly downwards. Unlike the tunnel they had arrived through, this felt entirely natural, jagged, and claustrophobic.

They stumbled onward for perhaps fifty feet, the passage widening slightly then narrowing again, the only sound their own ragged breaths and Levi's pained moans echoing unnervingly off the close walls. The faint green glow of moss provided just enough light to see the treacherous footing. Just as Elise began to despair, thinking the fissure simply dead-ended deeper in the rock, it opened abruptly into another space.

This wasn't a vast cavern like the sanctuary, but a much smaller, man-made chamber. Or at least, *man-altered*. It was roughly square, perhaps fifteen feet by fifteen feet, the walls bearing the unmistakable parallel scoring of drills and perhaps even the ragged scarring of dynamite charges from decades past. Against one wall lay a jumble of rusted metal – remnants of survey equipment, bent pitons, lengths of corroded chain, even the skeletal frame of what might have been a portable generator, long seized up. Tucked into a corner was a stack of rotted wooden crates, their contents spilled and decayed – canned goods burst open, unrecognizable organic sludge, tattered remnants of canvas and wool clothing being reclaimed by mold and slime.

And against the far wall, leaning incongruously against the drilled rock face, was a small, metal desk, surprisingly intact despite layers of rust and grime. On its surface sat a mildewed, leather-bound logbook, and beside it, a heavy-duty lantern, its glass cracked, its metal housing deeply oxidized.

"What... what is this place?" Elise breathed, shining her headlamp around the small, forgotten chamber. It felt like stumbling into a time capsule, a hidden pocket of failed human intrusion within the heart of the Stick-shí'nač's domain.

Nora looked around, her eyes wide, recognition dawning mixed with apprehension. "The stories... sometimes mentioned outsiders before. Prospectors, maybe. Loggers pushing too far. They spoke of tunnels dug, seeking gold perhaps, deep in the forbidden grounds. Tunnels that were... abandoned. Or," her voice lowered, "tunnels from which no one returned."

Boone, Elise realized with a jolt, hadn't fled into a random fissure. In his desperate flight, perhaps driven by instinct or a fragmented memory, he had found his way to this relic of a previous, failed human expedition. But had it offered him sanctuary? Or just a different kind of dead end? There was no sign of him, or the elder, within the small chamber itself. Had the struggle continued through another exit?

Her attention was drawn back to the metal desk, to the logbook lying there like a silent testament. Carefully, heart pounding with a mixture of dread and scholarly curiosity, Elise approached the desk. The leather cover of the logbook was stiff, warped by decades of damp, the pages within stained and fragile. Using the edge of her knife blade, she gently eased the cover open.

The first page was partially legible, written in a surprisingly neat, looping cursive script, the ink faded but still discernible in the focused beam of her headlamp.

"August 14th, 1973. Olympic Deep Exploration Project – Site Gamma. Entry Tunnel secured. Primary vein assessment begun. Dr. Peterson remains optimistic regarding mineral yield estimates, though frankly, the access challenges are proving… considerable. Strange pressure fluctuations noted within chamber – barometric, or something else? Also persistent low-frequency resonance recorded by Davies' equipment – source undetermined. Likely geological."

Olympic Deep Exploration Project. 1973. So, prospectors, or perhaps a more organized geological survey, pushing far deeper than official records ever indicated. They had blasted this chamber, set up equipment, seeking minerals.

Elise carefully turned the fragile page. The entries continued, chronicling the initial days of the exploration – drilling progress, sample analysis (disappointing yields, apparently), equipment malfunctions (frequent, blamed on dampness and 'magnetic anomalies'). But interspersed with the technical details were more personal, increasingly unnerving observations.

"August 17th, 1973. Davies reporting persistent equipment interference. Compass deviations now exceeding 15 degrees within main tunnel system. Strange… almost organic sounds reported from ventilation shaft late last night – animal, Peterson insists. I'm less certain. Feeling of being watched is… pervasive down here."

"August 21st, 1973. McClary failed to report back from northern survey tunnel Epsilon. Search party found his lamp smashed, rock pick discarded. No sign of him. Peterson suspects fall in unexplored section, but… odd scrape marks found on tunnel wall. Large. And those sounds again last

night, closer this time. Like... heavy breathing. Peterson ordered cessation of Epsilon exploration."

"August 24th, 1973. Morale plummeting. Yields negligible. Davies now convinced resonance isn't geological – believes it's bio-acoustic, possibly patterned. Peterson dismisses as fatigue-induced paranoia. Two more men refused tunnel duty today, claiming shadows move in the deep sections. Locked down generator fuel supply – paranoia breeding theft?"

"August 27th, 1973. They came last night. Not shadows. Massive... beings. Covered in hair. Attacked the main tunnel entrance near Site Beta where Peterson was inspecting core samples. Roars... incredible strength. Tore through the timber supports like matchsticks. Peterson... dragged away screaming. Davies opened fire with the emergency flare gun, drove them back temporarily. Sealed Beta tunnel with dynamite charge. Trapped? Or just cut off? God help us."

Elise's blood ran cold. It was their own story, mirrored four decades earlier. Intrusion. Strange occurrences. Disappearances. Then direct, violent attack. The pattern was horrifyingly consistent. These 'Deep Exploration' miners had encountered the Stick-shí'nač, suffered losses, and seemingly barricaded themselves deeper in.

She turned the page again, her hands trembling. The writing became more frantic, less neat.

"August 29th, 1973. Four days since Beta collapse. Davies, Miller, myself remain. Supplies low. Water rationed. Creatures patrol outside blast door – hear them scraping, pounding sometimes. The resonance... it's constant now, feels like it's inside my head. Miller claims he saw eyes watching through ventilation shaft – huge, glowing faintly. Is he cracking? Am I?"

"September 1st, 1973. Miller gone. Slipped out last night while Davies slept. Said he couldn't stand the waiting, the resonance. Said he'd try to find another way out, through the natural caves mentioned in the initial survey – the ones marked 'unstable/unexplored'. Fool. Went without light or water. Suicide."

"September 3rd, 1973. Just Davies and me. Fuel for lantern almost gone. Battery for recorder dead. The pounding on the blast door stopped yesterday. Silence now. Worse than the pounding. Davies thinks they've given up, moved on. I think... I think they're waiting. Or maybe they found another way in. That resonance... feels closer."

The final entry was barely legible, scrawled desperately across the page, the handwriting almost unrecognizable.

"September 4th? 5th? Light gone. Davies keeps humming. Strange tune. Says the stones whisper to him now. Says they showed him the way.

Went into Shaft Gamma-Prime an hour ago. Didn't take gear. Didn't say goodbye. Alone now. Hear scraping… in the walls? Or just my mind? Resonance… so loud… They're not gone. Oh God, they're…"

The entry ended there, trailing off into an ink smear, as if the writer's hand had been suddenly jerked away or lost strength.

Elise stared at the final words, horror washing over her in icy waves. They hadn't escaped. They had succumbed, one by one, to despair, madness, or the creatures themselves. This wasn't a refuge; it was a tomb. A testament to a previous generation of intruders who had met the same fate they now seemed destined for. The government cover-up Graves' files alluded to wasn't just about suppressing knowledge of the creatures; it was likely about suppressing the disastrous, fatal outcome of expeditions like this one. Kestrel knew. The dangers weren't just theoretical; they were historically documented, buried in forgotten logbooks like this one.

Nora had crept closer, peering over Elise's shoulder at the faded script, her face pale. "The Resonance," she whispered, touching a page gently. "The stones whispering… The elders spoke of this too. Said the deep places beneath the Hollow Ground held power that could fracture the mind, especially minds filled with fear or greed. Said the guardians sometimes used this power… drove outsiders mad."

Another layer of terror. Not just physical threat, but psychological manipulation? Was the 'resonance' geological, bio-acoustic, or something stranger, wielded by the creatures themselves? The spinning compass, the dead electronics… perhaps symptoms of the same deep-earth power?

Elise carefully closed the fragile logbook. This wasn't just a historical record; it was a vital piece of intelligence, corroborating Graves' hidden files, hinting at the depth of the cover-up, and suggesting the creatures possessed capabilities far beyond simple brute force. It explained the government's desire for secrecy, Kestrel's potentially ruthless methods. A sentient, potentially mind-influencing species living secretly beneath US soil – the geopolitical and scientific implications were world-shattering. No wonder they wanted it contained, controlled, silenced.

"We need to take this," Elise said decisively, tucking the logbook carefully inside her waterproof map case, alongside her own notes and the photos she'd taken. It felt like crucial evidence, perhaps the only testament that might survive them, proof of what they had faced, proof of the lies they had been fed.

But where could they take it? Boone was gone, presumably dead. Levi was fading fast. The tunnel they'd come through was sealed. The chamber felt like a sealed crypt. Was there another way out? The desperate final entries mentioned Shaft Gamma-Prime, natural caves… where Miller and Davies had supposedly gone to meet their doom.

Shining her light around the small chamber again, Elise noticed it – a narrow, darker opening in the far corner, partially obscured by the rusted generator frame. It wasn't clearly marked, looking more like a natural cave entrance than a blasted tunnel. Was this Shaft Gamma-Prime? The path to madness and death chosen by the doomed miners?

It was their only potential way forward, other than surrendering to starvation or the creatures. Another terrible gamble, into unexplored natural caves beneath the sanctuary, potentially leading deeper into the earth, or maybe, just maybe, towards an exit unforeseen by their captors.

As Elise contemplated this desperate possibility, Levi let out a low, rattling cough, his body convulsing weakly. Nora knelt beside him instantly, wiping his brow. His skin felt fiery hot now. His breathing was alarmingly shallow.

"He is fading, Elise," Nora whispered, her voice thick with sorrow. "The fever… it climbs. We must find warmth for him. Shelter deeper in, perhaps?"

The decision was made for them. Staying in the cold, damp chamber meant certain death for Levi, and likely slow starvation for them. Plunging into the unknown darkness of the natural cave passage offered the slimmest chance, however remote, however dangerous. Following the footsteps of the doomed 1973 expedition, armed with the terrifying knowledge contained in their buried files, Elise and Nora prepared to take Levi and venture deeper into the earth, hoping against hope for a path that led not to madness, but somehow, miraculously, back towards the light.

Chapter 25: Split Paths

The oppressive darkness of the natural cave passage swallowed them whole, a stark contrast to the ethereal glow of the sanctuary or the functional dimness of the miners' abandoned chamber. The air grew heavy, thick with the scent of wet earth, deep minerals, and something indefinably ancient – the smell of places untouched by sunlight for millennia. Their headlamp beams, kept on the lowest possible setting to conserve precious battery life, cut feeble cones through the blackness, revealing only dripping rock walls, treacherous footing littered with loose scree, and the endless, unnerving darkness ahead.

Progress was torturously slow, dictated entirely by Levi's worsening condition. He was largely unresponsive now, semiconscious at best, his body burning with fever despite the subterranean chill. Getting him through the narrow initial opening of Shaft Gamma-Prime had been another exhausting struggle, reopening wounds in Elise's own scraped hands and taxing Nora's wiry strength to its limit. Now, supporting his near-limp weight between them, they stumbled blindly forward into the unknown, following the path the doomed miners, Miller and Davies, had taken decades before.

Was this madness? Following men who had likely succumbed to insanity or the creatures? Elise wrestled with the question constantly, fear gnawing at her. But the alternative – remaining in the chamber to await starvation or the inevitable return of the Stick-shí'nač – felt like surrender. This blind plunge into the earth felt, paradoxically, like their only remaining active choice, however desperate.

Nora, moving with an innate sense of direction that seemed only partially reliant on the map Elise occasionally consulted (a map largely useless in these uncharted natural caves), seemed calmer now, perhaps drawing strength from the deep earth, from being closer to the primal forces her ancestors respected and feared. She moved steadily, supporting Levi's slumping form, her breathing even, her eyes scanning the darkness with watchful acceptance.

After what felt like hours navigating the winding, claustrophobic passage – sometimes crawling through low sections, sometimes wading through ankle-deep pools of frigid water, sometimes scrambling over smooth, water-worn boulders – the tunnel began to open up. The air grew slightly fresher, carrying the faintest hint of something different, something… organic?

They emerged into a series of larger interconnected caverns. These were clearly natural formations, sculpted by ancient water flows. Towering stalagmites reached up from the floor like stone teeth, meeting glistening stalactites dripping from the unseen ceiling high above. Vast curtains of flowstone draped the walls in milky white and ochre patterns. And weaving through it all, clinging to ledges and damp crevices, was the source of the organic scent – patches of the same strange, bioluminescent moss that lit the sanctuary, though dimmer here, casting only isolated pools of faint blue-green light in the overwhelming darkness. It was beautiful, otherworldly, yet utterly terrifying in its alien familiarity. They were still deep within the creature's domain, encountering the ecosystem that sustained its hidden world.

In one of the larger caverns, fed by a steady drip from the ceiling, was a clear, cold pool of water. They stopped here, gratefully replenishing their canteens, forcing sips past Levi's cracked lips. Nora gently bathed his feverish face with a dampened cloth, murmuring soothing words. He remained largely unresponsive, his breathing shallow and rattling.

While Nora tended to Levi, Elise swept her headlamp beam around the cavern, searching for any sign of the miners, Miller or Davies. Had they reached this far? Had they found water, only to succumb later? She saw nothing definitive – no human remains, no discarded equipment. But etched faintly onto one wall, near the water pool, was a single, desperate scratch mark – a crude arrow, pointing deeper into the cave system, accompanied by what looked like a frantically scrawled letter 'M'. Miller? Had he left a sign, hoping Davies or someone else might follow? A sign pointing towards escape, or just deeper into delusion?

Boone's absence was a constant, aching void. His pragmatic survival skills, his ability to read sign even in this alien environment, would have been invaluable. Elise missed his gruff presence, his cynical humour, even his arguments with Graves. Now, it was just her and Nora, two women from vastly different worlds, bound by shared trauma and the desperate responsibility of keeping Levi alive against impossible odds.

And the weight of the knowledge she carried – the buried files from Graves' pack, the miners' doomed logbook – pressed down on her. Kestrel's ruthless secrecy. The government cover-up dating back decades. The evidence of the creature's capture, dissection, and the chilling warnings ignored. The mission's true objective: 'asset recovery', possibly even 'live capture', with witnesses deemed expendable. It was a story that needed to be told, a truth that defied belief but demanded exposure. The scientific implications alone were staggering, world-altering. But interwoven with that was the story of deception, sacrifice, and the potentially catastrophic consequences of humanity's arrogant intrusion into places best left undisturbed.

As Levi rested, Elise pulled out her waterproof notebook and the precious logbook and documents she had retrieved. Using the last dregs of power in her nearly depleted headlamp, she began frantically copying key information, sketching the symbols, summarizing the autopsy findings, transcribing the desperate final entries from the 1973 logbook. Her handwriting was shaky, bordering on illegible, fueled by adrenaline and the fear that this might be her only chance, that these notes might be the only record left if they didn't make it out. Documenting felt like an act of defiance against the darkness, against Kestrel's intended silence, against the potential erasure of Boone's sacrifice, Jules' fate, Graves' complex culpability, Levi's suffering.

Nora watched her quietly for a while, her expression thoughtful. "You write down the sorrow," she observed softly. "Does it make the burden lighter?"

Elise looked up, surprised. "I... I don't know. Maybe. Mostly, I feel like... someone needs to know. What happened here. What these creatures are. What Kestrel did." She gestured towards the files. "They lied to us, Nora. They knew the danger. They might have even provoked it, years ago. People died then, just like now. It feels wrong for that to stay buried."

Nora considered this, her gaze drifting towards the darkness of the cave passages. "The world outside... your world... it consumes stories," she said slowly. "It twists them. Uses them. Sometimes, secrets are kept for a reason. Sometimes, knowledge itself is dangerous, especially knowledge of places like this, beings like the Stick-shí'nač." She looked back at Elise, her eyes holding ancient caution. "Bringing this truth out... it might save your world, or it might destroy this one. Are you prepared for that?"

Elise hadn't considered it that way. Her instinct was the scientist's imperative: observe, document, disseminate. But Nora was right. Exposing the existence of the Stick-shí'nač, revealing their hidden sanctuary, could trigger a global sensation, a scientific gold rush, military intervention, exploitation… a wave of intrusion far exceeding anything Kestrel had attempted, potentially leading to the destruction of the very species she now recognized as sentient, intelligent beings defending their home. Was preserving their secrecy, allowing them to continue existing undisturbed, the more ethical choice, even if it meant burying the truth about Kestrel and the lost lives?

The ethical dilemma warred with her visceral need for the truth to be known, for Boone's and Jules's sacrifices not to be in vain, for Kestrel and Graves to be held accountable. And for herself – if she survived, could she live with carrying this immense secret?

Before she could formulate an answer, Levi stirred, letting out a low, guttural moan that devolved into a wracking cough. His body convulsed, his breath catching, rattling horribly in his chest.

"He's worse," Nora stated grimly, already moving to support him, trying to clear his airway. "The infection… it settles deep. He needs to be out of this dampness. He needs medicine we do not have."

The immediate crisis snapped Elise out of her ethical debate. Levi was dying. Their time was running out faster than she realized. Staying here to document, debating the philosophical implications – it was a luxury they couldn't afford. Survival, stark and immediate, had to be the priority.

"Okay," Elise said, forcing decisiveness into her voice, carefully packing away the logbook and her notes. "Okay. We need to move. Try to find a way up, out. Towards breathable air, towards any chance of signaling." She looked at the faint arrow scrawled on the wall. "We follow Miller's path? See where it leads?"

Nora looked towards the passage indicated by the arrow, then back at Levi's struggling form, her expression torn. "This deep… the earth breathes," she murmured. "There may be air shafts. Openings to the surface, high on the slopes, hidden. Places even the guardians might not regularly use." It sounded like a thin hope, based more on geology and folklore than concrete knowledge.

"But Elise," Nora continued, her voice low, meeting Elise's eyes with painful intensity. "Levi... he slows us down. Terribly. Every passage we squeeze through, every climb... it risks him further. It risks *us*. Getting *him* out..." She paused, the unspoken words hanging heavy between them. "...might be impossible."

Elise understood the terrible calculus Nora was implying. Could the two of them move faster, travel further, have a better chance of reaching the surface and finding help, if they weren't burdened by Levi's near-limp form? Ethically abhorrent. Pragmatically... terrifyingly logical.

"No," Elise said fiercely, shaking her head, rejecting the thought before it could fully form. "We don't leave him. We got him this far. We get him out, or we don't get out. All of us." It felt like a necessary line to draw, a refusal to compromise their own humanity, even in the face of overwhelming despair. Leaving Levi behind would make them no better than Graves, prioritizing an objective – survival, in this case – over a life.

Nora searched Elise's face for a long moment, then nodded slowly, a flicker of respect in her eyes. "Together then," she agreed softly. "But we must be swift. And prepared." Prepared for the possibility that their loyalty might cost them everything.

With renewed, desperate purpose, they prepared to move again, bracing Levi between them. But as Elise took one last look around the cavern, her eyes fell on the hidden niche where she had quickly stashed the copied files and logbook, wrapped securely in waterproof material. The weight of that knowledge, the conflicting desire to expose it versus the potential consequences Nora had highlighted, felt immense.

A sudden idea struck her. A compromise, perhaps. A contingency.

Quickly, while Nora readjusted Levi's makeshift sling, Elise retrieved the packet. She looked around the cavern, finding a deep, dry crevice behind a large flowstone formation, high up, unlikely to be disturbed by water or casual passage. Working quickly, she wedged the packet deep into the crevice, covering the opening with loose stones and moss, camouflaging it.

She kept only her primary field notebook, containing her raw observations and a few key summaries, tucked securely inside her inner jacket pocket.

"What are you doing?" Nora asked, watching her.

"Insurance," Elise replied grimly. "If… if we don't make it… maybe someone else finds this cave someday. Maybe the truth won't stay buried forever. But bringing it out *now*…" She shook her head, recalling Nora's warning. "You're right. It's too dangerous. For them," she nodded towards the darkness that held the sanctuary, "and maybe for everyone."

Leaving the bulk of the evidence hidden felt like a concession, a partial surrender to the valley's secrecy, but also a pragmatic choice. Their priority now had to be survival, getting Levi out, getting *themselves* out. Documenting the full truth could wait. *If* there was an 'after'.

Nora simply nodded, accepting Elise's decision without comment.

"Okay," Elise said, taking a deep breath, turning towards the dark passage marked by Miller's desperate arrow. "Let's go. Together."

Supporting the increasingly unresponsive Levi between them, Elise and Nora plunged deeper into the earth, following the ghost of a doomed miner, leaving the buried files behind them like a ticking time bomb of hidden history. Their path forward was uncertain, fraught with peril, overshadowed by loss and the ever-present threat of the guardians. The split between documenting the past and surviving the present had been made, prioritizing life over legacy, at least for now. Whether it was the right choice, only the labyrinthine darkness ahead could tell.

Chapter 26: The Sacrifice

The passage marked by Miller's desperate arrow led them ever deeper into the bowels of the mountain, a twisting, disorienting labyrinth of natural caves and fissures. The faint patches of bioluminescent moss became scarcer, plunging them into near-absolute darkness relieved only by the weakening beams of their headlamps, now used sparingly, flicked on only to navigate treacherous footing or choose between diverging tunnels. The air grew heavier, colder, tasting of stone dust and immense, geological time. Water dripped incessantly, the sound echoing unnervingly, sometimes sounding like footsteps just behind them, sometimes like whispers just beyond the reach of their light.

Hours blurred into a monotonous cycle of struggle. Supporting Levi's dead weight between them became an almost unendurable agony for Elise and Nora. Their own bodies screamed with fatigue, muscles burning, joints aching. Their hands were raw from scraping against rock, their clothes soaked from wading through icy pools. Hunger gnawed constantly, a hollow ache amplifying their weakness and despair. They shared the last crumbs of their energy bars, rationing the final sips of filtered water from the cavern pool.

Levi himself was fading rapidly. His breathing was a shallow, wet rattle, his skin alarmingly hot to the touch despite the cave's chill. He rarely regained consciousness, and when he did, his eyes were vacant, unfocused, his occasional moans weaker, tinged with a finality that tore at Elise's heart. They were losing him. Despite their promise to stick together, despite their refusal to abandon him, the grim reality asserted itself with every stumbling step – they couldn't keep carrying him like this indefinitely, not in this terrain, not with their own strength failing.

Nora, drawing on reserves of stamina Elise couldn't fathom, navigated primarily by feel now, reading the subtle changes in air currents, the texture of the rock underfoot, the faintest echoes, seeking a path that felt like it led *upwards*, towards air, towards any potential escape. She seemed less reliant on the physical signs like Miller's arrow (they found no more) and more attuned to the deep earth's subtle language, a skill passed down through generations accustomed to navigating darkness both literal and metaphorical.

Late in what Elise guessed might be their fourth day underground since the attack on the ridge – time had lost all meaning – they reached a point of near collapse. They had entered a wider fissure, a deep crack in the mountain that seemed to ascend steeply, almost vertically in places, requiring actual climbing rather than just scrambling. Water streamed down the slick rock walls, making handholds treacherous. Looking up, far above, Elise could *just* perceive the faintest hint of lighter darkness, suggesting this shaft might eventually open to the surface, perhaps high on the mountainside. It was the first glimmer of real hope they'd had in days. But getting up there, especially with Levi, seemed physically impossible.

They slumped at the base of the vertical ascent, utterly spent, huddled together against the cascading cold water. Levi lay shivering violently despite his fever, his breathing a barely perceptible flutter. Elise checked his pulse again; it was frighteningly weak and erratic.

"We can't climb this," Elise stated bleakly, exhaustion making her voice flat, devoid of emotion. "Not carrying him. We can barely climb it ourselves."

Nora didn't reply immediately. She gently wiped Levi's face again, trying to clear his airway, offering him a last few drops of water which dribbled uselessly from the corner of his mouth. She looked at his still face, then up the seemingly insurmountable wet rock wall towards the faint promise of sky far above. Her expression was filled with a profound, weary sorrow.

"No," Nora agreed softly, finally. "We cannot take him further. Not like this."

The unspoken hung heavy between them again, the terrible pragmatic truth they had tried to deny.

Suddenly, Levi's eyes flickered open. But this time, there was a spark of lucidity within them, a moment of clarity breaking through the feverish fog. He looked from Elise's exhausted face to Nora's sorrowful one, then seemed to take in their surroundings – the dripping vertical shaft, the despair etched on their features. He tried to push himself up slightly, coughing weakly.

"Leave… me," he rasped, his voice a thin thread of sound, but his intent shockingly clear.

"No, Levi!" Elise protested instantly, kneeling beside him. "We're not leaving you. We'll rest here. We'll find a way."

Levi shook his head weakly, a ghost of his former pragmatic self surfacing. "No... way," he breathed, each word an effort. "Too weak... slowing you... down." He coughed again, a wracking, painful sound that sent tremors through his body. "You two... go. Climb. Get out."

"We made a promise, Levi," Nora said gently, her voice thick with emotion. "Together."

"Promise... broken," Levi whispered, a single tear tracing a path through the grime on his cheek. "My fault... the shot... broke truce." He seemed aware, now, of the consequences of his delirious action. Guilt flickered in his pain-filled eyes. "Shouldn't have... survived the ridge... Should be... me. Not Boone."

His lucidity, his acceptance of blame and his impending fate, was devastating. Elise choked back a sob, shaking her head mutely.

"Listen," Levi insisted, gripping Elise's wrist with surprising strength, his eyes locking onto hers, conveying desperate urgency. "Can hear... it. Still close. Heard it... back in the tunnels. Following. Waiting."

Elise and Nora froze, straining their ears. Over the sound of dripping water, was there something else? A faint scrape from further down the passage they'd just traversed? A low *huff* echoing from the darkness? Or was it just Levi's fevered perception, or their own paranoia? They couldn't be sure. But the *possibility* that one of the creatures had indeed followed them through the hidden passage, tracking them patiently, waiting for them to weaken, waiting for them to become trapped, sent a fresh wave of icy terror through Elise.

"It knows... we're here," Levi gasped, his breathing becoming more difficult. "Can't climb... with it behind you. Need... distraction. Time."

"What are you saying, Levi?" Elise asked, dread coiling in her stomach, understanding dawning even as she resisted it.

Levi looked up the vertical shaft towards the distant hint of hope, then back at Elise and Nora. A strange calmness settled over his features, replacing the pain and feverish anxiety. It was the look of a man who had made a final, terrible decision.

"Go," he repeated, his voice slightly stronger now, infused with resolve. "Climb. Fast. I'll... stay. Make noise. Draw... its attention. Buy... you time."

"No!" Elise cried, tears flowing freely now. "Levi, we can't! That's suicide!"

"Already dead," Levi whispered, offering a faint, ghastly smile. "Better… one than three. My choice, Elise. Debt… to pay. For Jules. For Boone." He squeezed her wrist again. "Tell them… if you make it… tell them I tried." Tried to survive, tried to help, and now, trying to atone.

Nora knelt beside him, placing a gentle hand on his forehead. "Your spirit will be remembered, Levi," she said softly, her voice filled with respect for his intended sacrifice. "May the ancestors guide you."

Elise wanted to argue, to refuse, to find another way. But looking at Levi's resolute expression, feeling the chilling possibility of the creature closing in behind them, seeing the impossible climb ahead… the brutal logic of his sacrifice was undeniable. He was right. He couldn't make the climb. Carrying him would doom them all. Staying behind offered their only chance, however slim. It was an act of desperate courage, a final assertion of agency in a situation that had stripped them of all control.

"Give me…" Levi gasped, nodding towards Elise's belt. "…bear spray. And… flare gun? Did Graves…?"

Elise remembered Graves packing a small, single-shot flare gun in his survival kit before the climb. Had it fallen? Had Graves dropped it before being taken? She quickly checked the meager pile of gear they still carried. Tucked into a side pocket of Levi's own pack, miraculously, was the small, orange flare gun and a single cartridge. Graves must have passed it to him, or perhaps Levi himself had taken it as a last resort contingency.

Wordlessly, heart aching, Elise handed Levi the bear spray canister and the loaded flare gun. His hands closed around them weakly but with purpose.

"Go now," he urged, his voice fading again, the effort costing him dearly. "Don't… look back. Climb."

Elise couldn't speak. She leaned down, briefly touched his feverish forehead, a gesture of farewell that felt agonizingly inadequate. Nora did the same, whispering a final blessing in Lushootseed.

Then, forcing down their grief, fueled by the terror behind and the desperate hope above, they turned towards the dripping rock wall. Finding the first handholds, testing their purchase on the slick surface, Elise started to climb, Nora close behind her. The ascent was terrifying, exhausting. Every upward pull felt like dragging lead weights, every foothold precarious. Water streamed down, soaking them, chilling them further, making the rock incredibly slippery. They dared not use their headlamps now, relying on the faint ambient light from above and their sense of touch, fingers searching desperately for purchase in the near-darkness.

Behind and below them, they heard Levi begin to make noise. Not screams of pain, but deliberate sounds. He banged the metal flare gun against the rock wall, creating sharp, echoing clangs. He let out weak shouts, coughs magnified into echoing barks in the confined shaft. He was deliberately drawing attention, announcing his presence, sacrificing his final moments of peace to lure whatever might be following towards him, away from them.

Elise gritted her teeth, tears blurring her vision, forcing herself to focus only on the next handhold, the next upward movement. Every foot gained felt like a victory hard-won, paid for by the sacrifice happening below. The sounds Levi made continued for several minutes – the banging, the shouts – then were abruptly cut off by a different sound drifting up from the bottom of the shaft.

A low, guttural roar, filled with predatory triumph. Followed by a sickening, wet tearing sound, and then... silence. A silence more profound, more horrifying, than Levi's desperate noise-making.

Elise choked back a sob, nearly losing her grip. Nora murmured something behind her, a prayer or a curse. Levi was gone. His sacrifice had been accepted. He had bought them time, paid his perceived debt.

Driven now by a grief-fueled desperation, knowing Levi's sacrifice demanded success, they climbed faster, heedless of scraped knuckles and straining muscles. The hint of light above grew stronger, closer. Cold, fresh air, tasting incredibly sweet after the stagnant cave atmosphere, washed down over them.

Finally, muscles screaming, lungs burning, Elise reached the top of the fissure. She hauled herself over the lip, collapsing onto a narrow ledge covered in hardy alpine moss and wind-battered heather. Nora scrambled up beside her a moment later.

They were out. Out of the suffocating darkness, out of the immediate trap. They were high on the mountainside, clinging to a precarious perch, the wind whipping around them, clouds scudding just overhead. Below them, the vast, rugged wilderness of the Olympic Mountains stretched out, valleys plunged in shadow, peaks hidden in mist. The scale was immense, intimidating, but it was open air.

They had escaped the depths. But looking back towards the dark opening of the fissure from which they had emerged, knowing what lay below – Levi's remains, the buried files, the hidden sanctuary, the hunting guardians – the feeling wasn't one of triumph, but of profound loss and lingering terror. Levi's sacrifice had bought them this chance, this breath of freedom. Now, somehow, they had to survive the surface, had to find a way down, a way back to a world that seemed impossibly distant and perhaps irrevocably changed by the knowledge they carried, even if the proof lay buried deep beneath the earth. The cost of their escape felt almost too high to bear.

Chapter 27: The Escape Route

The raw, biting wind whipping across the high mountain ledge was a physical shock after the stagnant stillness of the caves. It tore at Elise's already tattered clothing, threatened to pluck her from her precarious perch, and carried the chilling scent of snowfields and vast, empty space. But it also tasted clean, real, blessedly free of the subterranean taint of deep earth, decay, and stale fear. They had made it out of the labyrinth, purchased their freedom with Levi's horrific, courageous sacrifice. Collapsed on the narrow strip of alpine tundra, gasping for breath, muscles screaming in protest, Elise felt a wave of dizzying relief wash over her, so potent it was almost nauseating, immediately followed by a crushing undertow of grief and guilt.

Levi was gone. Boone was gone. Graves, Jules... lost to the valley, to the guardians, to the disastrous consequences of the Kestrel mission. Only she and Nora remained, two women clinging to the side of a hostile mountain, miles from anywhere resembling safety, pursued perhaps even now by the ancient powers whose sanctuary they had violated and whose wrath they had provoked. Survival felt less like a victory and more like a heavy, unwelcome burden.

Nora knelt beside Elise, her face turned into the wind, eyes closed, strands of dark hair whipping across her weathered features. She seemed to be gathering herself, perhaps offering a silent prayer to the wind, the mountain, the spirits of this place, acknowledging their escape while mourning the terrible cost. Her resilience was remarkable, rooted in a deep connection to this land that Elise could only dimly comprehend, a connection that encompassed both reverence and a stark understanding of its unforgiving nature.

After several minutes spent regaining their breath and battling the initial shock of emergence, the practicalities of their situation reasserted themselves. They were exposed, exhausted, dangerously low on supplies, and still deep within uncharted, hostile territory. Reaching the surface was only the first step; finding a viable path down, a route back towards civilization, was the next immense challenge.

"Which way?" Elise asked, her voice raspy, barely audible over the wind's howl. She pulled out her topographical map, trying to orient herself based on the surrounding peaks visible through breaks in the swirling mist, but without a functioning compass or GPS, pinpointing their exact location was difficult. They seemed to be high on the western flank of the main valley system, significantly south of where they had entered the Hollow Trail.

Nora scanned the landscape with narrowed eyes, reading the contours, the vegetation patterns, the subtle signs of weather and erosion with an expertise that made Elise's map reading feel like clumsy guesswork. "Down," Nora said finally, pointing not straight down the precipitous slope below them, but angling southwards along the mountainside. "That way avoids the worst cliff bands visible lower down. Follows… maybe an old game trail? Or water runoff channel? Leads towards the headwaters of what the loggers called Cougar Creek, I think. That drainage eventually flows west, out towards the Hoh River system. Towards roads. Far away, but… it is a path downwards that isn't straight back into the Hollow Ground."

It sounded plausible, a direction away from the heart of the danger, towards potential rescue, however distant. Trusting Nora's guidance implicitly now, they began the slow, arduous process of descent. Moving along the steep, exposed mountainside was nearly as treacherous as the climb out of the fissure. Loose scree shifted underfoot, threatening to send them sliding into oblivion. Dense thickets of subalpine fir and slide alder blocked their path, requiring exhausting detours or brutal push-throughs that tore at their clothes and skin. The wind buffeted them relentlessly, trying to pry them from the slope.

They moved with grim determination, conserving energy, communicating little, each lost in her own thoughts – grief for the fallen, fear of pursuit, the gnawing ache of hunger and exhaustion. Elise found her mind replaying the events underground, the glowing sanctuary, the creatures' intelligent eyes, Levi's final moments, Boone's desperate charge. The images were vivid, traumatic, yet overlaid with a persistent, troubling layer of scientific wonder. She had witnessed something extraordinary, world-altering. The desire to understand, to analyze, still warred with the primal urge to simply survive and forget. She clutched the small notebook in her pocket – her only remaining record – as if it were both a vital link and a terrible curse.

Nora seemed focused entirely on the path ahead, her connection to the land guiding her footsteps. She moved with a quiet grace, despite the difficulty, occasionally pausing to examine a bent twig, a disturbance in the moss, seemingly checking for signs of pursuit. Her expression remained somber, acknowledging the gravity of their situation, perhaps sensing the lingering presence of the guardians even here, beyond the immediate confines of the valley.

They traveled for hours, descending slowly, painfully, angling southwards along the rugged flank of the mountain range. The vegetation grew thicker as they lost elevation, transitioning from sparse alpine scrub back into dense coniferous forest, though still predominantly old-growth, untouched by logging. The air grew slightly warmer, the wind less ferocious beneath the canopy, but the forest brought its own challenges – poor visibility, tangled undergrowth, the constant feeling of being hemmed in, watched from the shadows.

By late afternoon, utterly depleted, staggering with fatigue, they stumbled into a small clearing bisected by a fast-flowing creek – likely the headwaters of the Cougar Creek drainage Nora had aimed for. The sound of rushing water felt like music after the silence of the caves and the howl of the wind. They collapsed onto the mossy bank, drinking deeply from the icy, clear water, the simple act feeling like a profound luxury.

It was here, while resting, gathering the last dregs of their strength, that Nora made another discovery. Poking through the dense ferns near the creek bank, investigating the remnants of what looked like an old trapper's lean-to, long since collapsed and decaying back into the forest floor, her foot struck something hard, metallic, hidden beneath the leaf litter.

Curious, she knelt and began clearing the debris. Elise crawled over to help. Partially buried in the damp earth was a length of heavy, rusted iron rail, like a section of narrow-gauge mining track. And beside it, almost completely overgrown, was the faint indentation of an old path or trackbed leading steeply uphill, away from the creek, towards a sheer rock face visible through the trees.

"Loggers," Nora breathed, running a hand over the cold, pitted metal. "Or miners, perhaps. From long ago. Before the park expansion, before the access roads washed out. They came this far, seeking timber, maybe gold."

Elise looked up towards the rock face the overgrown track seemed to lead to. "What were they hauling from up there? Seems like a dead end."

Nora followed her gaze, then her eyes widened slightly in recognition. "Not a dead end. A shortcut. Or… a way down." She pointed towards a specific feature on the rock face, a dark vertical line barely discernible through the intervening trees. "The Crevice," she said softly. "Another name from the old stories. Before my time, even my grandfather's time perhaps. They said the first loggers, or maybe railroad surveyors, looking for ways through these impassable mountains… they found a deep, narrow fissure cutting straight down through the rock formation. Almost vertical. Too steep for pack animals, too narrow for wagons. But passable for men on foot, carefully. They rigged it, some say, with ropes, maybe crude ladders, used it to descend quickly from the high country down towards the lower river valleys, bypassing miles of difficult terrain."

A vertical fissure? A logger's shortcut straight down? It sounded incredibly dangerous, potentially collapsed or impassable after decades, perhaps a century, of neglect. But it also represented the quickest possible route downwards, a direct line out of the high-altitude wilderness that currently imprisoned them.

"Could it still be passable?" Elise asked, hope warring with skepticism. "After all this time?"

Nora shrugged, uncertainty clouding her features. "The stories are vague. Some said it was cursed, haunted by the spirits of those who fell. Others said it was swallowed by rockfalls. No one I know has used it, or even knew exactly where it was. Just… a legend. But if that track leads there…" She stood up, decision hardening her face. "It is a chance. Perhaps our only chance to descend quickly, before…" She didn't need to finish the sentence. Before their strength gave out entirely, before infection claimed Levi fully in their memory, before the Stick-shí'nač decided their trespass extended beyond the valley and pursued them even here.

Fueled by this new, desperate hope, they left the relative comfort of the creek side and began following the faint, overgrown trackbed steeply uphill towards the rock face. Pushing through tangled salal and huckleberry bushes that had reclaimed the path, scrambling over fallen logs, they finally reached the base of the cliff.

And there it was. The Crevice. A deep, narrow fracture in the granite, like a wound sliced into the mountain's heart. It was perhaps only four or five feet wide at its entrance, plunging almost vertically downwards into shadow. Water trickled down one wall, feeding curtains of slick, green moss. Looking down into the blackness was like staring into an abyss.

But crucially, bolted into the rock on either side of the entrance, incredibly rusted but still present, were heavy iron rings – anchor points. And dangling down into the darkness from these rings, disappearing into the gloom below, were the rotten, frayed remnants of what looked like immensely thick, ancient ropes, possibly supplemented in places by segments of equally decayed wooden ladder rungs wedged between the narrow walls.

The logger's shortcut. Real. Terrifying. And potentially lethal.

"Can we climb down that?" Elise whispered, peering into the dark, narrow depths, feeling a wave of vertigo. It looked hundreds of feet deep, maybe more, disappearing into pitch blackness. The old ropes and ladders were clearly unusable, suicidal to trust. They would have to rely entirely on handholds and footholds on the slick, narrow rock walls themselves, rappelling or down-climbing in near darkness.

Nora examined the anchor rings, tested the rock around them. "The rock itself feels solid here," she assessed. "The fissure... it seems stable. But the climb..." She looked at Elise, acknowledging the immense risk. "It will require all our strength. All our focus. One slip..."

One slip meant falling into the abyss, joining the spirits the legends spoke of.

Yet, the alternative was trying to navigate miles of rugged, unknown wilderness downslope, a journey that could take days they didn't have, especially without supplies or reliable navigation. This vertical shaft, perilous as it was, offered a direct route down, potentially emerging hundreds, maybe thousands, of feet lower, closer to the river valleys, closer to potential escape.

They looked at each other, the unspoken question hanging in the air. Could they do it? After everything they had endured – the terror, the exhaustion, the grief – did they have enough left, physically and mentally, for one final, incredibly dangerous descent?

"Levi would want us to try," Elise said softly, invoking the memory of his sacrifice. "Boone too." It felt like the only way to honor them, to make their deaths mean something.

Nora took a deep breath, squared her shoulders, her connection to her ancestors, perhaps even to the spirits of this place, giving her strength. "Lead the way down, Elise," she said quietly. "My eyes are better in the dark. I will guide you from behind, tell you where the holds feel strongest."

Nodding, trying to quell the tremor in her hands, Elise took one last look back at the vast, imposing wilderness stretching out behind them, then turned towards the darkness of the Crevice. Securing the precious notebook inside her jacket, taking a firmer grip on her remaining resolve, she found the first handhold inside the narrow opening and began the perilous descent into the mountain's core, praying this final escape route wouldn't become their tomb. The climb downwards, inch by agonizing inch, into the cold, dark unknown, had begun.

Chapter 28: Forest Fire

The descent into the Crevice was a descent into another kind of hell, colder and darker than the subterranean sanctuary, yet terrifyingly immediate in its peril. The narrow fissure plunged downwards like a throat swallowing them into the mountain's core, the rock walls slick with perpetual moisture, coated in greasy moss that offered treacherous purchase. The only light came from their own failing headlamps, casting feeble, bouncing beams that emphasized the dizzying depth below and the suffocating narrowness surrounding them. Air, heavy with the chill of deep rock and the scent of mineral seepage, flowed sluggishly upwards, offering little comfort.

Every move was calculated, deliberate, excruciatingly slow. Hands, raw and bleeding from previous ordeals, scrabbled for purchase on tiny ledges and rough patches of granite, muscles screaming with the strain of supporting their own weight, plus the drag of their lightened but still awkward packs. Feet searched tentatively for footholds, testing dubious projections, scraping against the near-vertical walls. The rusted iron rings and rotten remnants of ancient ropes and ladders dangling near the entrance served only as mocking reminders of an easier passage long since decayed, forcing them to rely entirely on the treacherous rock itself.

Nora proved an invaluable guide, just as she promised. Descending slightly behind and above Elise, her eyes remarkably adept in the near darkness, she called out quiet instructions, her voice calm and steady despite the precariousness of their situation. "Left hand... higher... small crystal ledge..." "Right foot... deeper crack... test it first..." "Shift weight slowly... moss is thick there..." Her intimate knowledge of rock, honed by a lifetime navigating the rugged Olympics, translated into a lifeline for Elise, whose own climbing experience was minimal and whose nerves were stretched taut as aging climbing rope.

Hours bled together in a timeless agony of downward movement. Elise lost all sense of distance, of progress. Was it hundreds of feet? Thousands? The darkness below remained absolute, seeming to swallow the weak beams of their lights. Fear was a constant companion, a cold knot in her stomach – fear of slipping, fear of a handhold giving way, fear of dropping her precious light source into the abyss, fear of the darkness itself and what unseen things might lurk within its deepest recesses. The spirits of fallen loggers Nora had mentioned felt disturbingly plausible in this vertical tomb.

Compounding the physical strain was the psychological weight. Levi's sacrifice played on a loop in Elise's mind – his calm resolve, the desperate sounds from the bottom of the shaft, the final, horrifying silence. Boone's face, grim and determined as he charged into the fissure after the elder, haunted her vision in the flickering shadows. Had he truly bought them escape with his life? Or had the elder simply dealt with him and then allowed them to proceed, content to let the mountain itself claim them in this deathtrap? And the creature they'd briefly communicated with, the adolescent... its initial curiosity felt like a cruel mockery now, a prelude to the inevitable violence unleashed by Levi's panicked shot. Were others still pursuing them even now, waiting patiently at the bottom of this fissure? Every drip of water echoed like a footstep; every shift in the faint air currents felt like unseen breath.

Nora, though physically taxed, seemed less troubled by these psychological ghosts. Her focus was absolute, her connection to the climb, to the rock, seemingly pushing aside fear. Perhaps her worldview, steeped in stories of powerful spirits and the harsh realities of nature, allowed her to accept their precarious situation with a stoicism Elise envied but couldn't emulate. She climbed with a fluid efficiency, conserving energy, her presence a silent source of strength just above Elise.

After what felt like an eternity – perhaps six or seven hours of continuous, agonizing descent – Elise felt a subtle change in the air. It grew slightly warmer, less damp, and carried a new, alarming scent: smoke. Faint at first, then gradually strengthening, swirling upwards on the sluggish air currents within the Crevice.

"Nora," Elise rasped, pausing precariously, clinging to a narrow ledge, "do you smell that?"

Nora inhaled deeply. "Smoke," she confirmed, her voice tight with new apprehension. "Woodsmoke. Strong. From below."

Fire. In the wilderness surrounding the base of the Crevice? Wildfire was a constant threat in the dry late summer season, but the air hadn't felt particularly dry, and they'd had rain just days ago. Could it be a natural fire, sparked by lightning perhaps? Or something else? Given the unnatural occurrences they had experienced, Elise couldn't discount any possibility. Could the Stick-shí'nač use fire? It seemed unlikely, based on their primitive toolkit, but she no longer trusted the boundaries of 'likely'.

The smell of smoke grew stronger as they descended further, becoming acrid, biting at their throats, making their eyes water. It spurred them onward with renewed, albeit fearful, urgency. Fire could trap them in the Crevice from below, or it could represent... something else. Civilization? A logging camp? A rescue Dteam using signal fires? Hope, treacherous and perhaps foolish, flickered faintly amidst the fear.

Finally, agonizingly, the angle of the fissure began to lessen. The near-vertical descent eased into a steep, debris-choked scramble. And below them, visible now not as absolute darkness but as a flickering, orange-tinged haze, was the bottom. They were nearly there.

They practically slid the last twenty feet, muscles screaming, bodies bruised and battered, collapsing onto a jumbled pile of rock and earth at the base of the Crevice. They had emerged, not into open forest, but into another narrow, high-walled ravine, this one choked with dense undergrowth – ferns, devil's club, vine maple – and filled with swirling smoke that stung their eyes and lungs.

And through the smoke, they could see the source. Fire. Not just a campfire, but a significant forest fire, raging somewhere downslope, possibly across the entire lower valley floor towards which this ravine likely descended. Angry orange flames licked at the base of giant trees, casting terrifying, dancing shadows through the dense smoke. The roar and crackle of the inferno reached them even here, a hungry, destructive sound that replaced the silence of the caves with a new, immediate threat.

"God Almighty," Elise coughed, pulling the collar of her jacket up over her mouth and nose, trying to filter the acrid air. "The whole valley's on fire!"

Nora stood beside her, her face grim, scanning the burning landscape visible through the ravine mouth. "This is no natural fire," she stated firmly, pointing towards a section of the blaze where the flames seemed unnaturally contained, forming almost a straight line across the slope. "It feels... deliberate. Controlled, almost."

Deliberate? Elise stared, horrified. Who would deliberately set a fire this large in such remote wilderness? Loggers clearing land illegally? Unlikely, given the scale and location. Arsonists? Even less plausible. Could it be…? Could Kestrel, or the forces Graves represented, be involved? A fire could serve multiple purposes – destroying evidence, creating a plausible cover story for disappearances ('lost in the fire'), preventing pursuit by the creatures, or perhaps even acting as a containment measure, creating a burnt-out buffer zone around the AO Hollow. The thought was chilling, adding another layer of potential conspiracy and ruthlessness to the Kestrel operation.

Or, Nora's expression hinted at another, even more unsettling possibility. Could the Stick-shí'nač themselves have somehow started or manipulated the fire? As a final, desperate measure to cleanse their territory of the intruders? As a way to block pursuit? The ability seemed beyond them based on the tools Elise had seen, yet after everything she had witnessed, she couldn't entirely dismiss the possibility of powers she didn't comprehend.

Regardless of the cause, the fire presented an immediate, dire threat. While it raged downslope from them currently, the wind could shift, or the fire could race uphill through the dense canopy, trapping them between the inferno and the impassable Crevice they had just descended. They needed to move, get clear of the ravine, find a path away from the flames.

Stumbling out of the ravine mouth, they found themselves on a steep, forested slope overlooking what seemed to be the main channel of Cougar Creek below. The fire was primarily concentrated on the opposite bank and further downstream, forming a terrifying wall of orange and black cutting across the valley. Smoke billowed thick and grey, obscuring the sky, making breathing difficult even here, upwind of the main blaze. The heat radiating from the fire was already palpable.

Picking their way carefully downslope through the smoke-filled forest, aiming away from the fire, their progress was hampered by exhaustion and the disorienting conditions. The familiar landmarks were hidden, the air thick and stinging. Panic threatened to overwhelm Elise again – escaping the creatures only to perish in a wildfire felt like a particularly cruel twist of fate.

It was then that they heard it. A sound cutting through the roar of the fire, faint at first, then growing stronger. A rhythmic *whump-whump-whump*.

Helicopters.

Elise and Nora stopped, exchanging glances filled with a mixture of hope and profound apprehension. Helicopters meant people, meant potential rescue, meant contact with the outside world they had been so violently severed from. But after everything – the secrecy, Graves' buried files, the potentially deliberate nature of the fire – were these rescuers? Or something else?

They broke through the tree line onto a rocky bluff overlooking a bend in Cougar Creek, just upstream from where the fire raged most intensely. And they saw them. Not one, but three helicopters. Two were large, military-style craft – possibly Chinooks or similar heavy-lifters – hovering low over the valley further downstream, near the edge of the fire line. Men in what looked like HAZMAT suits or firefighter gear, but moving with military precision, were rappelling down, carrying equipment Elise couldn't identify.

The third helicopter was smaller, sleeker, painted a dark, unmarked grey. And it was heading directly towards them.

Hope surged, powerful and immediate. Rescue! They waved frantically, yelling, though their voices were lost in the wind and the noise. The helicopter spotted them, banked sharply, and approached the bluff, its rotors whipping up leaves and debris.

But as it drew closer, Elise's hope faltered, replaced by a chilling unease. The helicopter bore no markings – no Coast Guard insignia, no Forest Service logo, no Search and Rescue colours. Its windows were tinted dark, impenetrable. And the figure leaning out from the open side door wasn't waving in friendly recognition; they were aiming a long-lensed camera, or perhaps something else, directly at them.

The helicopter didn't land. It hovered twenty feet above the bluff, the downdraft nearly blasting Elise and Nora off their feet. The figure in the doorway, clad in dark tactical gear, face obscured by a helmet and visor, simply observed them for a long, unnerving moment. They weren't being offered a rescue rope; they were being assessed. Documented. Contained?

Elise thought of Graves' files again. *Neutralization authorized under extreme compromise conditions.* Were they considered 'compromised witnesses'?

Then, as suddenly as it arrived, the helicopter banked away, peeling off back towards the valley, joining the other aircraft hovering near the fire line downstream. It didn't communicate. It didn't offer aid. It simply observed, then departed, leaving them alone on the bluff, choking in the smoke, watching the deliberately managed fire rage below, understanding dawning with cold certainty.

This wasn't a rescue operation. It was a quarantine.

The helicopters weren't here to save survivors; they were here to manage the situation, contain the fallout, perhaps monitor the fire they may have even set themselves. The teams rappelling down weren't firefighters; they looked more like a specialized containment or clean-up crew. Kestrel, or whatever agency Graves truly worked for, was already on scene, locking down AO Hollow, ensuring the secrets within – both the creatures and the evidence of the disastrous expedition – remained buried, consumed by flame or official silence.

Elise looked at Nora, saw her own dawning horror reflected in the older woman's eyes. They had escaped the creature's grasp, survived the deadly descent, only to find themselves caught in a different kind of trap – a meticulously orchestrated cover-up. They weren't being rescued; they were being left behind, marooned between a burning forest and the silent, watching eyes of the agency determined to keep the valley's secrets buried. The outside world was here, but it offered no salvation, only confirmation of a conspiracy far deeper and more ruthless than Elise had ever imagined.

Chapter 29: Back to Silence

The stark realization that the helicopters signified not rescue, but quarantine, settled upon Elise and Nora like a shroud of freezing mist. Stranded on the rocky bluff, choked by smoke, watching the unmarked aircraft methodically manage the fire line below and deploy enigmatic crews in HAZMAT gear, hope curdled into a cold, pragmatic dread. They had escaped the clutches of the Stick-shí'nač, survived the deadly descent of the Crevice, only to be abandoned on the edge of a controlled inferno by the very forces presumably responsible for their expedition in the first place. They weren't survivors to be saved; they were loose ends to be potentially ignored, discredited, or, perhaps, eventually 'neutralized' if deemed necessary.

Exhaustion warred with a primal urge to flee. The fire below was a pressing danger, eating its way through the undergrowth, threatening to creep upslope. The hovering presence of the helicopters, distant but omniscient, felt like the eyes of prison guards. Their escape from the valley's heart had led them not to freedom, but to the perimeter of a meticulously controlled cage.

"We can't stay here," Elise rasped, shielding her stinging eyes from the smoke, her voice hoarse. "The fire... or *them*..." she nodded towards the distant helicopters.

Nora, her face grim, scanned the terrain downslope, away from the main blaze, looking for a viable path. "West," she decided, pointing towards a ridge that seemed less affected by the fire, leading away from Cougar Creek and deeper into the relatively untouched forests bordering the park proper. "Follow this ridge down. Away from the creek, away from their focus. Towards the Hoh River drainage. It's longer, harder. But safer than staying near... whatever this is."

It felt like plunging back into the wilderness, turning their backs on the semblance of civilization represented by the helicopters, but Nora's logic was sound. Remaining visible near the containment operation courted discovery and unknown consequences. Disappearing back into the anonymity of the vast forest, relying on their own depleted resources, felt paradoxically safer.

Summoning their last reserves of strength, fueled by adrenaline and the desperate need to evade both fire and the shadowy human forces below, they turned away from the burning valley and began another arduous trek. They followed the ridge Nora indicated, pushing through dense timber and tangled undergrowth, the acrid smell of smoke gradually receding behind them, replaced once more by the familiar scent of damp earth, cedar, and fir.

The next twenty-four hours blurred into a nightmare of stumbling exhaustion. They moved mechanically, putting one foot in front of the other, driven by sheer survival instinct. They had almost no food left – half an energy bar each, scavenged berries Nora identified as safe but barely caloric. Water, thankfully, was plentiful in the numerous small streams draining the western slopes. They slept fitfully, huddled together for warmth beneath the dripping canopy, starting at every forest sound, haunted by nightmares of giant shadows and falling rocks, waking with the names of the dead on their lips – Jules, Graves, Boone, Levi.

Elise's thoughts circled obsessively around the buried files, the miners' logbook hidden back in the cave. Had she done the right thing, leaving them? The notebook in her pocket felt simultaneously precious and dangerous, a fragment of truth in a sea of lies and unexplained phenomena. Could she protect even this partial record if she encountered the forces behind Kestrel?

Nora remained a pillar of quiet strength, navigating by instinct and ancestral knowledge, her endurance seemingly limitless despite the ordeal. She found edible roots Elise wouldn't have recognized, identified sheltered spots to rest, her presence a calming anchor in the vast, indifferent wilderness. Yet, Elise saw the profound sadness in her eyes, the weight of having witnessed the legends of her people manifest in such a devastating way, confirming their power while claiming the lives of those she had guided.

On the second day after escaping the Crevice, late in the afternoon, as they staggered through a section of slightly younger forest, showing signs of logging from decades past, they heard it again. Not helicopters this time. The distant, unmistakable sound of a chainsaw, followed by the crash of a falling tree. Civilization. Or at least, its encroaching edge.

Hope, cautious and fragile, returned. They pushed towards the sound, breaking through a final wall of dense salal bushes onto… a logging road. Wide, muddy, deeply rutted by heavy machinery, but undeniably a road. It felt like landing on solid ground after weeks adrift at sea. Tears streamed down Elise's face again, this time tears of sheer, overwhelming relief. Nora leaned against a tree, breathing heavily, a rare expression of exhausted satisfaction gracing her features.

They followed the road for perhaps an hour, their pace quickening despite their exhaustion. Around a bend, they saw it – a pickup truck parked haphazardly, tailgate down, belonging presumably to the loggers they'd heard. They weren't saved yet, but they were back in the world of roads, engines, potential communication.

As they approached the truck, hoping to find the loggers, ask for help, a ride, anything, another vehicle appeared, coming down the road towards them. Not a logging truck. A dark, late-model SUV, unmarked, windows tinted, tires splattered with mud. Chillingly familiar. It pulled up smoothly beside them, blocking their path.

Two figures emerged, moving with quiet, purposeful efficiency. They weren't loggers. They wore simple, practical outdoor clothing – canvas trousers, sturdy boots, dark jackets – but carried themselves with an air of trained competence that screamed agency, not forestry. They were men, mid-forties perhaps, nondescript features, short haircuts, eyes that assessed Elise and Nora coolly, impassively, betraying no surprise or concern.

"Dr. Elise Holloway? Ms. Nora Tallsalt?" the taller of the two men asked, his voice polite but devoid of warmth. It wasn't a question seeking confirmation; it was an identification. They knew who they were. They had been expected. Or perhaps, intercepted.

Elise felt her fragile hope evaporate, replaced by a cold dread. This wasn't a chance encounter. They were being met.

"Who... who are you?" Elise stammered, instinctively stepping closer to Nora.

"We're here to help," the man replied smoothly, offering a thin, unconvincing smile. "We understand you've had... a difficult time. There was a wildfire reported near the area you were surveying. We were dispatched as part of the incident support team."

Incident support team? Wildfire? It was the official narrative, presented calmly, professionally, designed to dismiss, to contain. No mention of the expedition, the creatures, the disappearances, the quarantine.

"Where are the others?" Elise asked, testing the waters, clinging to a sliver of hope that maybe Boone had somehow survived, been picked up. "Boone? Levi?"

The man's expression didn't flicker. "We have no reports of other individuals associated with your research permit being located at this time," he stated flatly. "Search and rescue efforts are ongoing, hampered by the fire. Mr. Graves' emergency beacon activated briefly near the fire zone before cutting out; his status is unknown, presumed casualty." A lie, woven seamlessly into the narrative. Graves hadn't activated the beacon; he'd been taken before he could. But they needed a plausible explanation for his disappearance linked to the fire.

"And Jules Jensen?" Elise pressed, desperation making her reckless. "He disappeared days before the fire."

The second man, shorter, stockier, stepped forward slightly. "Dr. Holloway, Ms. Tallsalt, you've both experienced significant trauma and exposure. It's understandable there might be some confusion. Official reports indicate Mr. Jensen became separated during severe weather conditions several days ago. Extensive searches yielded no results prior to the wildfire complicating efforts." Another lie, effortlessly delivered. Jules hadn't been lost in bad weather; he'd been taken, leaving behind blood and tracks.

They were rewriting the story, erasing the truth in real time. Elise felt a wave of helpless anger, but also caution. These men were calm, prepared, likely armed, representing the same organization that authorized 'neutralization'. Pushing back, arguing, revealing what she knew… it would be incredibly dangerous.

"We need to get you both back for medical evaluation and debriefing," the first man continued smoothly, gesturing towards the open rear door of the SUV. "Please, get in. You're safe now."

Safe? The word felt obscene. Elise exchanged a look with Nora. Nora's face was impassive, guarded, but her eyes conveyed a clear warning: *Be careful. Say little.* They had survived the guardians of the valley; now they faced the guardians of the secret.

Reluctantly, seeing no other immediate option – they were too weak to run, too isolated to seek alternative help – they allowed themselves to be ushered into the back of the SUV. The interior was clean, functional, smelling faintly of antiseptic. Childproof locks clicked shut as the doors closed, reinforcing the feeling of being contained, transported, processed.

The drive back towards Bluffs End felt surreal. They passed actual logging trucks now, saw signs of active forestry work, indicators of the normal world operating just miles from the quarantined nightmare they had escaped. The two men in the front seats said nothing, communicating occasionally via coded bursts on a discreet radio unit. They offered water and sealed nutritional bars, which Elise and Nora accepted gratefully, ravenous despite their apprehension.

As they approached Bluffs End, the familiar oppressive grey drizzle began to fall, washing the mud from the SUV, mirroring the bleakness Elise felt settling back over her spirit. The town looked exactly the same – damp, quiet, closed-in. But driving through it now felt different. The wary glances from the few locals they saw felt less like generic suspicion of outsiders and more like a fearful awareness, perhaps, of the strange comings and goings related to the valley, the disappearances, the hushed-up events. Did they suspect more than they let on? Tiedeman's General Store, The Fog Horn diner, The Loggers' Rest tavern – they slid past like set pieces in a play whose terrifying third act only Elise and Nora now truly understood.

They weren't taken back to the End of the Trail Motel. Instead, the SUV turned onto a secluded side road leading towards the misty bluffs overlooking the churning grey water of the Strait of Juan de Fuca. Hidden amongst the trees was a small cluster of nondescript buildings – prefabricated units, temporary-looking structures, surrounded by a discreet chain-link fence topped with security wire. A temporary command post? Kestrel's field base?

They were escorted inside one of the buildings. It was spartan, clinical – fluorescent lights hummed overhead, floors were bare linoleum, walls were institutional grey. They were separated immediately. Nora was led into one room, Elise into another.

Elise found herself in a small, windowless room containing only a metal table and two chairs. The door closed behind her with a soft but definitive click. She was left alone for perhaps twenty minutes, long enough for the adrenaline to fully drain, leaving her feeling utterly depleted, vulnerable, and terrified about what came next. Would they demand her notes? Question her relentlessly? Drug her? Discredit her? Worse?

Finally, the door opened and a different person entered. Not one of the men from the SUV. This was a woman, older, perhaps late fifties, dressed in a sharp, practical pantsuit, her grey hair cut short and severe. She carried a tablet computer and her eyes, behind sensible glasses, were sharp, intelligent, and radiated an unnerving calmness that felt more dangerous than overt hostility. She didn't introduce herself.

"Dr. Holloway," the woman began, her voice modulated, calm, devoid of inflection. She sat opposite Elise at the table. "Firstly, let me express the Kestrel Foundation's sincere regret regarding the loss of Mr. Jensen, Mr. Graves, Mr. Boone, and Mr. Clarke during what appears to have been an unfortunate series of tragic accidents compounded by the unforeseen wildfire." The official narrative, presented as established fact. "Your survival, and Ms. Tallsalt's, under such extreme circumstances is remarkable."

Elise said nothing, waiting, her heart pounding.

"We need to understand precisely what occurred," the woman continued, tapping briefly on her tablet. "For the official reports, insurance purposes, and to ensure lessons are learned for future environmental assessments in challenging terrains." She looked up, her gaze pinning Elise. "We have your preliminary field reports, transmitted by Mr. Graves before communications failed. Excellent work on the baseline ecological data." A pause. "However, subsequent events seem… confused. Likely due to trauma, exposure, malnutrition. Understandable."

She leaned forward slightly. "Tell me, Doctor, from your perspective… what *happened* after communications failed?"

It was the moment of truth. Elise's mind raced. Reveal everything? The creatures, the sanctuary, the files, the betrayal? Risk being declared delusional, hysterical, a 'compromised witness' needing containment or neutralization? Or play along? Stick to the fabricated narrative of accidents and wildfire, hoping to get out, hoping to preserve her partial notes, hoping for a chance to expose the truth later, somehow?

She thought of Boone's sacrifice. Levi's atonement. Nora's quiet wisdom. The sheer, undeniable reality of the Stick-shí'nač. The importance of the miners' logbook, the proof of the cover-up. The scientific imperative to reveal this hidden world, tempered by the ethical responsibility Nora had highlighted.

Taking a deep breath, trying to steady her trembling voice, Elise made her choice. Feigned confusion. Partial truths. Protect the core secret, protect herself, protect Nora, hoping for another chance.

"It... it all went wrong so fast," Elise began, pitching her voice to sound weak, traumatized, uncertain. "After the comms failed... we were blind. Then the storm hit," – there had been no major storm, but it fit the 'severe weather' narrative for Jules – "Jules got separated in the whiteout. We searched, but... couldn't find him. Then Graves insisted we push south. Boone argued... terrain was bad. Levi fell, broke his ribs." She recounted a version of events, weaving known facts with deliberate omissions and plausible distortions. She described getting lost, dwindling supplies, increasing desperation. She described finding the Crevice, the desperate climb down. She described seeing the fire, the helicopters. She painted a picture of tragic accidents, poor decisions under duress, the wilderness claiming its victims.

Crucially, she omitted any mention of the creatures, the nest, the sanctuary, Graves' files, the miners' logbook, the true nature of the conflict with Graves, or the circumstances of Boone's and Levi's final moments. She described finding Graves' beacon near the fire line, implying he'd made it that far before succumbing – supporting the official story. She portrayed Boone and Levi as getting separated during the chaotic descent or near the fire, their fates unknown but likely tragic casualties of the environment. It felt like a betrayal of their memory, sanitizing their sacrifices, but it felt necessary for survival.

The woman listened patiently, making occasional notes on her tablet, her expression unreadable. She asked clarifying questions, probing for inconsistencies, her calm demeanor a sharp counterpoint to Elise's feigned emotional fragility. Elise stuck to her story, focusing on disorientation, fear, exhaustion, letting trauma be the explanation for any vagueness. She offered her notebook readily when asked – the one containing only her sanitized field observations and deliberately vague entries about the 'difficult final days'. She mentioned nothing about the hidden packet of files back in the cave.

Finally, after nearly an hour, the woman seemed satisfied, or perhaps simply concluded Elise was too traumatized or broken to be an immediate threat, her account fitting plausibly enough within the framework Kestrel wished to establish.

"Thank you, Dr. Holloway," the woman said, standing up. "Your resilience is commendable. You've endured a terrible ordeal." The words sounded rehearsed, meaningless. "We'll arrange for medical checks for you and Ms. Tallsalt, then transport back to Seattle. A Kestrel representative will liaise regarding final reports and contractual obligations." She paused at the door. "Of course, given the sensitive nature of the Foundation's work, even standard environmental assessments, the non-disclosure agreement you signed remains strictly in effect. Discussing specifics of the mission, internal team dynamics, or locations with outside parties is… inadvisable. For everyone's security." A polite phrasing, but the underlying threat was unmistakable. Silence was not a request; it was a condition.

The door clicked shut again, leaving Elise alone in the sterile room, shaking uncontrollably, relief warring with self-loathing. She had survived the debriefing, maintained the façade. But the price was silence, complicity in the cover-up, the burying of the truth about the valley, the creatures, the lost men.

Later, after a cursory medical check by a tight-lipped doctor who seemed more interested in psychological stability than physical ailments, she was briefly reunited with Nora in a sterile transit lounge. Nora looked equally drained, equally guarded. They exchanged only a brief, knowing look – a shared understanding of the tightrope they had just walked, the necessary lies they had told. Nora, too, had clearly chosen silence, retreating behind the stoic mask of her cultural reticence, offering the Kestrel agents nothing they didn't already want to hear.

They were driven back to Seattle in another unmarked vehicle, dropped unceremoniously at Elise's apartment building in the late hours, given instructions for follow-up appointments, and left with the heavy weight of their enforced silence.

Elise stood on the rainy sidewalk, watching the vehicle disappear, the familiar cityscape feeling alien and distant after the raw intensity of the wilderness and the impossible wonders and horrors she had witnessed. She was back, ostensibly safe. But the silence imposed by Kestrel felt as confining, as dangerous, as the canyon walls or the watchful eyes of the Stick-shí'nač.

Upstairs, in the blessed normality of her apartment, she stripped off her filthy, torn clothes, showered for an hour, scrubbing away the grime but not the memories. She looked in the mirror and saw a stranger staring back – gaunt, haunted eyes, new lines etched around her mouth, the reflection of someone who had touched the edge of a different reality and returned irrevocably changed.

Later, sorting through the meager gear she'd managed to bring out, she found her field notebook. Flipping through the pages, the sanitized observations felt like a mockery. But tucked into a hidden pocket within the notebook's cover, something she'd transferred during a moment of panicked clarity in the caves, were two things: a single, high-resolution memory card containing the horrifying photos from the creature's nest and the Grove of Symbols, and one small, carefully folded printout – the final, desperate page from the 1973 miners' logbook.

Not everything was lost. Not everything was buried. A fragment of proof remained.

Her phone buzzed. A terse email from the Kestrel Foundation. Condolences again. Confirmation of final payment transfer. A reminder of confidentiality clauses. And an attachment: the 'Official Incident Report Summary'. It detailed tragic accidents, weather, wildfire. Boone's and Levi's names were listed as 'Missing, Presumed Deceased – Search Suspended'. Jules and Graves confirmed casualties claimed by the environment. No mention of creatures, anomalous findings, or organizational culpability. The official silence, codified, complete.

Elise felt a surge of cold fury. They wouldn't get away with it. Not completely. She wouldn't let them. The silence might be forced upon her now, but it wouldn't be permanent. The valley, the Stick-shí'nač, Boone, Levi… their stories deserved to be known. Somehow. Someday. The return to silence was just a pause, not an ending.

Chapter 30: The Hollow Truth

Months melted into a semblance of normalcy, a fragile veneer painted over the raw, unhealed trauma of AO Hollow. Elise returned to her life in Seattle, to the familiar routines of academia – lecturing undergraduates on primate morphology, analyzing decade-old data sets from Southeast Asian gibbons, attending departmental meetings where budget cuts and publication pressures felt simultaneously mundane and blessedly trivial compared to the life-and-death struggles she had endured. She went through the motions, functioned, even smiled occasionally, but felt profoundly adrift, haunted by memories that shimmered just beneath the surface of her carefully reconstructed reality.

The city felt different. The towering buildings seemed like fragile imitations of the ancient cedars. The bustling crowds felt like ephemeral ghosts compared to the solid, terrifying presence of the Stick-shí'nač. The everyday noises – traffic, sirens, construction – felt abrasive and meaningless after the profound silence of the Hollow and the resonant calls in the hidden sanctuary. She carried the wilderness within her, a secret landscape of terror and wonder that isolated her from the unsuspecting world around her.

Kestrel remained a silent, ominous presence in the periphery. True to their word, the final, substantial payment appeared in her bank account, blood money that sat untouched, feeling toxic. Occasional, encrypted emails arrived, requesting minor clarifications for 'final archival records' related to the ecological survey data she had submitted – gentle prods, perhaps, reminding her of their continued surveillance, ensuring her compliance with the NDA. She answered briefly, factually, playing the role of the cooperative, slightly traumatized survivor. She heard nothing about Nora, assuming the Tallsalt woman had retreated back into her own community, protected by generations of resilience and a deep cultural understanding that likely needed no external validation or debriefing. Elise respected her silence, sending only a single, carefully worded postcard expressing gratitude for her guidance, hoping it reached her across the divide of their shared, unspoken secret.

The official incident report became the accepted narrative. A tragic wilderness expedition gone wrong – poor planning, unforeseen weather, a devastating wildfire. Graves and Jensen were memorialized as unfortunate casualties. Boone and Levi joined the long, sad list of individuals 'missing, presumed deceased' in the vast, unforgiving wilderness of the Olympic National Park. Their names were briefly noted in outdoor adventure forums, cautionary tales mentioned in hiking guides, but the true circumstances of their disappearance, their sacrifice, remained buried beneath layers of official obfuscation and calculated silence. The cover-up held.

Elise wrestled daily with the weight of that silence. Guilt gnawed at her – guilt for surviving when others didn't, guilt for omitting the truth in the Kestrel debriefing, guilt for protecting the secret of the Stick-shí'nač even as she burned with the need to expose Kestrel's ruthlessness. Nora's words echoed constantly: *Bringing this truth out… it might save your world, or it might destroy this one.* The dilemma remained unresolved, a constant tension between the scientist's imperative to reveal and the reluctant guardian's burden to protect.

She tried writing. Pouring the experience onto paper, framing it as fiction, a way to process the trauma, to hint at the truth without directly violating the NDA or triggering Kestrel's potentially lethal response. But the words felt hollow, inadequate. How could fiction capture the sheer, visceral reality of standing before a nine-foot-tall guardian, the echoing horror of the nest, the ethereal beauty of the hidden sanctuary? The truth felt too immense, too strange, to be contained in metaphor.

Her scientific work suffered. Staring at charts of gibbon vocalization frequencies felt meaningless compared to the memory of the Stick-shí'nač's resonant hums. Analyzing primate social structures felt simplistic when confronted with the complex, hidden culture beneath the Hollow Ground. Her colleagues noted her distraction, her subdued presence, attributing it to the trauma of the expedition, offering condolences and space. She accepted their sympathy, letting the official narrative shield her secret isolation.

The memory card containing the photos of the nest and the Grove of Symbols, and the printout of the final page of the miners' logbook, remained hidden, tucked away with her field notebook in a fireproof safe buried deep within her cluttered apartment closet. Proof. Tangible fragments of the impossible truth. She looked at them occasionally, the images instantly transporting her back to the terror and wonder, reinforcing the reality of what she had experienced, steeling her resolve. She couldn't let it remain buried forever.

One rainy Seattle Saturday, months after her return, unable to bear the oppressive weight of the city and the secret any longer, Elise made a decision. She packed a small, sturdy backpack – not with scientific gear this time, but with essentials. Water, food, warm layers, a basic first-aid kit. And the hidden memory card and logbook page, sealed carefully against moisture. She drove north, leaving the city behind, heading back towards the looming, mist-shrouded peaks of the Olympic Peninsula.

She didn't drive all the way to Bluffs End. The thought of returning to that town, to the End of the Trail Motel, felt unbearable. Instead, she parked her car at a nondescript trailhead miles away, deep within a different section of the National Forest, an area she knew from previous, unrelated fieldwork. She hiked for several hours, pushing off-trail into a familiar stand of old-growth forest, seeking a specific location – a massive, uniquely shaped Douglas fir tree she had cataloged years before, notable for a deep, sheltered hollow near its base, hidden by ferns and decaying nurse logs.

Here, in the quiet solitude of the deep woods, miles from prying eyes or electronic surveillance, she carefully retrieved the memory card and the logbook page. She placed them inside a small, airtight, waterproof container, along with a brief, unsigned note summarizing the key findings – Kestrel's deception, the creature's existence and intelligence, the location of the hidden files she'd left in the cave, a plea for ethical consideration and protection should the sanctuary ever be rediscovered. She wrapped the container in multiple layers of protective material.

Then, reaching deep into the hollow at the base of the ancient fir, she buried the container beneath layers of soft earth, moss, and decaying wood, concealing it thoroughly, ensuring it was protected from the elements, hidden from casual discovery, yet locatable by someone who knew precisely where to look – namely, herself, or someone she might one day trust with the coordinates.

It felt like both a burial and a planting. Burying the immediate proof, complying, for now, with the enforced silence. But also planting a seed of truth, preserved, waiting for the right time, the right circumstances, to be unearthed. It was a compromise, a way to manage the unbearable weight of the secret while preserving the potential for future revelation. A promise to Boone, to Levi, to herself, that their story wouldn't be entirely erased.

Returning to her car as dusk settled, a fragile sense of peace settled over Elise, the first she had felt in months. She had taken an action, however small, however secret. She had created a contingency, honored the fallen, and bought herself time to decide the path forward.

Back in her apartment that night, she opened a fresh journal – not her field notes, but a personal one. On the first page, she began to write, not a fictionalized account, not a scientific treatise, but her own raw, unvarnished story, detailing everything she remembered, everything she felt, everything she suspected. The process was painful, cathartic, necessary.

She wrote for hours, filling page after page, the words pouring out – the arrival, the warnings, Graves' briefing, the growing unease, the silent grove, the tracks, Boone's tragic story, the blurry footage, Jules' horrifying disappearance, the clash of views, Nora's legends, the Grove of Symbols, the gruesome nest, the dead electronics, the clear sighting, the Hollow Trail, the terrifying climb, the impossible sanctuary, the fragile attempt at communication, the fatal shot, the chaotic attack, Boone's sacrifice, Levi's last stand, the treacherous descent, the fire, the chilling quarantine, the debriefing, the lies, the cover-up.

She wrote about the creatures, the Stick-shí'nač, wrestling with her understanding of them – not just as monsters or scientific curiosities, but as ancient, intelligent beings, guardians of a sacred place, capable of both terrifying violence and surprising restraint, complex subjects deserving of respect, not dissection or exploitation. She acknowledged their role in the deaths but placed the ultimate responsibility squarely on Kestrel's – and humanity's – arrogant intrusion and history of violence.

Finally, exhausted but strangely centered, she reached the end of her account, the present moment. She stared at the last blank lines on the page, then wrote her concluding thoughts, a declaration that felt both utterly personal and globally significant:

"They exist. The old stories are true, the dismissed evidence real. Deeper than folklore, stranger than science fiction, a civilization thrives in secret beneath the Hollow Ground. Kestrel knows. Elements within the

government have known for decades. They sought to contain, perhaps exploit, and ultimately, to bury the truth along with the bodies.

They failed. At least, partially. Graves is gone, his secrets partially unearthed. Jules, Boone, Levi... their sacrifices bought our escape, bought this fragmented record.

I carry their story, and the story of the First People, the Stick-shí'nač. I am silenced, for now. For my safety, for Nora's, perhaps even for the safety of the sanctuary itself, secrecy feels necessary. The outside world... it may not be ready. Its reaction – fear, greed, military intervention – could be catastrophic.

But they are not monsters. They are survivors. Intelligent, powerful, ancient guardians of a world increasingly encroached upon by ours. They responded to our intrusion, our violence, with violence of their own, yes. But they also showed restraint, curiosity, perhaps even a form of communication before fear and misunderstanding shattered the moment.

The ethical path forward is unclear. Exposure risks their destruction. Silence perpetuates Kestrel's impunity and buries the sacrifices made. The hidden files, the buried logbook, this journal... fragments of a truth too large, too dangerous, perhaps, for one person to hold.

But I know this: ***I will go back.*** *Not with weapons, not with secrets funded by shadowy foundations. But with respect, with caution, perhaps with knowledge gleaned from Nora's people, if they will share it. To understand. To apologize, if such a thing is possible. To bear witness, not as a conqueror or exploiter, but as a humble observer.*

Maybe there is a way to bridge the gap. Maybe communication is still possible. Or maybe the guardians will simply ensure I join the others lost to the Hollow Ground.

Either way, the silence cannot hold forever. The Hollow Truth must eventually surface. And my journey into that mystery is not over. It has only just begun."

Elise closed the journal, the final words echoing the determination solidifying within her. She had survived, she carried the secret, and she bore the responsibility. The path ahead was fraught with danger, both from human agencies and the ancient guardians themselves. But fear would no longer paralyze her. The scientist, the survivor, the reluctant witness – they were coalescing into something new. A protector, perhaps. An emissary, however unlikely. She owed it to the dead, to the living, and perhaps even to the Stick-shí'nač themselves, to try.

Epilogue: Dead Ends and Door Bolts

The cryptic email burrowed under Elise's skin, a persistent irritant beneath the already raw surface of her nerves. *Echoes persist. Vigilance required.* Was it Kestrel tightening the leash, a reminder veiled in poetic ambiguity? Or was it something else, a phantom reaching out from the conspiracy's tangled web? The uncertainty was almost worse than overt threat. It amplified the feeling of being watched, turning every shadow into a potential observer, every technological glitch into a possible sign of intrusion.

Sleep remained elusive. When exhaustion finally claimed her, the respite was brief, shattered by nightmares that dragged her back to the dripping darkness of the caves or the terrifying, luminous expanse of the hidden sanctuary. She saw Boone falling into shadow, heard Levi's final, desperate sounds, felt the ground tremble under the elder's roar. She woke gasping, heart pounding, the scent of moss and fear phantom-real in her sterile apartment air. The echo of the creatures' resonant hum sometimes seemed to linger, a subsonic thrum just below the threshold of hearing, making the floorboards vibrate, or perhaps that was just her own pulse hammering against the mattress.

During the day, she tried to maintain the façade. Lectured on primate evolution, graded papers on biomechanics, attended faculty meetings where debates about curriculum changes felt like absurdist theatre. But the focus wasn't there. Her mind kept circling back to the impossible truth she carried, the weight of the secret pressing down, making concentration feel like wading through thick mud. She caught colleagues glancing at her with concern, noticed the slight hesitation before they asked how she was *really* doing. She deflected with practiced vagueness – the trauma of the expedition, the wildfire, the lost colleagues. The official story provided a convenient shield, but it felt increasingly flimsy, transparent.

The small anomalies continued, too frequent, too specific to be dismissed as mere coincidence. Her office computer at the university began experiencing bizarre slowdowns whenever she tried accessing certain geological databases related to the Olympic Peninsula, or attempted searches using keywords like "uncharted drainage basin," "Project Backwoods," or even the name "Aris Thorne" – the Kestrel pathologist from the Goliath autopsy report. Pages would hang indefinitely, search queries would return inexplicable "server errors," or her entire system would require a forced reboot. The university IT department found no malware, blaming network traffic or aging hardware, but Elise knew better. It felt like sophisticated digital walls, specifically erected to block her inquiries, monitored by algorithms far beyond standard university security. Kestrel wasn't just watching her physical movements; they were policing her access to information, subtly reinforcing the boundaries of her confinement.

 The final straw came a week after the cryptic email. Returning late from the lab one evening, exhaustion making her less cautious than usual, she let herself into her apartment, tossing her keys onto the small entryway table. As she shrugged off her damp coat, a faint discrepancy caught her eye. A tiny smudge of mud, almost invisible, on the pristine white baseboard near the doorjamb, right where the chair she wedged under the knob usually rested. She hadn't noticed it that morning. She was meticulous about cleaning, especially since returning, needing the illusion of control over her environment. Had she tracked it in herself? Possible, given the perpetual Seattle damp. But something about its position, low down, slightly smeared, felt wrong.

 A cold dread washed over her. Moving slowly, deliberately, she knelt down, examining the smudge. It wasn't just mud; there seemed to be tiny fibers embedded within it, dark, synthetic. Then she scanned the area around the doorframe, her eyes sharp, the scientist's observational skills kicking into high gear, fueled now by adrenaline. And she saw it. A minuscule scratch on the metal doorplate near the lock mechanism, almost imperceptible unless you were looking for it. Fresh. Another tiny fiber, caught on the splintered edge of the scratch.

 Someone had been here. While she was out. Someone skilled enough to bypass the deadbolt and likely the chair wedge without leaving obvious signs, but perhaps hurried, or just slightly careless, leaving behind these minute traces. Kestrel. Confirming her suspicions, checking if she'd brought anything back, planting new listening devices? The thought made her skin crawl. Her sanctuary wasn't safe. It never had been.

 Panic threatened to overwhelm her, a suffocating wave urging her to run blindly out the door. She fought it down, forcing herself to breathe, to think rationally. Running wildly would achieve nothing, likely lead her straight into their hands. She needed a plan. She needed to disappear, properly this time. Staying silent wasn't enough; her very existence, her knowledge, was a threat Kestrel would eventually feel compelled to neutralize. The surveillance, the glitches, the likely intrusion into her apartment – they weren't just warnings anymore; they felt like the precursors to more decisive action.

That night, sleep was entirely forgotten. Fueled by black coffee and a desperate, cold clarity, Elise began systematically erasing herself. She started with the digital footprint. Using encrypted browsers accessed via public Wi-Fi hotspots miles from her usual haunts (changing locations constantly), she deleted social media profiles, closed unused online accounts, scrubbed cloud storage. She knew it was likely futile against Kestrel's resources, but it felt like a necessary ritual, severing ties. She backed up her essential, sanitized academic work onto multiple encrypted thumb drives, then reformatted her personal laptop's hard drive, wiping it clean. Her university computer would have to wait – tampering with it directly might trigger immediate alerts.

Next came the physical world. She gathered cash, withdrawn in small, random amounts from different ATMs over the preceding weeks, a paranoid precaution that now felt prescient. She packed her go-bag – not the one from the expedition, but a new, anonymous backpack purchased with cash. Inside went durable outdoor clothing, sturdy boots, a basic first-aid kit (replenished after the expedition), water purification tablets, high-energy food bars, a reliable compass (hoping it would work away from the valley's influence), detailed paper maps of Washington state and the Olympic Peninsula, and her small, essential field notebook. Finally, heart pounding, she retrieved the waterproof container holding the memory card and the logbook page from its hiding place. This, the core of the truth, the reason for her flight, went into a hidden pocket sewn into the backpack's lining.

She moved methodically through her apartment, destroying anything that could easily trace her movements or intentions. Credit card statements, bills, old journals, research notes related to Kestrel or the Olympics – all shredded, then soaked in water, reduced to illegible pulp. She kept only essential identification documents, tucking them away securely. She considered leaving a false trail – booking a flight she wouldn't take, sending misleading emails from a burner account – but decided against it. Kestrel was too sophisticated; clumsy misdirection might only confirm their suspicions faster. Better to simply vanish as cleanly as possible.

The hardest part was leaving behind the remnants of her life, the tangible connections to the person she had been before AO Hollow. Books accumulated over years, photographs holding cherished memories, research materials representing decades of work – all had to be abandoned. It felt like another kind of death, an erasure of her past self. But survival demanded it.

As dawn approached, casting long, grey shadows across the city, Elise took one last look around the apartment that was no longer hers. It felt hollowed out, stripped bare, reflecting the state of her own life. She left the key on the table, pulled the hood of an anonymous dark rain jacket over her head, hoisted the unfamiliar backpack, and slipped out the back entrance, melting into the pre-dawn anonymity of the awakening city.

Her first challenge was ditching her car. Driving it would leave an electronic trail Kestrel could easily follow. She drove several miles across town, parked it on a quiet residential street where it wouldn't immediately attract attention, wiped down the steering wheel and door handles, and walked away without looking back, merging into the flow of early morning commuters heading towards bus stops and light rail stations.

Public transport felt safer, anonymous. She rode a bus across town, paid cash, transferred to another line heading south, away from the Peninsula initially. She kept her head down, hood up, avoiding security cameras where possible, constantly scanning faces, looking for anyone paying undue attention. Every suited man, every person talking too intently into a phone, felt like a potential Kestrel agent. The paranoia was exhausting, but necessary.

She spent the day moving, never staying in one place too long. A few hours in a sprawling public library, hunched over maps in a quiet corner, planning a tentative route towards the Peninsula that avoided major highways and population centers. Lunch was a quick, cheap meal at a nondescript diner in a different part of the city, paid for with cash, eaten near the back exit. Another bus ride, then another, gradually circling back towards the Puget Sound ferry terminals, but choosing a smaller, less busy route, aiming for one of the islands first, a place to potentially disappear for a day or two, throw off immediate pursuit before making the final jump to the Peninsula.

Throughout the day, she resisted the urge to use any public computers, any traceable phones. Her burner phone remained off, its battery removed, tucked deep in her pack. Contacting Nora's intermediary was the next critical step, but it had to be done carefully, at the right time, from the right place, using the pre-agreed, low-tech method. They had established it during those brief, hushed conversations after the Kestrel debriefing, anticipating this possibility: a specific, innocuous message left within a particular, commonly found guidebook (a birdwatching guide, Elise recalled) shelved in the reference section of a designated small-town library on the Peninsula itself. A long shot, relying on the contact checking regularly, relying on the message not being discovered by others, but infinitely safer than any electronic communication.

As the afternoon wore on, the strain began to tell. Lack of sleep, constant vigilance, the gnawing uncertainty – it created a physical ache behind her eyes, a tremor in her hands. She found herself experiencing micro-flashbacks more frequently now, triggered by mundane things. The rumble of a passing truck became the sound of falling rock in the Crevice. The fleeting glimpse of a tall, dark-coated man disappearing around a corner morphed momentarily into the silhouette of the Stick-shí'nač on the ridge. The city, which should have felt safe through sheer population density, felt instead like a hostile wilderness of concrete and watchful eyes, every corner potentially concealing a threat.

She caught her reflection in a shop window – pale face, dark circles under haunted eyes, hunched posture – and barely recognized herself. The pragmatic, confident scientist was gone, replaced by a hunted fugitive. The transformation was chilling. Kestrel hadn't just silenced her; they were actively dismantling her, forcing her into a desperate, reactive existence.

As dusk began to settle, she found herself near the ferry terminal for Vashon Island. It felt like a plausible intermediate step – close enough to Seattle to be unassuming, yet offering a degree of separation, a place to potentially lay low for a night before heading further west towards the Peninsula library and the designated contact point. She paid cash for a walk-on ticket, joining the sparse line of commuters and island residents waiting for the next departure.

Standing on the ferry deck as the vessel pulled away from the Seattle skyline, the city lights glittering like cold jewels against the darkening, rain-bruised sky, Elise felt a profound sense of severance. She was cutting ties, burning bridges, stepping fully into the unknown. The wind whipped strands of hair across her face, carrying the salty tang of the Sound. She scanned the receding docks, the other passengers on deck, searching for any sign she had been followed. Nothing obvious. But Kestrel was good. Subtle. Patient. Were they already aware of her departure? Were agents waiting on the other side?

She clutched the railing, the cold metal biting into her fingers. The vast, dark water churning below felt symbolic. She was adrift, navigating treacherous currents, with dangers lurking both behind and ahead. Ahead lay the Olympic Peninsula, the source of her trauma but also potentially her only sanctuary, her only ally in Nora. Ahead lay the daunting task of retrieving the buried evidence, of confronting the Hollow Truth. Ahead lay the Stick-shí'nač, their hidden world, their inscrutable intentions.

Behind her lay Kestrel, relentless, powerful, determined to maintain their secrets at any cost.

Echoes persist. Vigilance required. The words resonated with new meaning now. The echoes weren't just memories; they were the consequences rippling outwards from AO Hollow. And vigilance wasn't just paranoia; it was the fundamental requirement for survival in a world where hidden giants guarded ancient secrets and shadowy organizations erased inconvenient truths. Her life as Dr. Elise Holloway, primate biologist, was effectively over. Her life as a fugitive, a keeper of impossible secrets, a potential catalyst for world-altering revelation or catastrophic conflict, had just begun. The ferry plowed onwards through the dark water, carrying her towards an uncertain future, towards the looming shadow of the Olympic mountains, towards the next chapter in her terrifying descent into the hollow ground.

As of this printing the *Bigfoot: Shadows in the Timberline* series continues with

Book Two: Echoes in Stone
Book Three: Thorne's Revenge

Printed in Great Britain
by Amazon